HATE
I ~~LOVE~~ YOU,
FULLER JAMES

Advance Praise for *I Hate You, Fuller James*

"Fun, refreshing, totally relatable!" —Lynn Rush, *NYT* & *USA Today* bestselling author

"I actually really love you, Fuller James. A lot." —Alex Evansley, author of *Love Scene, Take Two*

"Funny and heartwarming, *I Hate You, Fuller James* is sure to be your next favorite read…and book hangover." —Ali Novak, author of *My Life with the Walter Boys*

"Channeling a modern take on *She's All That*, *I Hate You, Fuller James* is the YA book you need this decade!" — Kristi McManus, Wattpad author

"*I Hate You, Fuller James* was a ride that I never wanted to get off. Prepare for a roller coaster of laughs, romance, and, most importantly, feels." —Rachel Meinke, *Along for the Ride*

"My heart is so full from *Fuller James*. Exciting, fresh, and full of all the feels!" —Sarah Ratliff, Wattpad author, Wattpad Star, and Watty Winner

I ~~LOVE~~ HATE YOU, FULLER JAMES

KELLY ANNE BLOUNT

Entangled Publishing, LLC
10940 S Parker Rd
Suite 327
Parker, CO 80134
rights@entangledpublishing.com

Crush is an imprint of Entangled Publishing, LLC.

Edited by Stacy Abrams and Judi Lauren
Cover design by Bree Archer
Cover photography by Olga Kan/Dreamstime

Manufactured in the United States of America

First Edition March 2020

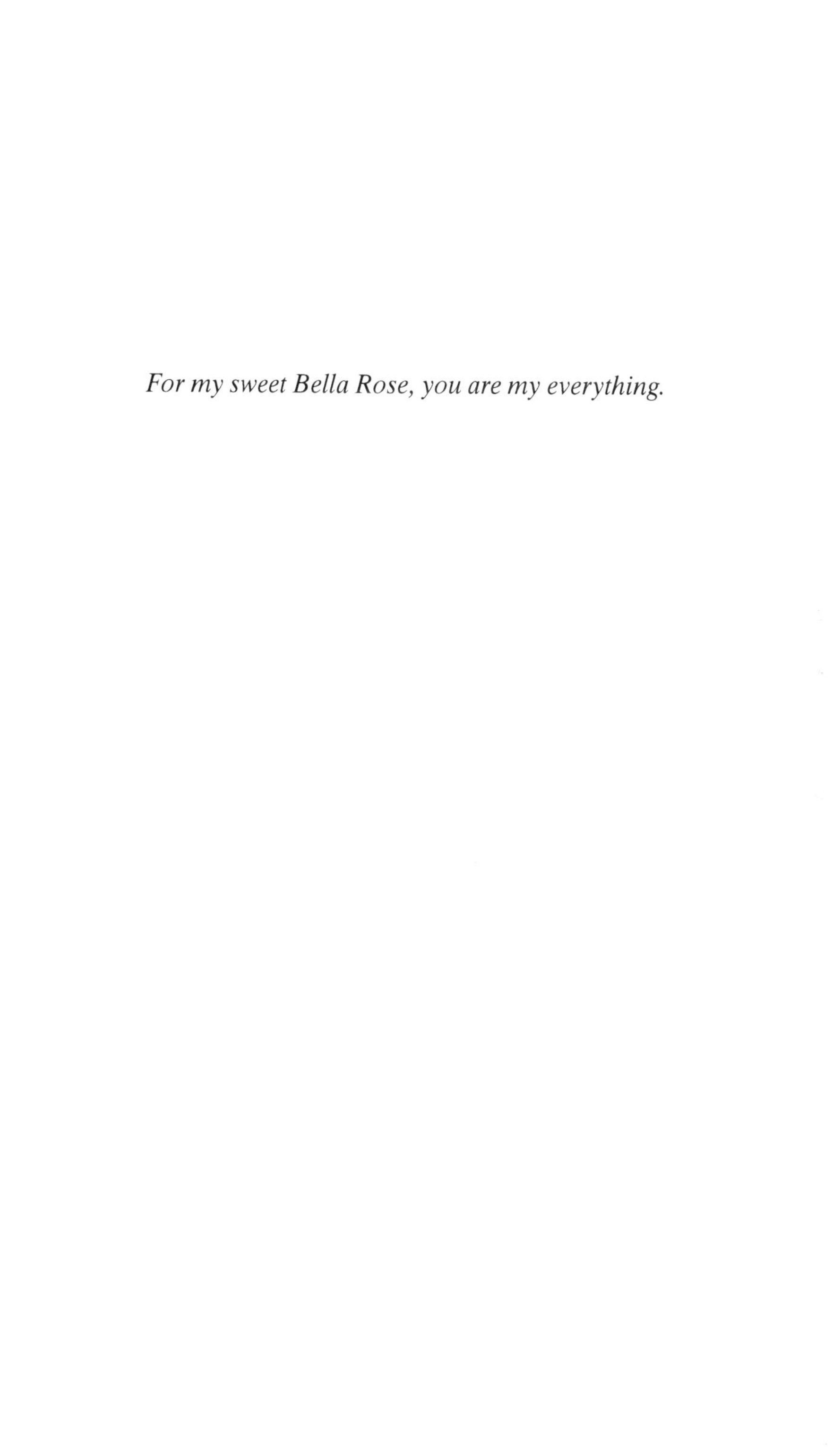

For my sweet Bella Rose, you are my everything.

Chapter One

Wren

"*Food fight!*" someone shouted behind me.

You've got to be kidding me, I thought as I scrambled to close my Calculus book. Hands fumbling, I tucked my calculator safely into my backpack, but by the time I'd turned around to grab my notebook, it was too late. Ranch-soaked lettuce splattered across my meticulous notes on differentiation and the homework assignment I'd started a few minutes ago. I ripped out the page and balled it up. Now I'd have to copy someone else's notes and redo the first five math problems.

The lunchroom buzzed with excitement as a group of freshmen got in on the action. They chucked their green beans at a group of girls sitting two tables away, who screeched and scrambled to their feet. A kid sitting in front of me dumped his casserole and cinnamon applesauce on the table and held up his tray as a shield. His fork clattered to the floor as I planned my escape. I wanted to get out of the cafeteria before things got totally out of hand.

Squelch.

Before I'd had a chance to move, a sticky substance landed on the back of my neck and slid beneath my shirt. My shoulders stiffened and heat prickled my skin. I didn't need to turn around to know who'd thrown it.

It was always the same group of guys who started crap like this.

"Seriously?" I shouted, spinning in my seat. My eyes immediately landed on Fuller freaking James, captain of the basketball team and the jerk responsible for my hideous nickname, "Wrentainer."

He'd given it to me in middle school after a humiliating incident during a school dance, and it had stuck. Five years had passed and I still had to put up with people reminiscing about the time my retainer flew out of my mouth and landed on Fuller's best friend.

"Come on, Wren," Fuller taunted. "You know you want to join us!"

He stood with a lopsided grin on his face and a glob of mashed potatoes in his hand. His blue eyes twinkled with mischief as he pushed his dark brown hair off his face with the back of his hand. He looked like he'd just stepped off the pages of an Abercrombie and Fitch catalog, right down to the perfectly pressed cargo shorts and maroon Magnolia Valley Cougars T-shirt that hugged his washboard abs. If I didn't detest him so much, I might have been impressed by his looks.

Emphasis on the word "might."

Fuller elbowed his teammate Marc, who dug his spoon into a container of yogurt and flung it at a group of freshmen.

Without thinking, I reached around to the back of my neck and scraped off a clump of the cold mashed spuds. Cocking my arm back, I flung the food at Fuller as hard as I could.

Instead of hitting the most obnoxious guy at our school, the potatoes landed square in the middle of his teammate's chest.

"Crap," I gasped.

Marc's lips parted and his eyebrows knitted together as he looked down at his shirt. With an aggressive swipe of his hand, he flung the mashed potatoes to the linoleum floor.

Fuller threw his head back in laughter. "Swing and a miss, Wren. Want to take another shot?" He held his arms open and winked at me. My heart fluttered for a second. *Ugh. Why are the cute ones always such jerks?*

I glared at him as I slid my backpack over my shoulder and stomped out of the cafeteria. I'd never lost my cool before, and I couldn't believe I'd thrown food at that jack wagon. Looking down at my gloppy hands, I exhaled through gritted teeth and made my way to the nearest bathroom.

The halls were empty, except for a sophomore with a laminated red pass in his hand. We passed each other a few steps before the girls' bathroom, the shiny floor squeaking under our sneakers.

"Hey, Wrentainer, you've got something on your back," he called over his shoulder with a chuckle before disappearing around the corner.

Balling my fists, I shoved the bathroom door open with the backs of my forearms. Per usual, the small room stank of cheap perfume, and paper towels overflowed from the trash can to the left of the sinks. I caught a glimpse of my scrunched-up face in the mirror.

I hated Fuller James.

No one else made my blood boil like him. When he wasn't throwing food in the lunchroom or making out with my ex–best friend right next to my locker, he was showboating on the basketball court and bragging about his stats. Fuller had such a big head, it was a miracle he could fit through the locker room door without getting stuck.

I cranked on the water and washed my sticky fingers. *What a jerk.* After they were sufficiently clean, I grabbed a handful of paper towels and headed into a stall.

Taking a breath, I tried to calm myself down before slipping off my shirt and wiping away as much of the mashed potato debris from my neck and upper back as possible. I still felt gross, but I tugged my shirt back on over my head.

I reached for the lock on the stall but froze when I heard my former best friend's nasally voice.

"Can you believe Fuller?" Marissa asked. "Throwing food in the cafeteria like a ten-year-old. Honestly, I don't know why I put up with him."

Pulling my hand back, I clutched my backpack to my chest and sat down on the edge of the toilet. The last thing I needed right now was a run-in with *her.*

"Because he's so damn hot?" Courtney laughed.

Courtney and Marissa were always together. As part of the popular clique, they wore only stilettos to school. I couldn't even begin to imagine hiking up to the third floor in those death contraptions.

"I heard he hooked up with Haleigh on Saturday night," Marissa said.

The jealousy in her voice was palpable. She and Fuller must have been on a break again. Keeping up with their relationship status required a degree in statistics, or at least some kind of master calendar.

"It's like he's shoving the breakup in your face," Courtney replied.

Silence. I could only assume they were putting on more lip gloss. Like they needed a seventh layer.

"Whatever," Marissa said. "That bitch will be yesterday's news. I can have him back anytime I want."

"I mean, duh," Courtney said.

Oh my gosh. Please stop talking and get out of here.

I couldn't believe I used to be friends with Marissa Stanton. We'd been inseparable in elementary school, but that all started to change in sixth grade. Marissa's parents went through a nasty divorce, and she quickly found out that she could manipulate them into giving her whatever she wanted. By the start of seventh grade, her whole personality had changed.

When we hung out, she spent most of the time asking me if I liked her hair or her clothes. She stopped wanting to stay in and make brownies or watch movies. Instead, when she wasn't obsessing about herself, she was fixated on Fuller James, the most popular guy at our school. When I didn't join in, she started to get annoyed with me. I could feel it building, but I didn't know what to do about it. I tried talking to her, but she didn't want to hear it. Instead, she started hanging out with Courtney more and me less.

Our friendship finally came to an end in seventh grade. She got boobs, while I got a retainer. To make matters worse, at the spring fling, Marc had asked me to dance. Normally, this would be a good thing. Unfortunately, I'd come down with a terrible cold and sneezed mid-dance. I can still remember the look of disgust on his face as my drool-laden retainer flew out of my mouth and rebounded off his light-blue dress shirt.

Marc never spoke to me again, but that wasn't nearly the worst of it.

As I fled the gym, I overheard Marissa telling everyone what happened. Even worse, I heard Fuller loudly exclaim the nickname that caused my classmates to howl with laughter, "Wren 'the Retainer' Carter," later shortened to "Wrentainer."

Marissa and Fuller started going out that night. He told her to stop being my friend, so she dropped me instantaneously. After that, I became an easy target for cheap laughs. To make matters worse, with Fuller at her side, she rocketed to the position of queen bee at our school. Between her relentless bullying and spreading gossip like wildfire, my remaining friends dropped me like a bad habit. No one wanted to get in her way, and by the end of the school year, no one wanted to be my friend.

Marissa's shrill laugh pulled me out of my painful trip down memory lane. It made me furious that I was stuck in this stupid bathroom stall, but the thought of facing Marissa made my stomach twist into knots. If at all possible, it was easier to stay out of her and Fuller's way.

"Oh, guess who Fuller nailed with those nasty mashed potatoes in the cafeteria today?" Marissa said.

"Who?" Courtney asked, smacking her lips together.

My chest constricted.

"Wrentainer," Marissa replied, bursting into laughter.

Courtney joined her. "She is *such* a loser. Can you believe that we used to be friends with her?"

My eyes stung as I prayed they wouldn't recognize my white, low-top Chuck Taylors under the stall. Blinking back the onslaught of tears that I refused to shed, I bit my lower lip and continued to clutch my bag.

"Ugh. We were so stupid." Marissa said. "Anyway, enough about *her*. This mascara is everything. It makes my eyelashes look, like, twice as long."

"I wish Mr. Ferguson would give us twice as long on our physics test next period." Marissa sighed. "I had to study for, like, four hours last night. I better get an A."

"Of course you will. You always ace his tests," Courtney assured her.

After an eternity, Marissa and Courtney grabbed their makeup and left the bathroom.

Letting out a sigh of relief, I stood and exited the stall.

My reflection stared back at me in the mirror hanging above the sink. The yellow painted concrete bricks in the bathroom felt like they were closing in around me. Turning on the tap, I splashed some cold water on my face and ignored the tight feeling in my chest.

As I patted my face dry with a scratchy paper towel, my thoughts drifted back to Fuller and the way he stood there taunting me with that irksome smile. Most girls would have thrown their panties at him instead of potatoes.

Worst of all, I knew that neither Fuller nor any of the guys on the basketball team would get in trouble for the food fight. They never did. Those guys practically walked on water, and they followed Fuller around like he was some kind of jock Pied Piper. Even my best friend, Brandon, who played point guard on the team, would succumb to Fuller's stupid antics from time to time.

Occasionally they'd pull a funny prank, like the time Fuller and Marc snuck out during last period and went to town with industrial-sized plastic wrap in the junior section of the parking lot. Brandon and a few of the other guys had helped them wrap dozens of cars. They made use of nearby light poles, which had acted as a makeshift barrier, completely sealing off the entire area. It looked like the cars had been quarantined by the Center for Disease Control and Prevention.

This wasn't one of those occasions, though. This time, Fuller had attacked *me* with potatoes. Biting my lip, I thought back to the tirade I went on yesterday after school. I'd caught Brandon on his way to basketball practice. With my hands on my hips, I'd urged him to stand up to Fuller. To tell him that one player didn't make a team and that all of Fuller's hotshot moves wouldn't mean a damn thing if the other team had a strong enough defense. Of course, Fuller happened to be walking by as I reached the height of my diatribe.

"Who died and elected you team captain?" The tone in his voice cut right through my confidence. Instead of responding,

I turned and practically ran in the opposite direction.

Looking at my reflection in the bathroom mirror, I cursed myself for lacking the confidence to confront Marissa and Fuller. I ran my tongue over my perfectly straight teeth. At least I'd come up with a secret nickname for him, Fuller "Fuller than a Bag of Manure" James or F.B.M. for short. Of course, I'd never say it out loud, but thinking about it always brought a smile to my face.

I considered talking to my uncle, the boys' basketball coach, about everything. It should have been easy. He was my dad's twin brother. Too bad they had completely different personalities. Sadly, I'd learned my lesson after the last time I'd confronted him. I tried to point out the injustice of treating Fuller and a few of the other guys on the basketball team differently, but I knew it was a lost cause. His response was typical: "Boys will be boys, Wren."

What a load of sexist crap. I knew plenty of boys who didn't act like jerks on a daily basis. Like Brandon and my other best friend, Dae.

When it all boiled down to the basics, the only thing my uncle, the head principal, and pretty much everyone else at our school cared about was winning another state title. We'd never won back-to-back championships, but with Fuller leading the team, our chances of going all the way again this year were strong.

The bell outside the bathroom rang. I had five minutes to grab my AP Literature book from my locker and get to class—class with Fuller. Luckily, he sat a few rows behind me and, once I got to class, I wouldn't have to see his face for at least forty-five minutes. I fished my phone out of my bag and sent Dae and Brandon a quick text message telling them what happened. We'd have a lot to talk about after school. Glancing at myself one last time in the mirror, I frowned. I'd missed a bit of mashed potato that was stuck to my ear.

I hate you, Fuller James.

• • •

As Mrs. Brewster wrote our homework on the board, I heard someone behind me giggle. When I stole a glance over my shoulder, I couldn't help but roll my eyes. Lyla Burkman was practically sitting in Fuller's lap, bent forward, with her cleavage on full display. *I guess Haleigh is out of the picture already.*

A small grin tugged at the corners of my lips for a fleeting moment. Marissa would be livid once she heard about Lyla flirting with Fuller. They were in the same clique, but Marissa always thought she was better than everybody else. This would definitely set her off.

Oblivious to the budding couple, Mrs. Brewster continued to write on the board. She was one of the nicest teachers at the school, but her disciplinary skills were weak at best. Most of the time, everyone respected her, but certain students still got chatty at the end of every class. Once, when she was writing on the board, Tiffany Neilson and Liam Mayor made out in the back row for two minutes and thirty-seven seconds. To this day, Mrs. Brewster still didn't know why the class had erupted in laughter.

Ignoring my classmates, I glanced at the clock and tried to nonchalantly sniff my T-shirt. At least I didn't smell like that nasty beef gravy they served with the mashed potatoes in the cafeteria. Even though the incident in the lunchroom had left me in a foul mood, class was a good distraction.

AP Lit was by far my favorite class. Yesterday, we'd finished reading *The Hate U Give* by Angie Thomas. It had immediately become one of my all-time favorite books. I'd loved it so much, I bought my own copy and filled the margins with notes. I'd also color coordinated florescent tabs with matching highlighters. That way, I could quickly locate the sections with important themes and my favorite quotes.

More giggles. This time louder. The rage that had been simmering since getting to class and seeing Fuller's stupid face began to boil.

I spun around in my seat and opened my mouth to say something, but nothing came out.

"Jealous much?" Lyla hissed.

You wish. I cursed myself for not being able to say the words out loud.

Fuller's eyes danced with amusement as he watched me squirm.

Why did he have to act like such a d-bag all the time? We were both seniors. By now, he should be smart enough to figure out how to act like a decent human being from time to time. Or at least pretend to.

Before I could turn around, Lyla rolled her eyes. "Loosen up, Wrentainer. It's not like you're ever going to be in the back of the class with a guy."

I thought I saw Fuller's smile falter for a moment, and then he was back to being obnoxiously handsome.

Mrs. Brewster cleared her throat. "If you three are done." She tapped the whiteboard. "You'll have two days to come up with a topic for your essay. Once I approve it, you can begin writing. You'll have one week to complete this paper." She set down the whiteboard marker. "Are there any questions?"

"Is that, like, one week from today or one week from the two days?" Lyla asked.

"One week after your topic is approved. That would make your paper due next Wednesday," Mrs. Brewster said, circling the due date in red dry erase marker on the whiteboard. "Any other questions?"

My mind raced. I'd already considered several topics for my paper. I'd typed up a list and had it tucked away in the front pocket of my binder. I wanted to go over my ideas one more time next period in study hall before I picked my favorite and ran it by Mrs. Brewster.

Several of my classmates groaned as they began shuffling dog-eared paperbacks into their backpacks. The girl sitting next to me sneezed into a tissue. I immediately grabbed the bottle of antibacterial hand sanitizer clipped on to my backpack and applied a liberal portion to my hands. I couldn't risk bringing any germs home to Gramps. He'd come down with a bad case of the flu last winter, and it had been really scary.

After rubbing the clear gel all over my hands, I waved them in the air and checked the clock mounted to the wall above Mrs. Brewster's head. One minute left, then study hall, where I'd have to start my math homework over again from scratch. *Stupid mashed potatoes. Scratch that. Stupid Fuller James.*

"Also, if you turn in your topic late, I'll deduct ten percent from your paper." Mrs. Brewster pushed her glasses back up the bridge of her long, thin nose. More groans erupted from behind me. "Oh, and, Wren, please see me before you leave class."

"Ooh," Fuller called from behind me. "Somebody's in trouble."

"Shut it, Fuller," I snapped. *Holy crap. I called him out.* I hated to admit it, but my constant lack of sleep had been playing a major role in my moodiness both during the day while I was at school and in the evenings when I was at home. Not that it mattered in this situation. Fuller was a complete jerk, and he deserved everything I threw at him.

Our eyes locked for several seconds before Lyla placed her hand on his leg.

Whatever. By next week, Lyla would be a distant memory in Fuller's black book. He and Marissa would probably be back together and we'd all have to be witness to their spit-swapping, over-the-top make-out sessions in between every class.

"Don't talk to him like that," Lyla sneered just loud enough for me to hear.

"Wren's agi-tatered," Fuller said, chuckling. "Get it?"

Liam, the varsity quarterback, burst out laughing. In the process, he knocked over his water bottle, which instantly soaked through the back of Jenny's shirt.

"Ugh," she screeched.

Mrs. Brewster put her hands on her hips. She looked like she was about to reprimand the boys, but before she could open her mouth, the bell rang.

Shaking my head, I stepped out of Jenny's way and shot a withering look at Fuller before making my way to Mrs. Brewster's desk. Two large bookshelves stood on either side. There were stacks of books overflowing from both, and smaller piles had started to accumulate on the top.

"Agi-tatered?" she asked as Fuller and the rest of the students filed out of the classroom.

I glanced down at her desk. There were papers and red pens covering every square inch. She must have been in the midst of grading essays from another class. "Yeah, Fuller thought it would be cute to throw mashed potatoes at lunch. He hit me in the back of the neck. I'm still sticky."

"Oh," she said, giving me a sympathetic nod. "Agi-tatered, as in the taters he threw at you."

"Yeah, apparently Fuller thinks starchy vegetables are funny," I said. "It's a bit of a stretch, but so are most things that involve thinking when it comes to Fuller James."

Mrs. Brewster picked up one of the pens on her desk. Tapping it against her open palm, she tilted her head to the side and said, "I have a favor to ask you."

"Sure, what's up?" I asked.

She stopped tapping the pen against her hand. "I need you to tutor someone in class for a couple of weeks."

I looked around at the empty desks. There were a few kids who struggled in class, but I didn't think anyone was failing. I mean, most of the time, if an AP class got too hard, kids would just switch to a regular class.

"Sure," I said, "happy to help."

"Great," Mrs. Brewster said. "I'll give you ten extra credit points on your paper in return. Plus, you two already have study hall together the last period of the day, so it should work perfectly."

"Okay, that sounds fair," I said, racking my brain. "Who do I need to work with?"

"Full—"

"No way," I said, waving my hands in front of me before she could finish saying his name. "He's seriously the worst!"

"Fuller James," she said, ignoring my frantic gestures. "You're my top student, and he really needs your help."

I crossed my arms and stared at Mrs. Brewster. "I'm not tutoring Fuller. I'm literally covered in food because of him."

Her dark hair framed her face perfectly. "I know he can be difficult, but—"

"Difficult? There are so many words I could use to describe him," I said, cutting her off. "But 'tutee' isn't ever going to be one of them."

Mrs. Brewster sighed. "He really needs your help, Wren."

Wow, I can't believe Fuller is failing. He's always so confident. I guess even the King of Magnolia Valley High has a few secrets.

"Wren?" Mrs. Brewster said, tilting her head to the side sympathetically.

"If it was anyone else, I'd do it in a second. Promise." I shook my head. "Plus, I'm sure there are other kids in class who can work with him. Why not ask Lyla?"

"If he doesn't bring his grade up, he won't be able to play basketball," Mrs. Brewster admitted. "And Coach is really worried." There it was, the real reason I'd been asked to tutor Fuller. My uncle knew I had great grades and that I used to tutor kids after school.

Too bad for him it would never happen.

"Perhaps you could try today and—"

I held up my hands, knowing my uncle would be disappointed in me. "I apologize for interrupting, but, Mrs. Brewster, I'd literally tutor anyone else in the class. I swear. But there is no way, no how, that I'd *ever* tutor Fuller James."

Chapter Two

Fuller

"I'm incredibly sorry, Principal Davis," I said, hanging my head in apparent shame and dropping my gaze to his desk. He and I were running through the same routine we always did. I'd apologize and he'd respond with something like, "I'm going to give you one more chance, son. Do you understand?" I'd agree, call him "sir," and all would be good until the next incident.

Normally, being called into the principal's office didn't bother me too much. I'd sit in the chair across from Principal Davis, where we'd usually end up talking about basketball and reliving the highlights of his high school career as the star center forward. We'd then move on to his time at the University of Virginia. We'd usually wrap up with how he could see a lot of himself in me.

But, this time, instead of it being the two of us, Coach and Wren Carter were here, too.

Coach Carter shook his head. "Fuller, we've been over

this before. In order to play, you have to be passing *all* your classes. We've made a lot of exceptions for you over the years, but this is one that you know we can't break."

My cheeks burned with embarrassment. It was bad enough Coach knew that my AP Lit grade had dropped to an F, but it was like rubbing salt in an open wound to have Wren find out, too. She was hands down the smartest kid in the entire school. I kept my gaze cast downward, on Principal Davis's desk. There was no way I could handle seeing a smug grin on Wren's face or, even worse, a look of pity. I'd never failed a class before. But, between the before school workouts, a full day of school, basketball practice, shooting hoops for an additional hour after practice ended, and hanging out with my little brother, I barely had enough time to eat and get a few hours of sleep, let alone read books and write AP Lit papers. I managed to keep up a 3.2 grade point average by getting most of my homework done and earning decent grades on tests, but that certainly wasn't high enough to earn any kind of academic scholarship.

I wanted to drop down to regular Lit, but my parents forbade me from doing it. "You aren't applying yourself, Fuller," my dad would say. "If you spent half as much time on your homework as you did on basketball and with the ladies, you'd be doing fine in school." Like he had a clue. He was an emergency room doctor with an eidetic memory. He was constantly at work and, unlike him, my only path to a full scholarship was basketball.

Plus, most people at school, including Wren, assumed I was a dumb jock. Who was I to prove them wrong?

I should have been able to coast through senior year, not have to worry about my spot on the team because of some English class that I'd never need again. Last time I checked, professional basketball players weren't worried about using proper APA citations when they were tearing up the court.

When I wasn't training, I spent time with my little brother. We watched *Deadpool* and read comic books together. Even though he knew the character Deadpool wasn't real, he always claimed he was going to be just like him when he grew up: indestructible. Instead, he was forced to deal with a diagnosis that had taken that dream from him and left him with an uncertain future.

A lump formed in the back of my throat whenever I thought about him. It wasn't fair. Here I was, voted athlete of the year by my peers, and my little brother was stuck in a body that couldn't even handle getting shoved in the hallway.

Fighting back the hot tears that welled up in my eyes, I pushed thoughts of Hudson to the back of my mind. I kept that part of my life private, and I certainly wasn't going to let Wren in on it. Speaking of Wren, my thoughts drifted to her copy of *The Hate U Give*. I'd spotted it on her desk today, cluttered with dozens of tabs and about a million notes in the margins. She'd probably already had her topic prepared for Mrs. Brewster and written half the paper. Me, on the other hand, well, I hadn't even had time to crack open the book.

Not that this or any other paper should even matter. If this basketball season went well, I'd win a scholarship to the University of Georgia to play basketball. That way my parents could focus on my little brother's medical bills.

A single session of physical therapy cost them ninety-five dollars. He had at least two sessions a week, every single week except during Christmas and one week during the summer when he went to a special camp for kids with serious medical conditions. The cost of those sessions, plus all his hospital bills, appointments with specialists, and trips to the emergency room for accidents, added up quickly. Even if my parents were to offer to help put me through college, I'd decided a long time ago that I wouldn't accept a single penny of their money when my brother's life was at stake.

To put it bleakly, if I didn't get a full scholarship, I wouldn't be able to afford to go to college.

Glancing up, my gaze fell on Wren. She sat two chairs over with her arms crossed and her lips pursed. She was so uptight she could produce a diamond if someone gave her a chunk of coal.

Her eyes had drifted to the bookcase to the right of Principal Davis's desk. At the top sat the basketball we'd won the state title with last year. All the guys on the team had signed it. The day we presented it to the principal, I thought he might actually cry. The school hadn't won a championship since *his* senior year, which had been over twenty years ago.

Sunlight streamed in through the window in the corner. I stole a glance, immediately wishing I was outside shooting free throws. There was a great court down the street from my house. Like the rest of Magnolia Valley, the basketball court was surrounded by the Blue Ridge Mountains of Western North Carolina, and the view was really incredible. I'd definitely miss it next year when I was playing for UGA.

Scratch that, *if* I was playing for UGA.

"Excuse me. I don't mean to interrupt, but why am I here?" Wren asked, dragging my mind from my happy place back to the depressing situation at hand. "I have a ton of homework, and I'd like to head back to study hall."

She refused to look at me. I couldn't blame her… Even though I wasn't the guilty party and nearly five years had passed, I still felt responsible for her hideous nickname. I'd never admit it, but I hadn't been brave enough to shut my classmates down when they were teasing Wren and calling her Wrentainer. I cared too much what they thought about me. Marissa was the one who came up with it, but I was the one who repeated it, loudly. I was the one who made all our classmates laugh. I was the reason Wren got bullied.

If it hadn't been for that night and the repercussions that

followed, I totally would have gone for Wren back in the day. Not only was she smart, but in middle school, she used to have a wicked sense of humor. I bet she still did. On top of that, she was pretty and not in that ten-pounds-of-makeup way like Marissa. Like today, her light brown hair was pulled back into a high ponytail, which accented her hazel eyes. She wasn't very tall, maybe five foot three at best, but her legs were long and lean from the countless hours she spent running around the track. *Thank you, cross-country team.*

Principal Davis cleared his throat, bringing me back to reality. "Wren, Coach tells me that you're refusing to tutor Fuller."

"It's not fair," Wren said quietly.

"Not exactly," the principal said, tapping on the screen of a tablet that sat on his desk.

When Wren's eyes landed on the video that he'd pulled up, her face turned ashen.

"It appears that the two of you were engaged in a food fight today in the cafeteria," Principal Davis said. He paused the video and zoomed in on Wren launching a handful of food in my direction.

His voice had taken on a serious tone, but I knew that we wouldn't get in trouble for the fight. It all made sense. The only reason he'd dragged Wren in here was to guilt her into tutoring me. She was hands down the best student in AP Lit, and we already had study hall together. Now that Principal Davis had some leverage over one of the smartest students in the entire school, he'd apply pressure.

I had his moves pegged.

Principal Davis looked directly at me and then Wren. "Normally, I'd hand down your punishments and not think twice about it, but today, I'm giving you two an ultimatum."

Wren's entire body tensed. "What about all the other kids involved in the food fight?" As far as I knew, she'd never been called to the principal's office or gotten into any kind of trouble at school. I wasn't sure if she was scared of earning a black mark on her record or just plain furious with me.

Probably the latter, since that was her default setting.

Mr. Davis straightened his tie and stole a quick glance at the game-winning basketball. "They'll be dealt with, Wren. Don't you worry. Now, you owe our custodians, Mr. Tillson and Miss Constance, an apology. That part is not debatable. And either you both agree to this tutoring arrangement, or you're both suspended for two days and given five days of detention."

"What?" Wren gasped.

"Was that not you throwing food in the lunch room today, Ms. Carter?" the principal asked. He arched an eyebrow and pointed to his tablet. "Or do my eyes deceive me?"

"It was me, but I..." Wren stopped speaking and looked down at her hands.

I watched as her fingers tightened and she dug her nails into her jeans.

"Wren, I'd hate for you to lose the opportunity to go to the STEM Academy Camp at UNC over winter break..." Mr. Davis sat back in his chair.

"Wait. What?" Her jaw fell open in disbelief.

Mr. Davis steepled his fingers. "Any record of suspension automatically revokes your spot in the program."

Wren didn't say anything. Instead, she just sat there, looking totally shell-shocked. I felt bad for her, but getting that scholarship was more important than some nerd camp.

Preparing myself to lay it on thick, I cleared my throat. "I've already started writing my apology to Mr. Tillson and Miss Constance. I'll deliver it to them today before practice and, if it's okay with Wren, I'd very much like to work with her in order to bring up my AP Lit grade. The guys on the team are counting on me, and I don't want to let them down."

"Thank you, Fuller," Principal Davis said.

Wren cringed.

Guilt washed over me, but that didn't matter. I had to look out for my family and myself right now. My entire future depended on it. Wren was so smart, she probably had ten scholarships all lined up for next year.

"Wren, I'm really sorry for throwing food at you today. I think…" I paused for dramatic effect. "I think that sometimes I act out because even though I try to be good at everything, the harsh reality is that I'm not. I'm flunking AP Lit, which means if I don't get a good grade on the next paper, I'm riding the bench in the season opener. Basketball means the world to me, and if you could please give me a chance, I promise to work hard and listen to everything you say."

The words sounded sincere as they left my lips and, to be honest, some of them were closer to the truth than I'd like to admit. Up until this year, I'd never struggled with my grades. But the mounting pressures had gotten to me.

After Coach had called my parents to let them know I *might* not get to play in the first game, they'd ripped into me. I vividly recalled the feeling of heat creeping up my neck and the tight knot forming in my stomach. I'd never felt more ashamed. Missing any of the upcoming games could risk my future at the University of Georgia, my dream school. The coach had come out to the State Championship game last season and, if the rumors were true, he planned to come out again to the season opener to watch me play. Missing the season opener could have a disastrous impact on my future.

Coach remained silent as Principal Davis let out a sigh. "Miss Carter, the choice is yours. Either suspension and detention or tutoring Mr. James until he brings his Lit grade up to at least a C, although an A or B would be preferred."

Wren stood and began pacing. "Suspension on my permanent record and losing my spot at the STEM Academy

Camp? No way."

"So, you'll agree to help Mr. James?" Coach interjected in a hopeful tone.

"Well, it's not like I have a choice," she responded. Her voice was full of anger. She shot me another look that would stop most guys dead in their tracks, her hazel eyes practically launching live grenades at me. I'd never seen her this riled up before, and even though I hated to admit it, she looked kind of hot, in an angry nerd kind of way.

"Thank you, sir," I said, standing to shake Principal Davis's and Coach's hands. "I promise this will never happen again."

"It had better not," Coach responded. He straightened the lanyard around his neck with his staff ID card hanging off the bottom.

Wren scowled as the corners of Coach's lips curled up into a triumphant smile.

The first time I found out Coach was her uncle, I thought I'd heard wrong. What were the odds? Either way, their next family dinner wasn't going to be a pleasant experience.

Principal Davis checked his watch. "Well, that's settled. You two can go to the library now. I've informed your study hall teacher that you'll be working together there until further notice."

Wren gave the principal and Coach a curt nod before storming out of the office.

"Fuller, wait for me outside the office," Coach said.

"Uh, sure." Was he going to chew me out in private?

Gathering my backpack, I thanked Mr. Davis and Coach before heading to the hallway.

But before I could get out of the office, I stumbled over an Algebra book in the middle of the floor.

"I'm so sorry, Fuller," the freshman apologized. He jumped out of his chair and scooped up the book. "Did you get suspended?" His eyes were wide open as he clutched it to his chest.

"What?" I asked, looking toward the door that led to the hallway.

"For the food fight," the kid said. "We got called down here twenty minutes ago." He pointed to five other students, all looking nervous.

"Oh, uh, you'll be fine," I called over my shoulder as I pushed through the office door.

A moment later, Coach joined me in the vacant hallway. "Fuller, I need you to keep this tutoring deal between you and Wren."

"What?" My eyebrows shot up in surprise. Not that I planned on telling anyone—it was embarrassing enough as it was—but why was he telling me to keep it a secret?

"Sophomore year, you were out for four games with a sprained ankle, remember? The team completely tanked and we lost our shot at State."

My gaze fell to the floor. "Yes, sir. I remember." What I remembered more than missing the game was the reason why… The day before, Hudson had taken a nasty fall during recess and broken his collarbone. My head was all over the place and, at practice the next day, I took a stupid misstep during a shooting drill and twisted my ankle. All I could think about was my little brother, and it all but destroyed the entire team's season. Without their leading scorer, they didn't stand a chance.

I tried to take a deep breath but failed. I had so much riding on me, it felt like an elephant sat on my chest and was refusing to budge.

"Well, we can't have that happen again. If your teammates think there's even a remote chance that you won't be playing in the season opener, it will give everyone a complex and could very well cost us the game and the championship.

Not to mention the fact that, if we lose a game or two, your chances at a full ride are going to go down significantly. To top it all off, if the UGA coach comes to watch you and you're riding the bench... Well, you can only imagine how that will look, right?"

"I'll keep it to myself, sir." Disappointment seeped into my core. For someone who was used to feeling like the king of the court, I suddenly had plummeted to feeling like the piece of gum stuck to the bottom of someone's shoe.

"Good. I'll speak with Wren after school." Coach placed his hand on my shoulder. "You really need to get it together, Fuller. Your entire future is on the line."

"Yes, sir." My chest constricted even more.

"Good. I'll see you at practice." He turned around and headed toward the gym, leaving me wincing from the verbal lashing.

Rubbing the back of my neck, I headed toward the library. *How could I let this happen? Failing a class? Coach and Principal Davis forcing Wren to tutor me and keep it a secret? I really screwed up...*

My eyes landed on her a moment later. She was standing beside the library doors with her back to me, digging through her book bag.

"Hey, Wren," I shouted, jogging toward her. "Wait up." *Damn, she really fills out those jeans.* I'd gone out with a girl on the track team a few times and her ass was nearly perfect. I wasn't sure how it was possible, but Wren's butt looked even better. I pictured her in the tiny shorts the track team wore.

Before I could fall any deeper into the world's most unexpected daydream, Wren spun around. She didn't say anything, but the way her eyes narrowed in on me, I could tell she was still plenty angry.

I grinned, trying to cover up how embarrassed I felt, and did my best impersonation of Principal Davis. "You were throwing food, too. Were you not?"

Instead of making her laugh, Wren put her hands on her hips. "Can we just get this over with?"

Catching movement out of the corner of my eye, I waited for a freshman to walk by us.

"Hey, u-uh, Fuller," the kid stammered. "Gonna take us to a state championship again?"

"You know it," I responded. The confidence in my voice masked the reality of riding the bench for the season. I kept smiling until he turned around and disappeared around a corner.

Even though I felt like a total loser, I had to keep up the charade. I needed to lay it on even thicker. "Come on, Wren. I promise to be a good student. If I'm not, I'll let you punish me." I winked at her.

"You're disgusting." Wren's face turned beet red, but not in the same way as the group of junior girls who waited around my locker every morning. Instead of wanting to rip off my clothes like my basketball groupies, she looked like she wanted to sock me in the face.

I had to admit, it was intriguing.

"If you're going to be my tutor, you might want to consider being a little bit nicer to me." I caught a whiff of her shampoo. She smelled like some kind of tropical flower. I imagined her prancing across the beach in a bikini, her long legs pumping and her feet flicking up sand. *Earth to Fuller. Knock it off!*

What had gotten into me? Was I sick? Had the possibility of getting kicked off the team made me delusional? Whatever it was, I needed to squash it. There was no way I'd ever crush on Wren. We had too much history and not the kind that anyone wanted to relive.

She scowled.

"It's not going to be that bad." I cocked my head to the

side and raised an eyebrow. "Plus, that punishment offer still stands."

"Punishment offer? You mean like how Zack Denver punished you on the court last year? He scored on you what, seven times before the first half of the season opener?" She didn't blink as she threw the statistic at me like nothing. "Or, punish as in when Nathan Dixon beat your free throw percentage by twenty-five points in the Sportsplex Summer Tournament?"

My eyebrows shot up in disbelief. "Seriously?"

"Did I stutter?" She drummed her fingers on her opposite arm.

Heat blasted up my neck. I wish I'd had some stats to throw back at her, but I didn't know anything about cross-country, and they certainly didn't hand out percentages for the number of books read in one sitting.

"Let's head to the library and get this over with," Wren said, spinning on her heel and leaving me in the middle of the hallway.

I stood there watching her stomp away in disgust.

"Dude, what was that?"

I spun around, making eye contact with Marc. His shirt was still stained from the mashed potatoes Wren had launched at him during lunch.

"Did you get called into Principal Davis's office?" I asked, trying to change the subject.

Marc chuckled. "Yeah, two days' detention. I get to serve them during lunch, though, so I don't have to miss practice. He showed me the video. I totally nailed that freshman with applesauce. Seriously, I wanted to ask him to email me a copy." He glanced over my shoulder, his eyebrows furrowing in confusion. "Anyways, why are you talking to Wren Carter? That girl hates you."

I turned around as Wren yanked open the large wooden

library doors and stormed inside.

"I'm not talking to her," I said defensively. Coach's words echoed in my ears, reminding me I needed to keep this a secret.

Marc jutted his chin out. "I totally heard you tell her she could punish you. Look, I know you and Marissa are on the outs, but how did you go from Haleigh and Lyla to Wrentainer?"

Before I could say anything, the library door flew back open and Wren stuck her head out and snapped, "Are you coming or—" She stopped talking when her eyes landed on Marc. Without another word, she disappeared back into the library.

"Ah, yeah. One second." My heart slammed in my chest as Marc's eyes narrowed in on mine. I hated lying to my teammate and one of my best friends.

"For real, are you seriously trying to hook up with her?" Marc asked, his left eyebrow raised. "Because she sounds like she wants to rip you a new one."

"She's totally into me," I lied. "And she's kinda hot." *At least that part is true.* The words tumbled out with ease.

"What?" Marc asked. "Who are you and what did you do with Fuller James? You do know that we're talking about Wrentainer, right? The same girl who spit her retainer at me in seventh grade?"

While I didn't correct him, I never had to lie about hooking up with girls before. In fact, I never had to even try when it came to the opposite sex. Well, except with Wren. But it wasn't like I'd ever tried to win her over.

"Hello?" Marc asked, waving his hands in front of my face. "Earth to Fuller."

Straightening up, I pushed back my shoulders and cracked my neck. "My bad, I'm, ah, thinking about practice."

"Okay, but don't change the subject," he persisted.

"What's the deal with you and Wren?"

I shrugged, trying to make what I was about to say as nonchalant as possible. "We have study hall together, so I figured after she did my math homework, I'd give her some one-on-one Fuller time. Maybe break in that AV room in the back. Come on, she's a hot nerd who's never even had a boyfriend." I clicked my tongue and winked. "We'll be making those stacks shake in no time." The words came out before I could stop myself, and I immediately regretted them. Even though I was being a complete dick, I desperately needed Marc to buy my excuse to hang out with Wren.

"You are so full of it," Marc responded.

Puffing out my chest, I stood my ground. "What, you don't believe me?"

"Nope," my teammate responded, shaking his head. "There's no way you'd go after a girl like Wren. Plus, she literally hates you."

I could feel my heartbeat ringing in my ears. "All right then, I'll prove it."

"Prove that Wren Carter actually likes you?" Marc asked. "How?"

"I bet you that by our first game, Wren Carter will be in the stands cheering for me."

No, no, no. Stop it! What are you doing?

Marc rolled his eyes. "She's always in the stands. That girl loves basketball more than ninety-nine percent of the kids at this school."

"Okay, okay," I said, realizing how deep I'd dug this hole. "I bet she'll show up at the first game as my girlfriend." *Girlfriend?* Why was I making things impossible for myself? "I'll dump her in the parking lot afterward. Your consequence for losing the bet is to pick up the pieces and convince her to go to the Fall Harvest Dance with you."

My chest tightened as the words left my mouth. Sure, I

could be a cocky jerk, but I'd never do something like that to her—or anyone. *Then why the heck did you just say it?*

"You're brutal," Marc said with a chuckle.

I laughed, trying not to let my friend in on the fact that I was lying. "*And* you have to give me your *Deadpool* comic book collection."

Marc tilted his head to the side. "Now you're bringing Hudson into this?"

"He loves *Deadpool* and you know it." Even though the bet was a terrible idea, I thought about the massive smile the comic books would bring to my little brother's face. He always wanted to be like the superhero who could withstand any type of injury. With his diagnosis, it made sense.

"Are you chickening out?" I asked, desperate for him to back off. He loved his comic book collection. There's no way he'd risk it and go through with this stupid bet.

"No way; this bet is too easy to walk away from. It is so on," Marc said.

My chest constricted so tight I could barely breathe.

"But," he continued, "getting her to show up as your girlfriend… You could totally fake that, and I'm not giving up my *Deadpool* comics that easily."

I cleared my throat and tried to appear nonchalant. "Okay, what do you have in mind?"

"I'm thinking three things. First, prove that you two are hooking up. A picture will work. Nothing graphic, 'cause I don't want to see all of that. Second, there needs to be some kind of public display of affection. I need to witness it, or it doesn't count. Otherwise, how will I know you're really going through with everything? Three, she needs to show up at the game as your girlfriend. As in, wearing your letterman jacket, the whole nine yards."

I gulped. I was totally going to lose this bet. I said a silent prayer that the consequence wouldn't be something I couldn't handle.

"If, or should I say, *when* you lose, you'll have to wear Ryan's Halloween costume from last year to school for picture day or until you get sent to Principal Davis's office." Marc grinned. "Sound good?"

Shit, shit, shit! It's not too late. Fall on your sword! I repeat, fall on your sword! Coach will get over you spilling the beans.

"Unless you're the one chickening out?" He arched an eyebrow.

"The mesh wrestling singlet?" I asked, mentally recalling the costume. "That thing is made for a ten-year-old." That singlet left nothing to the imagination. I was confident, but was I *that* confident? Wren would totally freak out if she saw me wearing it.

Hmmm… That might actually work in my favor.

Before I could get lost down that rabbit hole, Marc cleared his throat. "Do we have a deal or are you ready to admit you're full of it?" Marc grinned, holding out his hand.

Before I could stop myself, I grabbed his hand and shook it. "It's a deal."

Chapter Three

Wren

Fuller sat across the table from me. He'd emptied out his backpack and surprise, surprise, he didn't have his copy of *The Hate U Give.* All he had was his laptop and a notebook. He literally didn't even have a pen or pencil. "Where's your book?"

He shrugged and grinned. "I must have left it at home. Hey, how did you know all of those statistics off the top of your head?"

"I'm good with numbers, and I really like basketball." My admission was simple, but Fuller still looked at me like I'd just solved one of the Navier-Stokes Equations.

The library was quiet. Besides us, the only other person in there was Mrs. Parsons, the librarian. She'd won some kind of grant and was unloading a huge box of new books. I'd even helped her select some of them. She knew how much I loved reading and asked for my input on new material from time to time.

"Anyway," I said, "do you want to go grab an extra book from Mrs. Brewster's classroom?"

"Nah, let's share yours." He didn't wait for an objection; instead, he got up from the table and made his way to my side.

I flinched as his leg bumped into mine. "Can you watch what you're doing?"

"My bad." Fuller pushed his dark hair off his face. His deep blue eyes locked with mine and refused to budge. "You really don't like me, huh?" He offered a lopsided smile, but it faltered.

"Not particularly." I wanted to say so much more, but the words refused to come out. Fuller James was literally the last person I'd ever choose to spend time with. He all but ruined my life five years ago, he walked around the halls of Magnolia Valley High like he was untouchable, and he never had to face any real consequences for acting like an arrogant jerk. He was always getting a free pass from one of our teachers or even the principal. Today was probably the only time he'd ever been forced to do something he didn't want to while in the halls of our school.

"Ouch." He held his hands to his chest and grimaced. "That hurt." But instead of being serious, he laughed it off. Everything was a joke to him and his dumb friends. "Now, what do I need to do to get you to write my paper?"

"I knew this was a stupid idea. I'd rather take the suspension and lose my spot at STEM camp." I picked up my backpack and slung it over my shoulder.

Fuller's cheeks turned dark red and his mouth opened, but nothing came out. For the first time since getting beat by our rivals last year, he actually looked shocked. "I was just kidding, Wren. Hold up."

Mrs. Parsons looked over at us and held a finger to her lips. "This is the library, not the playground."

I expected Fuller to burst out laughing at the notion

that we were behaving like we were at a playground, but he immediately stopped talking. It didn't matter though; I'd had enough.

Fuller caught up to me and held out his hands. "Wait, Wren," he whispered. "Don't go. Please." His voice had a slight quaver.

Crossing my arms over my chest, I shook my head. "Why not? You're just going to treat this like a joke. Why should I waste my time working with you?"

"I'm sorry. I was just joking around." Fuller dropped his gaze, his eyes actually looking remorseful. "I didn't think," Fuller said, his dark lashes sweeping up. "Please stay."

I stood with my feet planted but remained silent. I really didn't want a suspension or detention on my permanent record. More importantly, I really wanted to go to STEM camp. I'd won a spot there due to my grades and a heartfelt essay. There was no way my parents could afford the hefty seven-hundred-dollar price tag otherwise. Plus, everyone who got into the camp was awarded a certificate for four free science textbooks at college next year. That was worth at least four hundred dollars.

"Wren?"

"Fine." The hesitation in my voice was unmistakable. "But only if you take this seriously."

"I promise." His tone had completely transformed. He sounded sincere.

"If that changes, I'm out." I sat back down at the table. "For real." I didn't need to waste my time on a dumb jock, but I'd seen a different side of him in the library. Maybe there was more than met the eye when it came to Fuller James?

He nodded. "Understood."

I pulled out my laptop and binder. "All right. First question…have you read the book?"

Fuller winced.

Surprise, surprise. "I'll take that as a no. Break it up into chunks. Take nine chapters tonight and tomorrow, and eight on Thursday. You'll obviously need to turn in your topic before then, but if you get the majority of the reading done, I'll help you. Deal?"

"I'll do my best." Fuller's voice didn't sound nearly as confident as it had a few minutes ago.

"To get you started, I want you to think about these themes as you're reading." I paused and waited for Fuller to get out his laptop. "Racism and police brutality, the importance community plays in one's upbringing, dueling identities, and racial injustice."

His fingers moved over the keyboard painfully slowly. Waiting for him to finish, my gaze drifted to his muscular biceps. According to two sophomore girls who sat behind me at lunch, Fuller worked out constantly. He allegedly spent hours before and after school lifting weights, running, and shooting free throws. Whatever he was doing, it was obviously working.

"Okay, got it." Fuller looked up and caught me staring. The corners of his lips twitched, but he didn't say anything.

Heat crept up the back of my neck and pooled in my cheeks. Luckily, before I could die of embarrassment, Fuller's phone buzzed.

He looked down to check it. He didn't even worry that Mrs. Parsons would see him and take it away. His brazen confidence was beyond irritating.

"Okay, well, I'm going to get started on my apology note to Mr. Tillson and Miss Constance, and then I've got to tackle my Calculus homework. There's really nothing more I can help you with until you do some of the reading." I reached into my backpack and pulled out a notebook and my calculator. If I could get the letter and my homework done before the bell rang, I'd have time to go for a long run when I got home from school. After getting dragged into the principal's office and being forced to deal with Fuller this afternoon, I'd need it to blow off some steam.

Fuller's jaw dropped.

"What? Did you want me to sit here with you and read the book out loud?"

Recoiling, Fuller's eyebrows knit together. "Fair enough."

"Remember, nine chapters tonight." I softened my tone and paused, mentally reflecting on his time-consuming workout schedule. "But, if you're short on time or too tired, I recommend checking out the audiobook. You can listen to it on your phone or your laptop. Mrs. Parsons can help get you set up and you can start listening to it now."

Fuller's eyes lit up. "Really?"

"Yeah, I listen to books all the time. Especially during training and cross-country season. Helps pass the time during long runs." What I didn't tell him was that I started listening to them in seventh grade, after Marissa stopped talking to me and Fuller's nickname for me had stuck.

I escaped into those books for hours on end. Getting lost in new worlds, falling in love with shapeshifters, and wishing I could go back in time, become a vampire, or somehow magically escape into the pages.

With a fresh reminder of Fuller's obnoxious ways, I closed my laptop and shoved it into my backpack. "Anyway, like I said, I'm going to get started on my homework. Somehow the first five problems aren't legible anymore. They're covered in lettuce and ranch."

Fuller flinched. "Yeah, sorry about that."

I didn't respond. What could I say? It wasn't like I forgave him. Plus, I still had to track down someone from Calculus to copy today's notes.

"Okay, well, I'm going to go check on the audiobook situation. Thanks for telling me about that. I'm not the fastest reader. If I'm lucky, I might even be able to get a chapter in before practice." Fuller packed up and headed over to the librarian's desk. "See you here tomorrow?"

"All right," I said, not looking up.

Thirty math problems and one box of grape and strawberry Nerds later, the bell rang. Glancing up, I was surprised to see Fuller still at the circular librarian's desk. They must have been having problems with the audiobook. Normally, I would have headed over to help, but Fuller and Mrs. Parsons could figure this one out without me.

"Hey, Wren. Can we talk for a moment?"

I spun around, coming face-to-face with my uncle.

"I think you said everything you needed to in the principal's office." I knew I sounded disrespectful, but I was angry. If I wasn't his niece, there's no way I would have gotten saddled with tutoring Fuller.

"Listen, kid. I'm sorry about earlier. I know this isn't how you want to spend your study hall, but Fuller really needs your help." He glanced over his shoulder at Fuller and Mrs. Parsons. "If he gets kicked off the team, he can kiss any chances at a scholarship goodbye, and there's no way we'd be able to make it back to the state championship without him. That would really hurt him and the rest of the team, too."

I grimaced. I definitely didn't want any of the other guys on the team to have to pay for Fuller's bad grades. But it wasn't my fault he'd earned them in the first place.

"Listen, I have a favor to ask." He looked around, as if he was checking to make sure no one was listening in on our conversation.

"*Another* one?" I crossed my arms.

"This is the last one, I promise." He lowered his voice. "Can you keep this whole mandatory tutoring duty and Fuller's failing grade to yourself?"

My nose scrunched up. Why did my uncle want to keep

things so hush-hush?

"The thing is, when Fuller missed a few games before, the team took a nosedive. Even though he's a bit full of himself, the other guys really look up to him and rely on him to be their leader. If word gets out that he might not play, it could start to mess with their heads. Doubt could creep in. It could have a very negative impact on the season. Plus, the one bad grade is practically irrelevant. After working with the smartest student at Magnolia Valley High, I'm sure he'll be back up to passing in no time."

I slowly let out a deep breath.

"And…it would mean a lot to me."

My heart hammered in my chest. *Mean a lot to him? You know what would mean a lot to* me? *Never having to spend five seconds alone with Fuller James, let alone ongoing tutoring sessions! What if it takes him until graduation to boost his grade?*

"It's not like we're friends, though. What excuse do you want me to give people to explain why we're hanging out during study hall?"

A line formed on his forehead as he pressed his lips together. "Maybe just say that, since you're in the same class, you're just doing your homework together?"

"Like people will believe that," I scoffed.

"Please, Wren." My uncle sounded desperate.

"Fine. I'll just tell people we're working on our AP Lit papers because we have study hall at the same time. That's at least partially true." Why Fuller couldn't just switch to regular senior Lit was beyond me. I felt a bit guilty, but it wasn't my fault he was struggling in an AP class. I mean, I'm not good at riding a skateboard, therefore, I wouldn't try out for the World Roller Games.

I know my strengths and my weaknesses. Fuller the jock should know his, too.

"Thanks, sweetheart. You're the best," my uncle said with a smile. He checked his watch. "I better head to the gym and get ready for practice. Thanks again, Wren."

After he left, I stood still for several seconds. Did I just agree to keep a secret on Fuller's behalf? All so the boys' basketball team wouldn't have a complex over their star player getting benched?

Sure, he averaged twenty-five points a game, but so what? Why couldn't TyShaun or Marc step it up? They weren't as skilled with the ball as Fuller, but between the two of them, they should be able to improve their averages this season.

Before I could pick apart what had just happened, I felt the familiar buzz of my phone from the back of my book bag.

Seeing as school hours were over and we could use our phones without getting into trouble, I unzipped my backpack and unlocked the screen.

Dae: Meet me in the hallway.

Me: Which one?

Dae: Outside the library.

I slipped my backpack straps over my shoulders and headed out into the hallway. Dae stood on the other side with his arms crossed.

"What's up?" I couldn't hide the surprise in my voice. "How did you know I was in there and not study hall?"

"Got out of class a few minutes early and saw you in there with—"

"Hey, Dae." Two junior girls walked by, batting their eyelashes at him.

"Hey." He smiled politely but turned his attention back toward me immediately.

"But Dae." I did my best to imitate the girls. "Pay

attention to us."

Hot, but down-to-earth and not interested in being part of the popular crew, Dae had a lot of admirers at our school. But, after having his heart trampled last summer by his ex-girlfriend, Eva, he'd sworn off dating anyone new until he got to college.

"Yeah, yeah. Very funny. But seriously," Dae said, lowering his voice, "not the important part of this conversation. Why in the world were you sitting next to F.B.M. in the library?" He looked like he'd just downed a large gulp of sour milk. "Have you lost your mind? Do you need me to take you to the hospital or something?"

"Oh, um, I..." The hallway buzzed with students, including a group of sophomore guys who all had their phones out. One of them narrowly missed an open locker.

"Hello? Earth to Wren? Why were you with Fuller James?" Dae waved his hand in front of my face.

"Not here. Let's talk in the car." I wasn't sure how to handle what had just happened with my uncle. Everyone in school knew I detested Fuller. How was I going to explain hanging out with him during our last period if I didn't tell the truth? Also, how would I put up with him one-on-one for an hour a day?

Not only had he given me the world's worst nickname, he'd dated Marissa on and off since seventh grade. I knew he wasn't responsible for turning my best friend against me, but he hadn't exactly helped the situation. He was the reason I'd given up on being friends with girls after Marissa, Courtney, and practically every other girl in my class started making fun of me. I couldn't trust that my own gender wouldn't throw me under the bus the next time a guy like Fuller James gave them the opportunity.

I shook my head and cursed myself for getting in that stupid food fight. Spending time with Fuller was like a constant reminder of how, in a single night, I'd become the laughingstock of our middle school and lost my best friend.

On top of having to lie and being forced to work with Fuller, I thought about the extra time I'd have to spend doing homework every night, since my study hall had been hijacked. I could handle it, but it was more than annoying.

Dae and I walked side by side as we made our way through the crowded hall and into the crisp fall air. The leaves had started to change, and the towering oak and maple trees on the mountains surrounding our school had transformed from serene greens to vibrant reds, yellows, and oranges. Thankful for the unspoken understanding that came from being best friends for five years, I walked next to Dae in silence until we got to my car.

"Okay, spill it."

I inserted the key in the ignition and exhaled slowly.

Dae shook his head. "Spill. It."

I knew I had just promised my uncle that I wasn't going to tell anyone, but Dae wasn't just anyone. He'd keep my secret. "So, you know how when you were meeting with Mr. Norman during lunch, there was that food fight? Well, I kind of lost it..."

"Yeah." Dae's voice was laden with confusion. "You texted me and told me that you nailed Marc with the mashed potatoes. Which I'm sure he totally deserved. But what does that have to do with Fuller?"

"Principal Davis called Fuller and me into his office after AP Lit. He had video of me chucking mashed potatoes at Fuller but accidentally hitting Marc." Saying the words aloud made me realize how childish the entire situation was and how easy it would have been to avoid.

"Uh-oh."

Even though the car was in park, I gripped the steering wheel. "He gave me an ultimatum. Suspension and detention, which would mean losing my spot at STEM camp, or…"

"Or what?" Dae turned toward me, his dark brown eyes not leaving my face.

"Before I tell you, you've got to promise not to tell anyone else about this, Dae. I mean it, I haven't even told Brandon yet." I released the wheel and cracked my knuckles.

"Promise. Now what's going on?"

"I could face suspension, detention, and missing STEM camp, or tutor Fuller James." As the words left my lips, my gaze fell on Marissa and Courtney getting into Marissa's car. Last year, when she'd gotten her license, her parents had surprised her with a BMW convertible. Sure, a few kids at our school drove really nice cars, but with Marissa, she was constantly shoving it in everyone's face and making fun of classmates who drove old beaters. She was the epitome of spoiled rotten.

"Wait, what?" Dae shook his head. "Either get suspended or tutor Fuller? That's complete crap."

Marissa peeled out of her parking spot and sped off toward the exit, her blond hair flying in the air behind her.

"Tell me about it. To make it worse, my uncle was in the principal's office with us. He totally guilt-tripped me. If Fuller doesn't play, the team is going to pay the price and their chances of winning State practically disappear." Saying his name left a bitter taste in my mouth. "There was no way I could say no with him in there." I crossed my arms over my chest. "So, yeah. I had to decide between detention and suspension or tutoring Fuller until he brings his grade up."

"Wow…" Dae sat in the passenger's seat, looking at a complete loss for words.

"And there's more." I frowned. "My uncle doesn't want me to tell anyone."

"Keep the tutoring sessions secret? Why?" Dae asked.

"He doesn't want the other guys on the team getting

psyched out about the possibility of their star player riding the bench or even getting kicked off the team. He said it could cost Fuller and some of the other guys a scholarship." Thanks to my grandpa, I loved watching basketball, especially our high school team, and I certainly didn't want to do anything that would hurt the other guys… But, when it came down to it, did I love it enough to put up with Fuller James?

"Wow…" Dae's dark brown eyes met mine. "That's… To be honest, I don't even know what to say."

"I know, right? It's totally not fair. I mean, I know I shouldn't have thrown the mashed potatoes, but Fuller and his teammates, minus Brandon, are always pulling stupid crap like that, and they never get in trouble. At least, not real trouble. I do it once and *bam*! I'm stuck deciding if I want a permanent mark on my record and screwing STEM camp, or tutoring the most arrogant boy in the entire school. Not to mention, the person responsible for giving me the worst nickname ever. I mean, he hasn't even started reading *The Hate U Give*, and our topics are due in two days." My chest rose and fell dramatically. "He didn't even have a pen or a pencil with him. Who does that?"

"Take a deep breath," Dae instructed. "He's a total douche, but let's put things into perspective. What's the end goal?"

I let my head fall back against the headrest. "I have to tutor him until he brings his grade up to at least a C minus. He should be able to do that with good grades on this paper and a few assignments."

Dae grabbed my hand. "That should take only, what, like a week or two?"

"There's only a week and a half until the season opener." I closed my eyes and rubbed my face.

"That's only nine days." Dae squeezed my hand. "You can totally handle nine days."

"You're right. It's not that long." Even though it would feel like an eternity, if Fuller did the work and brought up his grade, I'd be rid of him before the first game. "As long as he brings his grade up. Otherwise, we're going to have to come up with a backup plan; there's no way I'm going to get saddled with tutoring him for the foreseeable future."

"Let's stick with the nine-day goal. That means spending forty-five minutes a day with him for nine days, so that comes to, what?" Dae stared at the ceiling of my car, attempting to solve the math problem in his head.

"Six hours and forty-five minutes," I said, letting my arms fall to my sides.

"See, that's less than seven hours. That's not even one full school day. You can totally handle that, right?"

"I guess."

"Focus on getting through it, one day at a time, and then you'll never have to talk to him again," Dae said with a smile. "Except when you're yelling at him from the stands. Plus, you and I both know that you want them to win the state championship again."

"Yeah. You're right, Dae. Thanks for the pep talk." If Fuller acted like a decent human being, I'd survive the next nine days. On the other hand, if he continued to slack off and act like a moron, there's no way he'd bring his grade up in time, and my uncle would be majorly disappointed in me.

Even worse, I'd be stuck with Fuller James for who knew how long.

Now *that* would be a nightmare.

Chapter Four

Fuller

The shrill sound from Coach's whistle echoed against the gym walls. "Warm-up time. Ten laps."

Some of the guys groaned, but I didn't care. Running around the gym helped clear my head. Which, after working with Wren today, I really needed. I'd never felt so guilty in my entire life. Making a stupid bet that could end only one way—badly.

Plus, I was still furious with myself for letting my grade slip down to an F in the first place. I could make a list of excuses, but it came down to one thing, I simply didn't have time to read everything the teachers assigned us, do all my homework, go to practice, and work out in my spare time. At least Wren had told me about those audiobook things. I'd be able to listen to the book tonight after practice.

I started out slow, the gym floor squeaking under my sneakers, but I quickly picked up the pace. Most mornings, I got up at five o'clock and ran outside for an hour before heading back to the house, showering, and going to school to shoot buckets until seven thirty. I was usually the only one in the gym at that time. It was my sanctuary.

Now I'd gone and messed everything up. My chest tightened as I thought about sitting on the bench instead of playing in the game.

A hand on my shoulder caused me to flinch. Turning around, I came face-to-face with TyShaun, who had caught up to me, taking matching strides. "You really think you're going to score with Wrentainer?"

Every muscle in my body tensed. "What did you just say?"

"You and Wrentainer? Magnolia Valley's newest couple?"

I grimaced, forcing myself to inhale and exhale slowly before responding.

"Well?" TyShaun pressed. "What happened? Did you hit your head on something last night?" He stared into my eyes. "Do you have a concussion?"

"That bet was supposed to stay between Marc and me." I picked up the pace, leaving TyShaun several steps behind me.

"Hold up, hold up." His shoes squeaked as he caught up with me. "You're telling me that you don't have some kind of head trauma? You're *actually* into her?"

My muscles started to burn as my quads and hamstrings pumped. "No head trauma. But keep your voice down." Crap. How could Marc blab about this to TyShaun? We had been friends since kindergarten. TyShaun and I were friends, too, but I didn't trust him like I did Marc.

TyShaun shook his head. "You're going after Wrentainer, but you don't want anyone to know?"

"Whatever, she's got legs for days and her face isn't bad, either. Plus, she'll help pass the time until Marissa and I get back together." My throat felt thick. I hated lying anywhere, but it was the absolute worst to lie while on the court. After all, the gym was like my church. It was practically sacrilegious to lie here. But I couldn't help myself. It had been only a few hours and I was already in too deep. Failing a class, being forced to work with Wren, the bet, what was next?

I wanted to clear the air. Tell my teammates what was really going on and promise them that I'd have it taken care of before the season started, but I'd given Coach my word. I wouldn't let him or the guys down.

That's when it dawned on me—the perfect excuse. "And she's Coach's niece. He'd definitely bench me if he found out."

TyShaun nodded. "Ah, that makes sense. All right, all right. I won't say anything to anyone else. Your somewhat disturbing secret is safe with me."

"Thanks, Ty." I hoped he was done talking about Wren, but that dream went down the toilet two seconds later. "So, you two are hooking up during study hall? In the library?" He had a big grin on his face. "That's ballsy. Even for you."

I shook my head and focused on my stride. Hopefully TyShaun would get the hint and stop asking me about Wren. The chances weren't great, though; we'd talked about previous hookups. If this wasn't a massive lie, it wouldn't be any different. While I hadn't told any of the guys on the team about it, I planned on dropping the charade next year at college. Sure, I still wanted to go out and meet girls, but I wasn't going to brag about my conquests in the locker room. It made me sound immature, and it left me feeling a little sick.

Brandon jogged past us, but he didn't seem to be paying attention. *Thank goodness.* He and Wren were close. He wouldn't hesitate to tell her the moment practice was over, and then she'd definitely refuse to work with me. I'd be royally screwed.

TyShaun raised an eyebrow. "Listen, whatever you want to do is your business. But if you're going through some kind of quarter-life crisis, let me know. We can get you help." He threw his head back and laughed. "The team would fall apart without you, bro. So you do whatever, or *whoever*, you need to in order to keep in top form."

Instead of responding, I shoved him and sprinted forward.

The rest of practice flew by. By the time Coach told us to hit the showers, I was sweaty and exhausted. I'd given it my all, like I always did, and even though I normally stayed for at least an hour afterward to shoot baskets, I had to head home and get going on my homework.

Plus, I needed to do some brainstorming and figure out a way to get out of the bet without giving up my secret or destroying my pride.

Coach blew his whistle. "Fuller, I need to talk to you for a minute."

"Yes, sir." I jogged over to him.

The rest of the guys walked by me. Marc made sure to spin around once Coach's back was to him. He mouthed "Wrentainer" and made stupid kissing motions, then burst into laughter, and TyShaun joined in.

Good thing my face was already red from practice. These two were obviously going to humiliate me every chance they got. I'd have to take it, though. I couldn't risk anyone else finding out.

"How did the tutoring session go today?" Coach's face looked pensive, like he was preparing for me to tell him Wren had already given up on me.

"Good, sir. Wren gave me several areas to focus on while brainstorming the topic for our next Lit paper. She's really smart and helpful." I might be laying it on a little thick, but every word I uttered was true. That made the guilt of the bet sting a little less.

He kept his arms planted firmly across his chest. "You know this is serious, right? If you don't bring your grade up, you're riding the bench."

"Yes, sir. I understand."

Coach gave me a curt nod. "That's all."

"Thank you, sir." I turned around and headed for the locker room.

"You aren't staying late to shoot free throws tonight?" Coach arched an eyebrow.

I shrugged. "Actually, I'm going to head home. I've got to read nine chapters of a book, or um, listen to it, and I have math homework, too."

Coach's expression softened. "I'm glad to hear you're taking this to heart, Fuller."

• • •

The scent of garlic bread floated across the kitchen table. My stomach promptly grumbled in response.

The light gray walls in the dining room were cluttered with family photos. Enshrined forever were happy trips to Yellowstone National Park and framed pictures from a vacation to Washington, D.C. My parents always insisted on taking family photos, some serious and others totally goofy, every time we went somewhere new. They had rows of homemade scrapbooks lining the bookshelves in their bedroom and offices.

"How was school today, honey?" Mom passed me a large bowl of pasta.

"Good." I scooped several heaping servings onto my plate, burying the blue flower design in the center.

My little brother giggled from across the table, his light brown eyes flashing with interest. He took after our mom in the looks department, and I took after my dad.

Clearing his throat, Dad caught Mom's gaze. "Hudson, can you do us a favor and grab the pitcher of lemonade from the refrigerator?"

He scrunched up his nose and grinned. "You're in so much trouble."

"Hudson," Mom said in a firm voice. "Lemonade, now."

Getting off his chair, his little feet hit the floor. "I know. I know. I'll take my time."

As soon as he disappeared around the corner, Mom and Dad turned toward me.

"Fuller, how could you be doing so poorly in AP Literature class? You've never failed a class before!" Mom's eyes were wide and her brow furrowed.

Of course Principal Davis would let them know... It couldn't have been a complete surprise to them. They'd been on me when my grade dropped from a B to a C and again when it went from C to a D, but I'd promised to bring it up. A promise, it turns out, that I couldn't keep.

"I—I—" Unable to come up with an excuse, I let my head fall. The homemade bunny salt-and-pepper shakers in the middle of the wooden table didn't offer any brilliant answers, so I remained quiet.

"I don't want to hear excuses. This is your only AP class." My dad frowned. "Principal Davis told us that Coach's niece will be tutoring you until you've raised your grade back up."

"Yes, sir." I struggled to get the words out. Not only were my parents upset with me, but I'd made a terrible bet that could end up hurting someone who didn't deserve it.

"We want a daily report. Details of what you covered in class, what you did in your tutoring session, and a rundown of your homework." Dad crossed his arms. He looked at me like Coach had before I left practice.

Shoulders drooping, I replied. "Yes, sir."

"You need to set a better example for your little brother."

Mom's words stung. She was right.

"Yes, ma'am."

Hudson walked back into the room with a glass pitcher balanced in between his small hands. "Are you done being disappointed in Fuller?" He pressed his lips together, trying to suppress a grin.

"Your brother is going to do much better in school," Mom said, shooting me a look that could stop a freight train in its tracks. "Isn't that right, Fuller?"

"Yes, ma'am."

Hudson poured himself a glass of lemonade. "Do you have a lot of homework tonight or can we play some Fortnite?"

Without looking, I could feel my dad's eyes burn into me.

I shook my head. "Sorry, buddy. I have a lot of reading to do. Rain check?"

His little shoulders slumped. "Okay." I hated disappointing my parents, but I hated letting my brother down even more.

After covering my pasta in Dad's homemade spaghetti sauce and adding a heaping portion of baked asparagus to my plate, I tucked into my food. Grateful for the chewing-induced silence, I ate my meal as quickly as possible.

Less than ten minutes later, I excused myself and headed up to my room with my backpack slung over my shoulder.

My bedroom walls were covered in posters of my favorite basketball players. Everyone from Michael Jordan to LeBron James. One day I wanted to be on a poster, posing in my NBA jersey, being a role model for kids across the world.

But first, homework.

I grabbed my laptop and flipped open the cover. All I needed to do was read over the themes that Wren had given me during study hall and then binge listen to the book. I figured I could do push-ups and sit-ups while listening, maybe even knock out some of my math homework.

"Crap." I frantically scrolled through my open document. My notes were nowhere to be found. Somehow they'd disappeared. *Always save your work.* My elementary school computer teacher's words rung in my head. After trying every trick I knew, I sighed in frustration. There was only one option left: ask Wren. I mean, if I didn't report back to her on the topics she'd given me, I'd be totally screwed. She'd probably march right into Principal Davis's office and demand that he suspend both of us.

I picked up my phone, but quickly realized that I didn't have her number. *Instagram, she's got to have an Instagram account.* After typing her name into the app, her account popped up. *Dang it.* It was set to private.

My finger hovered over the follow button. If anyone found out that I followed Wren, everyone in school would go nuts. *Whatever, I can follow her and then unfollow her as soon as she sends me the themes.* I tapped the blue follow button and waited. Five minutes passed, then ten, then fifteen. I checked the time and exhaled. I couldn't wait much longer. If I did, I'd have to stay up until three in the morning listening to the book.

I cursed myself for not paying better attention to Wren. I remembered racism was one of the themes, but what were the others? Something about community injustice? No, that wasn't right…

Pacing back and forth in my room, I laid out my options. Someone else could have similar notes, but would they be the same as Wren's? Probably not. If I had to spend time studying, I needed to focus on the right topics. Otherwise, it could be a massive waste of time. I could call Brandon and ask for her number, but that would bring up too many questions. I couldn't call Coach and ask him—that would all but be admitting that I hadn't taken our first tutoring session seriously.

It became painfully clear. My only option would be to go over to her house.

Assuming she still lived in the same place. I'd been in the car with Marissa before when we'd passed it; Marissa had pointed it out and laughed. The memory made my skin prickle. Marissa could be really mean when she wanted to be.

"Okay, it's no big deal. I'll head over there. Ask her in person, write them down in my phone, and head back home. I can be in and out in five minutes." The pep talk didn't leave me any more prepared for what I had to do.

Clomping down the stairs, I headed into the kitchen. "Mom, is it okay if I head over to my tutor's house to grab some notes?"

She arched an eyebrow. "Why do you need to go over there to get notes?"

"Computer glitch," I explained. My cheeks felt hot. This was not the best way to convince my parents that I was turning my AP Lit grade around. "It'll take only a few minutes."

"All right, as long as this isn't a social visit."

"A social visit? Yeah right. More like being sent to detention."

She frowned, a crease forming across her brow. "Okay, don't be out long."

"Thanks, Mom." I grabbed my keys and headed out the front door.

It took only five minutes to get to her house, a small ranch with white siding and a brick front. Purple flowers hung in baskets on either side of the bright red front door.

I got out of my car and locked the doors behind me.

"Fuller? Is that you?"

I spun around, coming face-to-face with TyShaun and his dog Bear. *Crap!* I forgot he lived in this neighborhood, too.

"What are you doing?" he asked, looking up toward the house.

"Oh, ah, I'm—" Stammering, I struggled to come up with an excuse.

A massive grin spread across his face. "Are you seriously paying Wrentainer a booty call?"

Cocking my head to the side, I shrugged. "She can't get enough of me, what can I say?" My stomach twisted into a knot as guilt settled in my stomach like a brick sinking to the bottom of a lake. I was a terrible person.

TyShaun punched me in the shoulder. "You're a dog, you know that, right?"

Bear lifted his head into the air and barked.

"You're right, Bear," TyShaun said, petting his dog's head. "He's not a dog, he's a total catfish."

My nose wrinkled. "I'm a catfish?" My mind drifted to the show where people pretended to be one thing in order to get someone to like them, but in real life, they were the complete opposite.

Well, I was pretending, but I wasn't trying to get with Wren in real life.

"Yeah, you're a bottom feeder." TyShaun burst out into laughter. "We won't keep you any longer. Go get her, champ."

Swallowing the lump in my throat, I forced a fake smile and winked. "See you tomorrow, Ty."

I'm totally going to hell.

Chapter Five

Wren

"Got it," I shouted, heading toward the front door. *Who in the world would be stopping by so late?* Dae and Brandon were the only people who ever came to hang out with me, and they were both doing homework. Mom and Dad rarely had unplanned visitors, and it certainly wasn't for Gramps.

"You've got to be kidding me." My voice came out in a whisper as I peeked through the peephole.

Thanks to Fuller's antics and my momentary lack of impulse control, my parents had sat me down at the dinner table and told me about the phone call they'd received from Principal Davis. They couldn't believe I'd participated in a food fight at school. They told me that they'd thanked Principal Davis for his leniency and promised to talk to me about the incident.

After hearing how disappointed they were and that they couldn't believe I'd risked my spot at STEM camp, I wanted to disappear into my room and never come out. Luckily, since it was the first time I'd ever gotten into trouble, they didn't ground me.

The doorbell rang for a second time.

"Wren? Can you get the door?" My mom's voice called out from the office. "I'm in the middle of something for work."

"Yeah, I got it." I grabbed the brass handle and swung open the door. "Geez! Impatient much?"

Fuller stood on the other side. He shifted his weight from his right to left foot. His shoulders were slumped and there was a slight crease across his forehead. He didn't say anything, instead, he simply stood there, looking back at me. Behind him, the sun had set, but streaks of orange were still visible over the mountains.

"Why are you here?" The words came out sharper than I intended.

"Oh, um, well, I went to look over the themes you told me to pay attention to while I was listening to the book tonight and something happened to the document. Somehow I lost all the notes."

Grabbing the themes wasn't a big deal, but watching Fuller squirm on my porch was beyond worthwhile. So, instead of inviting him in, I decided to push it even further. "Didn't you save it?"

He opened his mouth but then closed it and shook his head. "I thought if I stopped over here that I could, I mean, that you could tell me them again and I could text them to myself? That way I won't lose them."

"Wren, who's your friend?"

I spun around and practically bumped into Gramps.

"Hey, wait. Is that Fuller James? The best player Magnolia Valley High has seen in over two decades?"

Instantly straightening up, Fuller puffed out his chest and grinned broadly. "Yes, sir. At your service."

Gramps looked at me, his blue eyes wide with excitement.

"Ah, yeah, Gramps. This is Fuller. We have a class together and he needs a copy of my Lit notes." I turned toward Fuller. "I'll be right back."

I started to close the door, but Gramps put his hand out and stopped it from shutting. "Aren't you going to invite your friend in?"

"Yeah, Wren. Aren't you going to invite me in?" Fuller arched an eyebrow and gave me a wry smile. He was obviously doing it to spite me.

"Fuller, would you like to come in?" My jaw clenched, and the words came out clipped. The last thing I wanted to do was invite him into our house.

"That would be great, thanks." He pushed his hair back with his hand.

He'd gone from sad sack to Mr. Cocky in less than a minute.

Gramps led Fuller to our kitchen table and offered him a glass of sweet tea.

"Here, use some of this," I said, handing Fuller a bottle of hand sanitizer. "Gramps is getting over a bad cold."

He rubbed his hands together and flapped them in the air for a few seconds before sitting down.

The circular oak table stood in a small nook off the kitchen. There were paintings of the Appalachian Mountains on the walls and a wooden sign that read, "Carter Family." I'd made it with my mom at a painting party last year. While it wasn't the most artistic thing ever, the memories of making it together were beyond special.

Fuller looked at me and then Gramps. "You have a very nice house."

"Why, thank you, son. Wren's mom and dad have really made this place a lovely home." Gramps smiled, the corners of his eyes crinkling.

I prayed that Fuller hadn't seen the parade of school

pictures my parents displayed on the hallway wall. I'd gone through some super awkward phases, including the time in kindergarten when I'd cut my own bangs. They were so short, they literally stuck straight out in the photo. Dae and Brandon still gave me crap about that picture. That was okay, though, because I'd seen their school pictures, and third grade wasn't very kind to them, either.

"I'll get the sweet tea." I pulled out a chair for my grandfather. "Why don't you two talk basketball for a while?"

That's all it took for them to start trading stats from their favorite players and who they thought would win the NBA championship this year. I hadn't heard Gramps this lucid while talking to a stranger in a long time. My heart melted as I stood in the doorway and listened to them. Gramps let out a few chuckles and recalled facts that I thought he'd lost for good. Fuller's arrogance had completely dissipated and had been replaced with someone who appeared gentle and caring.

Brandon mentioned something to me once about Fuller's little brother being in the hospital a lot. Maybe he was better with little kids and grandparents than he was with people his own age.

I set down two glasses of chilled raspberry tea. "Here you go. I'm going to grab something for Fuller. I'll be right back." My voice had lost its edge. Seeing Gramps so happy had made my night.

Gramps nodded and then turned his attention back to Fuller. "So, who's your favorite player?"

I raced to my room and grabbed my laptop. Flipping the top, I quickly pulled up the document I'd been working on during study hall. Gramps was doing okay right now, but I knew better than anyone that that could change any moment. Over the past twenty-four months, he'd gone from living independently to moving in with my family. My dad worked from home and was able to keep an eye on him during the day. Mom and I usually took over at night, making sure Gramps had everything he needed. Recently, I found myself waking up between two and three in the morning to the television blaring in the family room, Gramps cursing the remote for not working. I'd usually put on ESPN or an old basketball game and curl up on the couch as he dozed in his favorite recliner.

My mom would ask time and time again why I didn't wake her. He was her dad, and she wanted to take care of him. I always had the same rebuttal. She had a job to go to the next morning. I could always take a nap after school if I was feeling tired.

I emailed the document to myself and shut my laptop. I could forward it to Fuller. That would be the quickest way to get him out of the house.

As I came around the corner, I heard Gramps ask Fuller, "Who's your favorite player?"

Fuller's brow furrowed. "It's a tie between Michael Jordan and LeBron James."

"Ah, those are two great players. I like Stephen Curry the best. But, that Charles Barkley, he was really something in his day." Gramps chuckled. "He's got a big personality too. Big Chuck."

I placed my hand gently on his shoulder. "Hey, Gramps. I hate to break up the fun, but Fuller has to go."

"Oh, I can stay—"

I shot Fuller a look that could sink a ship. He froze for several seconds before standing. "Wren's right. I have a lot of homework and should get going. It was very nice meeting you, sir. I hope to see you in the stands during the upcoming season."

"Oh, do you play basketball?" Gramps asked. His face was serene, completely unaware that he had known who

Fuller was only a few minutes ago.

"Um, yes, sir."

Fuller's manners caught me off guard.

"It was nice meeting you, sir."

"You, too." Gramps picked up his iced tea and took a long swig. "Have a good night, kids."

Fuller followed me outside. He remained silent as I closed the door behind us.

"What's your email?" I held my phone in my hands and waited.

As he rattled off his school email address, I typed it into my phone. When he was done, I pressed send.

"Okay, I sent you an email with the themes. Check and make sure it came through."

Fuller reached for his phone. "Oh… I um, I don't have my school email on here. I check it only from my laptop."

Of course you don't.

He raked his teeth over his lower lip. "Is there any way you could text it to me?"

Even though the sky was dark, I could see Fuller's cheeks turn a deep shade of pink. He stole a glance over his shoulder, scanning the street.

I turned my gaze in his direction. *What is he looking at?*

I copied the themes from my email and then opened up my messenger app. "Yeah, what's your number?"

My fingers flew across the screen as he rattled off a series of digits. A few seconds later, the text went through.

"Got it." He slid his phone back into his pocket and checked over his shoulder again.

The realization hit me like an anvil falling from the sky in an old-time cartoon. "Are you that embarrassed to be standing in my driveway?" The words tumbled out of my lips before I had time to weigh the consequences.

Fuller held up his hands. "No, no, not at all."

"Then why do you keep looking behind you? Are you afraid someone's going to see you and tell your friends that you're hanging out with Wrentainer?" My chest rose and fell as anger coiled in my stomach.

He opened his mouth to respond, but nothing came out.

Figures. I rolled my eyes. "Whatever, Fuller. I've got to go. I'll see you tomorrow."

"Wren, wait."

But I didn't. Instead, I turned around, went back into the house, and slammed the door behind me. *Ugh, I can't believe I had to spend another*—I checked my phone for the time—*fifteen minutes with that jerk. I should start charging him overtime.*

Yeah right, like any amount of money would ever make up for being forced to tutor Fuller James.

"Hey, Wren. Who were you talking to outside?"

I linked my arm around my grandpa's and walked him back to the kitchen table. "No one, Gramps. Let's finish our iced tea."

Chapter Six

Fuller

"Did you do the reading last night?" Wren grabbed a small bottle of hand sanitizer that was connected to her backpack and squirted some in her hands.

I flinched. Wren's voice was void of emotion and interest. She was clearly still pissed at me. I couldn't tell her the real reason I was looking over my shoulder last night, that I was on the lookout for TyShaun, who knew about the stupid bet I'd made with Marc. Ugh.

I hated that TyShaun had probably already told Marc about my visit to Wren's. Shoot, I should have told him to take a picture. That might have counted as proof for the first part of my bet… No. Screw that. I needed to find a way out of the bet, not figure out how to fulfill it.

Plus, there's no way Marc would accept a picture of me standing in her driveway. He wanted proof that Wren and I were hooking up. I swallowed the lump in my throat. No how, no way, would that picture *ever* happen. This situation sucked, and I was the only one to blame. And I hated myself for it.

"Um, Fuller?" Wren drummed her fingers on the table. "Did you do the reading last night?"

"Yeah, sorry. I got a lot done. Thanks for the audiobook tip." I couldn't believe no one had ever told me about audiobooks before. It made getting through the reading assignments ten times easier. Plus, I could multitask, could shoot hoops or run while listening.

I'd actually borrowed Hudson's library card and logged on to the public library's website last night. In five minutes, I'd downloaded the audiobook of LeBron James's biography and placed my name on the waiting list for Angie Thomas's second book, *On the Come Up.* What would my teammates think if they found out that I was listening to books that weren't assigned by a teacher? "Fuller the Jock" becomes "Fuller the Nerd." A small smile played on my lips.

"You're welcome." Wren sat across from me with her arms folded over her chest. Her eyes refused to meet mine.

"Listen, about last night… I tried following you on Instagram," I started, unsure of where to take the conversation. "You didn't accept me—"

She held her hands up, cutting me off. "I don't want to hear any stupid excuses. You were obviously embarrassed to be at my house last night. It's not like I expected anything different. You're Fuller James, Homecoming King and captain of the basketball team. Why would you want to be seen with *Wrentainer*?"

She emphasized the terrible nickname. It wasn't that she was putting herself down, but pointing out that others, including me, had done it countless times. I frowned as a queasy feeling settled in my stomach. "I know that's what it looked like, but I promise you, that's not what happened."

Wren's knuckles turned white, and she hugged her body

tighter. "Whatever, it's not like I wanted you there, either."

Ouch. That stung.

I wasn't trying to get with Wren or anything, but her hatred for me was a stark reminder of the consequences of acting like a cocky asshole. "I swear to you, Wren. Last night may have looked bad, but it's not what you think." *Not that I can tell you* why *it's not what you think, but it isn't…*

She didn't respond.

Clearing my throat, I tried to change the subject. "I really liked meeting your grandpa. He seems like a great guy. He sure loves basketball, huh?" Her body tensed even more as soon as I mentioned him.

She didn't answer. Instead, she just looked away.

"How long has he been living with your family?"

She inhaled slowly. "Two years."

"He seems really happy." I wasn't sure if that was the right thing to say, but I was being honest with Wren, and it felt good.

"He is, most of the time." Her voice got softer. "Sometimes he has…episodes. It can be pretty tough to calm him down."

Her honesty reverberated through me. "That sounds difficult."

"It can be, but there isn't another option. We're not going to send him to a nursing home. Not when he's happy and safe living with us. I know one day…" She paused. "One day that will probably be the reality, but for now, he's staying with us."

We sat in silence for several minutes.

"I-I know what it's like. To live with someone who's sick," I said quietly.

Wren's expression softened.

I certainly didn't plan on baring my soul to her, but I felt safe, and deep down, I knew she wouldn't tell anyone. "My little brother, he's got a condition. It's called brittle bone disease. He's extra susceptible to getting hurt." Saying the words out loud felt freeing. Besides Marc, I didn't talk about Hudson with anyone else. Well, I'd told Marissa once, but she'd somehow turned the conversation around and made it about her.

Even though I didn't know Wren well, I already knew she would never do that or blab about it to half the school. "I don't have a lot of free time, but when I do, I spend most of it with him."

Wren's sympathetic hazel eyes locked onto mine. "That must be really tough. For him, I mean."

"He's a good kid. He's got a great sense of humor, too. It's gotten him through a lot of rough times. The hardest thing is when people find out that he's my brother, but they don't know about his medical condition. They all assume he's a basketball prodigy. When he tells them that he doesn't play sports, things can get..." I trailed off. "Well, let me put it this way, most people these days don't have any manners or common decency."

Wren finally let her arms fall from her chest. "That sucks."

"Yeah, but he's developed a thick skin when it comes to stupid people and their comments. I think being a huge fan of Deadpool has helped."

Wren chuckled. "Deadpool? Shouldn't he be more into Spider-Man or Thor? Something a little more kid-friendly?"

Was she a Marvel fan? I wondered if she was just into the movies or if she was hardcore and into the comics. "Eh, not really, but my parents got over it once they saw the positive impact it was having on him."

"That's pretty cool," Wren responded. "I'm a big superhero fan. Marvel, DC, you name it and I've read the comics and probably watched it."

"Yeah, Deadpool is indestructible and he doesn't give a crap what anyone else thinks of him. Sometimes Hudson calls me Weasel." I grinned.

"Weasel as in the bartender?" Wren asked.

"Yeah, he says I'm the guy he can tell all his problems to." A warm sensation surged through my heart. "The best part, though, is that he has a new favorite song. It's from the first movie, and he's obsessed with it."

Wren bit her lower lip and smiled. "I'm afraid to ask."

"'Shoop' by Salt-N-Pepa." I closed my eyes and laughed. "You should hear him rapping it. It's hilarious."

"He's got good taste in music." A chuckle escaped Wren's lips, but she quickly brought her hand to her mouth, quelling the proof that she might have actually been enjoying talking to me.

We sat in silence for a few seconds, both of us still smiling. "I meant it, though, what I said earlier about meeting your grandpa. He seems like a great guy."

Wren didn't respond. She got this faraway look in her eyes. Then she reached up and tucked a strand of hair behind her ear.

"Does he have…um, memory issues?"

Her head moved up and down slowly. I felt myself pulled into her eyes, warm pools of emerald with flecks of gold. Why hadn't I noticed how pretty her eyes were before? Had they changed colors? I swear they were a light brown earlier. We'd learned about eye color during a genetics lesson in biology, that they had something to do with incomplete dominance. Either way, Wren's eyes either looked different colors in different lighting or they straight-up changed color.

"My great-aunt has Alzheimer's disease. She lives in a memory care facility now." Shocked by my own openness, I continued to talk. "It was really hard on the family, but it's the safest place for her."

Wren looked down at the table. "My grandma died three years ago. Gramps started forgetting little things shortly after that. We went from having him over for NBA games and dinner every night to moving him into our spare bedroom in just under six months."

"That's a lot to take on."

She shrugged. "When things get tough, you have two options. Pass the buck or stand up to the plate and go to bat for the person you love. The decision was simple."

Wow. I had no idea what Wren dealt with on a daily basis. To make it worse, she had to deal with our classmates bullying her. The night we'd stood on the dance floor five years ago came crashing back. I felt like such an asshole. If I hadn't uttered Marissa's nickname for Wren so loudly, it might never have caught on. Or, maybe if I hadn't been such a jerk, I could have told Marissa and my friends to stop calling her Wrentainer. But no, I was too worried about maintaining my popular status.

It felt like a ton of bricks had been dropped on my chest. I had been a gigantic jerk to her five years ago and here I was, doing it again. I needed to figure out a way to make things right, pronto.

"I don't know how you handle it all… Taking care of your grandpa, getting perfect grades, taking every AP possible… That's a lot to deal with."

"I'm sure you've made sacrifices for your little brother."

I thought back to the countless hours my parents spent with him at appointments or by his bed in the hospital. I was there, too, but it was hard during the basketball season. I constantly balanced feelings of guilt and pride. Guilt that my brother had been cursed with a terrible medical condition and pride in myself for working so hard to accomplish my basketball goals. It left me with a sinking sensation in my gut.

"I always feel like I'm not doing enough." I was never this honest or open with anyone, but I meant every word that I was saying to her. It was like she had a superpower, one that blasted through my shields and let her into the most personal inner folds of my life.

Wren shrugged. "You do what you can for family. They're the most important people in the world."

"You're right." Wow. I never thought I'd have anything in common with Wren besides basketball. But here we were, two completely different people, with a tragic commonality. Sick family members we'd do anything to help.

I tilted my chair backward and laced my hands behind my head. "Your gramps knows a ton about basketball. That's pretty cool. Do you guys watch a lot of games together?" According to Brandon, Wren knew the sport better than just about anyone. She even kept stats for him. Like, proper stats during every game.

Wren smiled. "Yeah, I love watching games with him. It's like getting transported back in time. He's so lucid and with it during the games, kind of like he was when you two were talking last night—well, at least in the beginning. He used to take me to all the high school games and even some college ones when I was a little girl. We'd share popcorn, M&Ms, and a soda. He taught me how to keep stats and everything. It was really special. I go to all our games, I mean, the school games, but it's too hard on him." She paused, blinking slowly. "But we still watch them together, every Saturday morning. I pop popcorn, get a bag of M&Ms, and have a soda waiting for him. It's our special time together."

"Wow, that's really...amazing of you, Wren."

"It's no big deal. I love spending time with my grandpa." Her cheeks had taken on a pink hue. "It's so hard to see him struggle. He forgets words and he confuses my mom and me a lot. I try not to let it get me down, but it's hard. And, lately... Lately, he's been getting up in the middle of the night. Thankfully, I'm a really light sleeper, so as soon as I hear his door open, I get up and figure out the best way to help him."

"I'm sorry you have to go through that. I bet you're really tired." I cringed internally as I said the word "bet."

"Yeah, well. What can you do, except keep on going?" Wren glanced down at her hands. "Plus, it's only sleep. I can make up for it in college, right?" She gave me a sad smile.

"You're right." I found myself wanting to reach out to her. Pull her into my arms. *Dude. What are you thinking? Get a grip!*

"Anyway," Wren said, digging her worn personal copy of *The Hate U Give* out of her backpack. It looked like she'd added more fluorescent Post-it notes. "We should probably talk about the book." Her voice was softer, unlike the beginning of our tutoring session. Scratch that, for the first time ever, she didn't sound like she resented having to work with me.

"Yeah, I read, well, listened to ten chapters." I grinned, knowing it would impress her. "You would know that if you looked at my text messages."

Wren placed her hand on her backpack. That must be where she kept her phone. "Yeah, about that…"

"Not a big deal. But yeah, yours truly listened to ten chapters." Bragging about doing my schoolwork? Trying to impress Wren Carter? Did I get transported into a different dimension?

She arched an eyebrow. "Seriously? You really listened to ten chapters last night?" She paused, studying my face. "You better not be lying to me, James."

"Cross my heart and hope to die." I made an *X* over my chest. "Well, I listened to seven chapters last night and three this morning." Plopping my backpack onto the table, I slid out my laptop and flipped it open. "Once I started listening, I actually had a hard time stopping. The book is incredible."

Wren's eyebrows knit together. "You really think so? You're not doing this to try to score suck-up points with your tutor, are you?"

"Honestly, yes. Oh, I mean, yes to the book being amazing. Not yes that I'm trying to score brownie points with you." I chuckled. "The themes were really helpful, too." I opened up the Word doc that I'd typed notes into last night. "I put a few thoughts down here and even came up with an idea for the topic of my paper."

Mrs. Parsons walked by us and smiled. The weird thing was, I don't think I ever saw her teeth when she smiled. It was something my little brother constantly pointed out. When people smile, they either show their top teeth, bottom teeth, both, or no teeth at all. Sometimes, when we'd watch movies together at home, we would bet on what type of smile people had. Whoever won got a handful of Sour Skittles, his favorite snack.

"Not bad." Wren still had her eyes glued to the Word document on my computer. "I think Mrs. Brewster will be happy with your proposed topic."

Pride swelled in my chest. For the first time in what felt like forever, someone was impressed with me for my ideas, not for how I handled a basketball.

"Angie Thomas's Use of Symbolism to Highlight Racism and Police Brutality in Society. It really spoke to me. Everything from the moment Khalil picks up the hairbrush to *The Fresh Prince of Bel-Air*." I felt confident in what I was saying. I could only hope Wren and Mrs. Brewster agreed.

"Very powerful." Wren nodded in agreement. "Angie Thomas is hands down one of the most influential authors of our time. She wields words like the Samurai wielded their katana swords."

"Definitely." Damn, speaking of having a way with words. Wren always sounded so smart. "Did you know that part of Darth Vader's helmet was inspired by the samurai?"

She tilted her head to the side. "Are you making that up?"

"No." I chuckled. "The neck part on his costume was inspired by the samurai's helmet."

"Interesting." Her eyes met mine. It looked like she was going to smile, like a legit authentic smile, not the type Marissa would plaster across her face.

"So, ah, I was, um, thinking of stopping by Mrs. Brewster's classroom before practice started. Maybe she'll sign off on it early, and I can have an extra day to work on the paper. After I finish listening to the book, I'm going to make an outline. I was hoping you could go over it with me? Make sure I didn't miss anything important or include anything that doesn't need to be in there?"

Wren's nose wrinkled. I'd never noticed how cute she looked when she did that.

I never noticed a lot of things about Wren...

"What? What's with the look?" The corners of my lips twitched. "You don't want to review my outline?"

"Of course I'll review your outline. It's, ah, I guess I'm surprised." Wren picked up a pen and tapped it against her open palm.

I cocked my head to the side. "Surprised that a slacker actually came through and did the work he said he'd do?"

"Your words, not mine." Finally, she returned the smile.

She was a top-row-teeth smiler. My favorite kind.

"Listen, I was thinking—" But before I could finish the sentence, my phone buzzed. At the same time, Wren's phone started vibrating from somewhere in her backpack.

"That's weird," she murmured.

I guess she didn't get many texts during the day. I thought I'd turned all my notifications off after lunch. Mrs. Brewster was a stickler about phones—if she caught anyone even looking at theirs, she'd take it and wouldn't give it back until you had a signed note from your parents. Since being assigned to work with Wren yesterday, I decided keeping it in my bookbag until the end of the day was probably the safest plan. Neither of us needed to get into any more trouble than we were already in.

Wren reached into her backpack as I unlocked my phone. As soon as I tapped on the notification, my jaw dropped. An anonymous Instagram account, famous for posting gossip, had tagged Wren and me in a picture together. I was standing in her driveway, grinning like a fool. The caption read, "Hookup Alert: Wrentainer lets Fuller James spend the night at her house!"

Wren's gasp was audible. By the time I looked up, she was standing and pointing a shaky finger at me. "Did you do this? Is this the reason you kept looking over your shoulder?"

"No." I shook my head. "I swear, Wren. I didn't have anything to do with this post."

Before I could defend myself any further, TyShaun popped his head into the library. "Wow. You two can't seem to get enough of each other!" He winked before throwing his head back and laughing. "I'm surprised I didn't find you in the AV room." He bent his elbows and brought his arms toward his body in a repetitive motion.

"Shut up, TyShaun." Wren's voice quaked.

Shit. My mind floated back to last night, when I'd bumped into him outside of Wren's house. He must have been the one to take the picture and send it to the gossip IG account.

"The picture is out there." TyShaun continued laughing, slapping his hand on the side of the door. "You can't hide your relationship forever." He held up one finger and winked.

Oh no. He and Marc must have counted this as step one. My guilty conscience crumbled under the pressure. I opened my mouth to tell TyShaun to screw off, but Wren beat me to it.

"We aren't in a relationship!" Wren's eyes were glossy.

"You act like this isn't helping your reputation," TyShaun

said. “Whoever posted that did you a favor, Wrentainer!”

The librarian stomped toward TyShaun with a scowl on her face. “This is a library, not the mall. Get to class, Mr. Adams. *Now.*”

TyShaun winked at me before disappearing around the door. “See ya later, FullTainer.”

I balled up my fists. He was damn lucky we were teammates.

By the time I turned my attention back to Wren, she was shoving her book into her backpack. Her hands shook as she attempted to zip it shut.

“Wren, wait.” I reached across the table, but she pulled back. With tears streaming down her face, she snatched her backpack off the table and bolted toward the doors.

Chapter Seven

Wren

The halls were empty, but that would change as soon as the bell rang. Panicking, I raced to my locker. If I could move quick enough, I'd be able to get all of my books and make it to my car before anyone noticed me.

My fingers trembled as I fumbled with the lock on my locker. Finally, it clicked, allowing me to open the door and grab my books. There was a small mirror stuck to the inside of the locker door, something left by its previous tenant. My tear-soaked face stared back at me. Luckily, my mascara hadn't run down my cheeks—yet. I grabbed a tissue and dabbed it carefully underneath my eyes before slamming my locker shut.

How could I let myself be so stupid? Baring my soul to him? Telling him about Gramps? Fuller had always been a jerk, and this only made that point crystal clear. This would be the *last* time I let him hurt me.

Brinnnggggggg. The sound of the final bell of the day

echoed throughout the empty hallway. Crap. I'd taken too long. With my arms full of books, I put my head down and continued toward the doors leading to the parking lot.

"Wren! Wren, wait up!"

I didn't turn around. I never wanted to speak to Fuller James again. He might not have taken the picture or even been the one to post it, but I knew he had something to do with it. It explained why he kept glancing over his shoulder. He had clearly been looking for whoever took the picture.

Worst of all, he hadn't even tried to deny it, he'd only told TyShaun to shut up.

A hand touched my shoulder. "Wren, please. Talk to me."

I stopped, juggling the textbooks in my arms. "I'm sure this is all some kind of joke to you, but I will not be made the laughingstock of our school again." My voice cracked. "Unlike some other girls, I don't get off on the fact that people think we hooked up!"

"I swear, I didn't—"

I didn't let him finish his sentence. Instead, I pushed past him, bumping against his arm in the process. That's all it took to send my pile of books flying. They scattered on the linoleum floor with audible *thump*s.

Fuller scrambled to help me pick them up as classmates walked by, whispering and laughing.

"Get away from me! I don't need your help." The anger in my voice was palpable.

"Trouble in paradise?"

Could this moment get any worse?

I spun around to find Marissa staring me down. She tapped her stiletto-clad foot. Courtney stood behind her with a wicked grin on her face.

"Get away from me, Marissa." Fuller's voice was low and came out like a growl. "I don't want anything to do with you right now."

Her perfectly shaped eyebrows went up, but only for a second before her face twisted into a sneer. "That wasn't what you were saying two weeks ago."

Instead of responding, I grabbed my books from Fuller's arms and raced down the hallway. Marissa's cackles chased after me.

As I made my way outside, I sucked in the fresh air. *You're almost to your car. You only need to hang on for a few more seconds.*

Brandon waved at me from the first row of the parking lot.

I loved my friends, but right now, I didn't want to talk to anyone. I needed to go home, get into bed, and pull the comforter over my head.

As soon as I got closer, Brandon frowned. His blue eyes instantly filled with concern. "What's wrong?"

Unable to hold it in any longer, my chest heaved, and a fresh round of tears ran down my cheeks.

"Oh my gosh! What happened?" Brandon grabbed my books and opened up his car door. "Here, come sit down."

"Y-Y-You're going to be late for practice." I choked on the words as they left my lips.

"I don't care. Get in and tell me what happened."

Once I sat down in the passenger's seat, I completely lost it. I worked hard for my perfect GPA, had two awesome best friends, I took care of my grandpa as best as I could—I was a good person, damn it. But somehow Fuller, TyShaun, Marissa, and an anonymous Instagram account managed to make me feel like I was completely worthless. I'd never even had sex with anyone, but now, half the school thought I was sleeping with Fuller James. *Yeah right, like I'd ever stoop to that level of sleaze!*

Several minutes passed before I was able to pull back and show Brandon the post.

As soon as his blue eyes landed on the picture, his face turned as red as his hair.

"H-H-He came over to get some notes. You know, for tutoring. He came in, talked to my grandpa about basketball, but when he left, he...he was acting weird. He kept looking over his shoulder. I asked him about it today during study hall. He said it wasn't what it looked like. Then, boom. This picture is posted."

I tapped on the comment bubble. "There's already fifty-one comments. Everyone is making fun of him for being at my house. I think he set the whole thing up. I don't know what his endgame is, though—people are making fun of him as much as they're making fun of me. It wouldn't be so bad, but right before the post went up, we'd had this long talk about Gramps and his little brother. For just a minute, I thought there was more to him than just his jerkwad cocky attitude, and I let my guard down." I shook my head. "Talk about being gullible."

"You are not gullible, Wren." Brandon's eyes narrowed in on my phone. "That stupid account is always messing with people," he grumbled.

I wiped my cheeks with the backs of my hands.

"You know what? Screw Fuller. He's an ass. You know it, I know it. The whole world knows it." Brandon's cheeks were red again. "He thinks he's untouchable."

I nodded. I'd never met someone so cocky in my entire life.

"I'm going to confront him. He obviously didn't take the picture, but I bet he knows who posted it. He needs to get that crap taken down and tell TyShaun, his friends, and especially that witch Marissa to leave you alone. You don't deserve this, Wren."

Sniffling, I reached out and placed my hand on Brandon's forearm. "Thanks, Brand, but please don't."

A small spark lit in my core. I needed to fight this battle head on. I never stood up for myself, and it was time that changed.

Brandon placed his other hand on top of mine. "Are you sure? I don't want to fight your battles, but I want to be there for you. Plus, I'm about to go see that asshole, and it's going to be really hard holding my tongue."

"I'm sure. Thank you, though." I squeezed his hand.

"If you change your mind…"

Wrapping my arms around Brandon, I hugged him again. "You and Dae will be the first to know, I promise." Looking down at my phone, I sighed. "You better get to practice. I don't want you to have to run extra laps because of me."

"Can I drop you off at your car first?"

I let out a small sigh, thankful for my friends. "That would be really nice. Thanks, Brand."

My phone buzzed as Brandon slid his car into drive.

DAE: Are you okay?

DAE: I just saw the picture and that stupid freaking caption.

DAE: I already reported it.

DAE: But since there isn't any nudity or anything, I don't know if Instagram will take it down.

ME: I'll be okay…

DAE: Do you want to talk about it?

ME: In a bit.

ME: Brand is giving me a ride to my car.

ME: I need to clear my head on the drive home.

DAE: Of course.

I really do have the best friends.

...

By the time I got home, my phone had blown up. More than twenty people had tagged me in the post's comments, and Fuller had sent me five text messages. Five!

Sighing, I opened the app and looked at the picture one last time. While some of the comments were hurtful and rude, a lot pointed out how creepy it was that someone was taking secret photos of Fuller and me. Others pointed out that the picture didn't mean anything.

Someone even said, "He could have been out for a run and ran into her. Why would you assume anything else? Desperate much?" That one made me smile.

Deciding I didn't need to see anything else, I blocked the anonymous gossip account and switched to my text messages.

FULLER: I'm sorry.
FULLER: I promise, I'll find out who took that picture and get it taken down.
FULLER: I know you don't have any reason to believe me.
FULLER: But, I swear, I'm not this big of an asshole.
FULLER: I'd never tell someone we were hooking up.
FULLER: Please just let me know that you're okay.

Even though I hated thinking about middle school, my mind floated back to the night after our seventh-grade dance. Marissa had come over to my house, but instead of comforting me after I humiliated myself by spitting out my retainer, she flat out told me we couldn't be friends anymore. "Listen, Fuller and I are a thing now, and he doesn't think you and I should be friends anymore." I remember the air whooshing out of my lungs.

She didn't say anything else to me that night. She called her mom, asked to get picked up, and then she turned around and walked out of my front door and, more importantly, my life.

I'd tried calling and texting her, but she refused to talk to me. At school, she straight-up pretended like I didn't exist, minus when she was calling me Wrentainer. Thank goodness Dae moved to town that same year. He was new, and I was in desperate need of a friend who didn't think Marissa and Fuller were the world's cutest couple. Plus, like me, he loved basketball. We immediately became friends. After he and Brandon were paired up for a social studies project, Brandon quickly became part of our crew. Turns out, Brandon and Dae both had little sisters in the same fifth-grade class and they became friends, too.

It was almost like it was meant to be.

Dae was the one who got me into running cross-country. He used to be on the boys' team, but a knee injury left him on the sidelines this past season. He was looking forward to dominating in javelin for the upcoming track season in the spring, and I'd be right there cheering him on.

Back in the day, the three of us would shoot hoops after school for hours, hang out at Floats, the local ice cream parlor, eat the most delicious Korean food you'd ever imagine at Dae's house, and spend our weekends watching basketball games on Brandon's massive flat-screen.

That's when it hit me. I'd made a vow in Brandon's car to start standing up for myself, but did I really mean it? I was sick and tired of walking on eggshells around Marissa, Fuller, or anyone at school. I'd been a victim for five years. That was five too many.

Brandon was right, screw them and whoever ran that gossip account. I was done being pushed around, breaking down in tears. From this point forward, I was going to tell them all how I really felt.

I sniffed and blinked away the tears. I'd stand up for myself and live my life. I wasn't going to start initiating fistfights in the parking lot, but if Marissa dared to laugh at me again, I'd tell her to shove it. As for Fuller, even though I wanted to quit working with him, I'd finish tutoring him and then never speak to him again. We'd be done in two weeks, max. After that, there'd be only eight months left of high school. Eight months, then a summer with my friends, STEM camp, and finally college.

I'd escape Marissa, Fuller, TyShaun, and all their immature stunts once and for all.

I turned off my phone and grabbed my backpack, my body buzzing with confidence. I felt like I'd chugged a Red Bull or something, like I could break my personal best running a mile. Gathering my books in my arms, I glanced at myself in the rearview mirror. "You can do this, Wren."

Juggling my books, I managed to slide my key into the front door and push it open.

"Wrenny." My grandpa met me at the front door with a massive smile. "How was school today?" He was wearing the sweater I'd gotten him for his birthday. It was navy with maroon stripes.

"Hey, Gramps. You look really nice today." I set everything down on the long, skinny wooden table inside the door and gave him a hug. He smelled like Old Spice. He'd used the same cologne as long as I could remember. "School was okay. How was your day?"

"Oh, you know. I helped your dad make lunch. We had tomato soup and grilled cheese." He rubbed his stomach. "It was deeeelicious."

"Mmm, my favorite." During his lucid moments, it felt like the good old days again—back when he and Grandma used to live down the block and I'd go to their house every day after school. I loved it. There was always fresh fruit or carrot sticks with a side of ranch waiting for me when I got there. I'd sit at the kitchen table and race through my homework, even though Grandma always made me go back and double-check it. Sunny days meant long walks and games outside together. Rainy days were for blanket forts and watching movies. Most nights, my parents would pick me up after they got home from work, but Fridays were my favorite because I always got to sleep over.

The memories tugged at my heartstrings.

Gramps nodded. "I know. That's why I saved you half a sandwich and some soup. Want to warm it up and watch some basketball?"

"Sure, do you know if Mom's running late?" I asked, recalling that I hadn't seen her car in the driveway.

"She's staying late at work and your dad said he's still full from lunch. So, what do you say to dinner and a game with your ole Gramps?"

Even though I had at least three hours of homework, I didn't care. I could do it after dinner. Spending time with my grandpa was more important. "Let's do it. Want to watch the 1998 championship game between the Bulls and the Jazz?"

Gramps's eyes lit up. "Do I ever!"

"Awesome. Let me go drop off this stuff in my room. I'll be right out."

"Oh, Wren, how's your new friend? That good ball player who came over the other night."

I froze. Grandpa usually struggled to remember meeting new people, but here he was asking about Fuller like it was no big deal.

"Oh, um. He's fine. He's at practice right now with Uncle Chuck."

"He's a nice boy. I really liked talking to him. He knows a lot about basketball. You should have him over again."

"Sounds like a plan, Gramps." My heart sank. I hated lying, but there was no way I'd *ever* let Fuller James back into my house.

Chapter Eight

Fuller

"What the hell, Fuller?"

Someone shoved me from behind with so much force that I flew forward several feet and almost crashed into the gym floor.

Spinning around, I put my fists up and got ready to confront whoever had pushed me. "Damn, Brandon! What's your problem?"

"Did you have anything to do with that picture?" Brandon's nostrils flared as his eyes narrowed in on mine. I'd never seen him this angry before.

"Seriously?"

"Do I look like I'm joking?" Brandon practically growled as he spoke. With each passing second, his face turned a brighter shade of red.

I glanced over my shoulder. A few of the other guys had entered the gym. Practice had been delayed by half an hour due to a minor flood in the boys' locker rooms. Unfortunately,

I couldn't find TyShaun anywhere, and Marissa didn't pick up when I called her. I had a sinking feeling in my gut that she was involved. Feeling helpless, I was stuck waiting until practice started to be able to do anything about that stupid picture.

"Did you?" Brandon demanded. He wasn't as tall or as muscular as me, but he'd shoved me with as much strength as an NFL linebacker.

"No." I lowered my voice so no one else would hear what we were talking about. "I swear. I didn't have anything to do with it."

Brandon didn't budge; instead, he reached out and poked me in the chest. "You better figure out who did and get them to take it down."

"I'm working on it, *Brandon*." I emphasized the two syllables in his name as I said them. I shouldn't have spoken to him that way—he was a teammate and he didn't have anything to do with the bet—but he was all up in my face. More importantly, I didn't want anyone else on the team to know something was up. The quicker I ended this conversation, the better.

Brandon glared and me and spoke through a clenched jaw. "Wren is the best person I know. She doesn't need someone like *you* bringing her down. So you, Marissa, and whoever else are screwing with her need to stop."

"Back off. I'll handle it. And for your information—"

The shrill sound of Coach's whistle erupted on the opposite side of the gym. "Fuller, Brandon, is there a problem?"

"No, sir," we both responded in unison.

"Good. We're already behind. Get those fifteen laps started." He blew his whistle again, not taking his eyes off us.

Soon the echoes of shoes squeaking on the gymnasium floor rang in my ears. My heart rate picked up quicker than normal. My run-in with Brandon had left a knot in my stomach. I wouldn't admit it to him, but I'd already planned on confronting TyShaun. Since Coach had given us an extra five laps, I'd have plenty of time to do it.

Slowing my pace, I waited for TyShaun to catch up. But before I could say something, Marc jogged up alongside me. "Nice job on pulling off the first part of the bet. I almost didn't count it, but that stupid grin you had on your face sealed the deal." He slapped me on the back before putting his head down and sprinting forward. My pulse raced and my mouth went dry.

A moment later, TyShaun passed me. I matched his stride and ran alongside him for a full lap, trying to calm down, before I opened my mouth. "I know it was you."

TyShaun rolled his eyes and picked up the pace, leaving me behind.

Pushing my body, I caught up with him in a matter of seconds. The backs of my calves burned as we raced around the outer loop of the gym. "I know you took that photo, so you need to tell whoever runs that Instagram account to take it down. *Now.*"

He laughed. "Now? Are you serious? Coach isn't going to let me skip out of laps to go slide into someone's DMs."

I bumped into his shoulder, shoving him to the left. "I'm serious, TyShaun. I don't care what you need to do, but you have to tell whoever posted that picture to take it down immediately. Or else."

"Are you threatening me?" He threw his head back and laughed. "Over Wrentainer? Man, you've got it bad for that weirdo."

Clenching my fists, it took everything in me to stop myself from punching my teammate in the face. TyShaun never used to pull crap like this. He'd changed a lot since he'd started hanging out with Marissa. She was like a poison that contaminated everyone it came into contact with.

I winced. How pathetic was I for dating her for so long?

"Thinking about your girl?" TyShaun's voice brought me back to reality.

"Get it down or I'll give Coach the pictures of you doing keg stands at Marc's party last weekend."

TyShaun's smile vanished. "Are you serious?"

"And if you mention this bet to anyone, not only will I give Coach those pictures, but I'll figure out who runs that anonymous account and I'll send them the pictures of you sucking face with Chantel Williams." It was a well-kept secret that TyShaun had been hooking up with his older brother's girlfriend, but I'd accidentally caught them in the act once. I was acting like a punk by threatening him, and I needed to stop, but this was for Wren.

His eyes narrowed in on mine. "You're an asshole. You know that, Fuller?"

"Do it. Now." I didn't need to say anything else. The next time we passed the locker room, TyShaun told Coach that he'd be right back. He clutched his stomach, mocking a queasy feeling.

As he disappeared through the locker room doors, I put my head down and focused on the warm-up. My arms and legs pumped in unison for the remaining laps. By the time I'd reached number fifteen, TyShaun had reemerged. He gave me a subtle nod before circling up around Coach.

Good. Problem solved.

Coach instructed us to begin a series of passing drills. The guys broke up into pairs. Luckily, Jacob was on vacation today, so we had an odd number of guys on the court.

"Coach, I need to use the bathroom real quick. I'll be right back."

Coach frowned. "First TyShaun, now you? Is there a bug going around or something?"

"Ate something at lunch that isn't sitting right." I'd been lying way too much lately. But there was no way I could be honest with Coach about what was going on. Especially because it involved a nasty rumor being spread about his niece. People believed anything that went up on that stupid Instagram account, and the last thing Wren deserved was for our classmates to be gossiping about her, especially since it was my fault.

Brow furrowed, he nodded.

I raced into the locker room and opened up my locker. Fishing out my phone, I quickly opened up Instagram and looked for the post. It was gone. Thank goodness.

Pulling up my texts, I typed out a message to Wren.

ME: It's down.

My fingers flew across the keyboard. Even though I knew it was him, I couldn't admit that TyShaun was the one who took the photo. That could lead her to confronting him, and even though I threatened him with exposing pictures of him and Chantel, he might still blab about the bet. I'd already hurt Wren enough. I couldn't stand the thought of seeing her cry again.

Nobody deserved to feel like that, ever.

ME: I'm so sorry.

The messages read, "Delivered," but not, "Read."

The door opened, causing my heart to jump. I shut my locker door, tucked the phone into my waistband, and ducked into a bathroom stall. If anyone caught me on my cell phone during practice and told Coach, I'd be running laps for the rest of the night.

Whoever it was left a few seconds later. To be safe, I stayed in the stall, standing next to the toilet and looking at my phone. *Come on, Wren. Write me back.* Feeling desperate, I typed out another message but quickly deleted it. *There's nothing else you can do. Time to suck it up and go back to practice. You can deal with the fallout once you get home.*

I left the stall and headed back to my locker. Unfortunately, my little pep talk didn't work, not even a little bit. Wren's tear-soaked face was still on my mind. After checking for a response one more time and coming up empty, I reluctantly turned off my phone and shoved it back in my locker.

The intensity of the situation and emptiness of the locker room suddenly felt as though they were crushing my lungs. I dropped to my knees and sucked in the stale air that smelled of body odor and bleach. My heart hammered in my chest and the room started to tilt. Shit, was I having a panic attack or something? Closing my eyes, I forced myself to take several deep breaths. Finally, after what seemed like an eternity, everything stopped spinning.

"Get it together, Fuller." My voice sounded hoarse.

Clearing my throat, I got up, pulled the locker room door open, and was met with a rush of cool air.

"Feeling better, son?" Coach stood with a basketball tucked under his arm. His eyes were full of concern, and a deep line had formed across his forehead.

Before I could respond, my stomach clenched. I raised my hand to my mouth, but it was too late. My partially digested lunch splashed all over Coach's shoes.

Chapter Nine

WREN

"Remember, your papers are due on Wednesday. That's two days from now." Mrs. Brewster pointed to a reminder she'd written in red marker in the corner of the whiteboard.

The bell rang.

Mrs. Brewster frowned and looked up at the clock. "Wren and Fuller, I need to speak to both of you before you leave."

"Ooh," someone from behind me cooed.

I spun around in my seat and stared down Lyla. "Seriously? You're going to be that immature?" My classmate immediately looked down at her desk, her cheeks turning dark pink.

Another classmate made kissy sounds.

"Shut up, Eric. Wren and I are friends. Nothing more and nothing less." Fuller said it loud enough for everyone in the room to hear, including Mrs. Brewster.

Did he really stand up and justify himself? And call me his friend? It was about the most un-Fuller-like thing I'd ever seen him do. He actually stood up for the right reason and didn't go along with it for a stupid laugh.

Whatever. One time doesn't make F.B.M. a hero. Before I could second-guess myself or my feelings about this new hero Fuller, Mrs. Brewster cleared her throat.

"Class is dismissed." Mrs. Brewster shook her head and pressed her thin lips together in disappointment. They were coated in dark burgundy lipstick that matched her ill-fitting blazer.

Tapping my fingers on the desk, I ignored the snickers from the kids in my class. Fuller would probably receive some heat from his teammates, minus Brandon, for his declaration that we were friends. But everyone in the room, including me, knew that he was lying. Fuller James and I would never be friends.

That didn't stop me from thinking about him though… My mind kept jumping back to our conversation about Gramps and Fuller's little brother, Hudson. He'd been so genuine and real during that moment. Nothing like the cocky show-off he portrayed himself to be on the court and in the hallways. If he was like that all the time, I actually *could* picture us being friends.

A tight feeling clenched at my chest, making it difficult to take a deep breath. Too bad he'd never be that person. A few glimpses here and there would never be enough.

I waited for everyone to leave before getting up. A few people gave me looks as they walked by, but I ignored them. I assumed that everyone had seen the post on the gossip account. Over three thousand people followed the account, and most of the Magnolia Valley High School population checked it for news at least once a day. It was all the underclass students talked about. The photo of Fuller and me had popped up a few more places over the weekend, but all of them had been taken down by this morning.

"Miss Carter, you did an excellent job." Mrs. Brewster handed me my paper with a bright red A+ marked at the top. I'd earned 100 percent on the paper, but that had been bumped up to 110 percent, thanks to the extra credit points I earned for agreeing to tutor Fuller.

Speaking of whom, Fuller stood next to me. I caught him tensing up as Mrs. Brewster praised me. Turning in my assignments early felt good. I loved crossing them off in my planner.

"I'm checking in to see how your paper is coming along, Mr. James." Mrs. Brewster pushed up her black-rimmed glasses with her pointer finger. She must have left her contacts at home today. She didn't usually wear glasses.

I hadn't spoken to Fuller since Friday. Mrs. Brewster had been impressed with his hypothesis, but I didn't have any idea if he worked on his paper over the weekend. All I knew was that he'd texted me seven times, but I hadn't responded. Somehow, he'd managed to get the picture down from the gossip account, but he didn't elaborate as to how in his messages. I didn't care, either. I just wanted to be done with my tutoring duty as soon as possible.

Fuller reached into his backpack and pulled out a stack of papers clipped together in the left-hand corner. "Yes, ma'am. I've written the first draft. I planned on going over it with Wren today in study hall—I want to make sure I'm on the right track before I go through and add a few more details and fully edit it."

Mrs. Brewster accepted the papers from Fuller's outstretched hand. She took a few minutes to read over what he'd written. "Miss Carter, Mr. James did this work himself, yes?"

"Yes, ma'am." Like I'd ever do his work for him.

With a nod of approval, she handed the assignment back to Fuller. "Very nice, Mr. James. Your citations need a bit of work, but that's easy. Overall, I'm impressed. It seems that Miss Carter has had a very good effect on you. Maybe you two should continue your study hall sessions together for the rest of the year."

Neither Fuller nor I responded, but my insides screamed "NO!"

"Is there something wrong?" Mrs. Brewster raised an eyebrow.

"No, ma'am," I responded. "Anxious to get to study hall, that's all."

Her gaze passed from Fuller's face to mine. "All right then. Well, I don't want to keep the two of you any longer."

"Thank you, Mrs. Brewster." Fuller placed his paper back into his backpack.

"See you tomorrow, Mrs. Brewster." My heart started racing in my chest. I was hoping to pop out of class ahead of Fuller and meet him in the library moments before the bell rang. Instead, I'd have to walk down the hallway with him now. Not only would it be awkward and uncomfortable, it would surely elicit comments from our classmates.

I'd prepared myself for this moment, though. Well, standing up for myself, not walking down the hall with Fuller. I'd practiced walking more confidently and I'd even thought up a few comebacks if anyone gave me crap. If I could work up the courage to use them, I'd be golden.

Earlier today, a freshman I stood next to in the lunch line flat out asked me why I was embarrassed to be seen with Fuller James. Her eyes wide in disbelief, she went on to tell me that he was the cutest guy in school and that, if he were to show up on her doorstep, she'd invite him in for a make-out session.

The old me would have ignored her, but the new me, the me who stood up for herself, told the random freshman who'd butted her head into my business that Fuller was the last guy on the planet I'd ever want to make out with. The expression on her face was priceless. It was like I'd told her that the Tooth Fairy wasn't real.

She didn't say anything to me the rest of the time we were in line together.

Now, as Fuller and I entered the hallway, people's eyes were immediately on us. As I predicted, I could hear them whispering. A few even pointed. Instead of letting my head hang down, though, I pushed my shoulders back and held my chin high as I made my way to the library.

Fuller walked alongside me but remained silent.

Once we finally reached the library and sat down at our regular table, Fuller opened his mouth. "Wren, listen. I'm really sorry about last week."

"Are you?" My tone was sharp, and the library was quieter than usual. I looked over my shoulder, expecting to see Mrs. Parsons with a scowl on her face. Strangely enough, she was nowhere to be seen. The two sophomore girls who helped her put away books on Monday afternoons weren't around either. *Weird.*

Fuller pushed his hair back and straightened out his retro Magnolia Valley basketball shirt. "I swear, I had no idea that someone took that picture of us."

"How did you get them to take it down?" That question had been bugging me all weekend. Obviously, Fuller was part of the popular crowd, but I always assumed whoever posted on the anonymous Instagram account wasn't part of his crew. I'd always secretly thought it was someone like Charlie, a junior who was kind of a sleaze but somehow maintained connections with all the major cliques on campus. I could be wrong, though.

"I'd rather not say."

"You'd rather not say? What's that supposed to mean? Who are you protecting? TyShaun? Marissa?" I could feel my cheeks getting hot.

Instead of the bemused look Fuller typically sported, his eyebrows knit together in concern. "No. Why? Did someone tell you that?"

I shook my head. "Why don't you admit what actually happened?"

Fuller's blue eyes met mine. He placed both his hands on the table, fingers splayed. "I can't, and even though it's probably the last thing you want to hear from me, trust me, I handled it. And it won't happen again."

Leaning back in my chair, I held his gaze. I could see how girls would get lost in his blue orbs. They were like the sea on a calm day. "You know what? Fine. I don't care. Not about that stupid photo *or* you. Let's go over your paper and get this stupid tutoring session done with."

Fuller flinched. "Tell you what. Don't worry about the paper. I'll ask someone else to look it over. You don't need to waste any more time working with me."

He stood up and pushed in his chair.

"Oh, I got this for you." He slid a box of grape and strawberry Nerds across the table. "And this is for your grandpa." Fuller tossed a plastic-wrapped DVD on the table in front of me. "It's one of the best NBA games ever played. Game seven. Boston Celtics versus the St. Louis Hawks. It went into double overtime." Fuller zipped up his backpack and slung it over his shoulder. "I thought he'd enjoy watching it."

Temporarily forgetting my anger, I reached forward and picked up the box of my favorite candy and the DVD case. "Where did you find this?" I asked in awe.

"The Nerds? At Walmart."

"No, the DVD. I've only ever seen clips of this game online. I've never been able to watch the whole thing with the original commentary."

Fuller shifted his weight. "Oh, I found it on eBay. I ordered it the night I met your grandpa. It came in the mail on Saturday."

Tingles shot from my core to my fingertips. Fuller was right. This was easily one of the top NBA games of all time.

"Thanks for helping me, Wren." Fuller tapped the chair with his hand. "It might not seem like it, but I really do appreciate it."

I picked up the DVD case and turned it over. My grandpa would love it.

"Fuller. Wait."

He paused as he reached for the door.

"Come back. Sit."

Fuller hesitated.

"I'm sorry I was so rough on you. If you say you didn't have anything to do with the picture, I believe you." I turned the DVD over in my hands. "Can I see your paper?"

His eyes lit up. "Really?"

"Yeah, really." I gave him a small smile.

Fuller grinned as he pulled the chair out and sat next to me. I caught a whiff of his cologne. Since when did he wear cologne to school? He smelled like the forest after it rained. Fresh and enticing. Shaking my head, I pushed how good he smelled to the back of my mind and focused on the task at hand—serving as his tutor.

He riffled through his backpack and pulled out the same paper he'd given to Mrs. Brewster. "I worked on it all day on Saturday." He handed me the paper. "It might be complete garbage."

"Mrs. Brewster didn't think it was." I accepted the paper and, for the next several minutes, I read every word Fuller had written. His thesis and introduction were solid. The body of his paper needed a little tightening up and his citations definitely could use some help, but otherwise, he'd done a good job.

"What do you think?" Fuller's voice was full of doubt.

"It's solid." I set the paper down but kept my hand on it. "In fact, I'm impressed."

Fuller exhaled, his shoulders finding their way back to a relaxed position. "You've got no idea how much of a relief that is to hear. That website you sent me last week helped a lot. The organizational tips are key. I think that's been a big part of why I've struggled in Mrs. Brewster's class this year. I've been writing papers without any sense of organization. That…and I hadn't been reading the books." The corners of his lips quirked into a coy smile.

Fuller pulled his chair closer to the table. "I know there's definitely some room for improvement. I don't think I did the citations right, but I'm hoping I'm close?"

After opening my laptop, I grabbed a note card and permanent marker. "You can use this website as a guide to everything APA. But, for quick reference, these are the three citations I use the most." I scribbled down sample one-, two-, and three- author citations. "Here."

"Wow. How did you memorize all of those?"

I tapped my temple with my pointer finger. "Good memory."

Fuller's lips curved into a small smile as he looked over the note card. "Did you use your last name for all the examples?"

"Yup." I cocked my head to the side and held the card out in my hand. "Look, it's my citation cheat sheet. Use it or lose it." He was definitely giving me a hard time, but he wasn't being arrogant. The genuine Fuller had reemerged.

He snatched the card from my grasp and chuckled as he held it against his chest. "It's mine now. All mine."

I found myself smiling for the first time in days.

"Be honest, what else needs work?" Fuller asked,

pointing to his paper.

"You get a bit wordy in some of your sentences." I admitted. "Like this one for example. 'Angie Thomas does a brilliant job of using Khalil's hairbrush as a symbol throughout *The Hate U Give*, for example, it is used to represent the mindset that police believe all black teenagers pose a threat and have guns in their vehicles, if it were a white teen in the same circumstances, it's doubtful the police officer would have pulled his gun, let alone discharged it.'"

Fuller clenched his teeth. "Yeah. That *is* kind of a long sentence."

"Break it up a bit and make each point clear. 'Angie Thomas does a brilliant job using symbolism throughout her debut novel, *The Hate U Give.*' That reinforces your thesis. Then you could say something like, 'She uses Khalil's hairbrush to prove that the police have a distrust of Khalil and young black men. The police officer automatically assumes that Khalil has a gun and is willing to use it. It is doubtful that the same police officer would have pulled his gun, let alone discharged it, if he'd stopped a white teenager.' Then, I'd add in a line about Angie Thomas demonstrating how racism and police brutality are inevitably linked.'"

"Wow. You're really good at this. Do you care if I write that down?"

"Not at all."

Fuller grabbed a pen from his backpack and began scribbling notes into a notebook.

It was the first time he'd come to study hall with more than his laptop.

"I need to go through my paper and do this to, like, all of it." Fuller inhaled slowly and ran a hand through his hair. "Do you think I'll be able to fix all these issues and the citations in two days?"

"Definitely."

Fuller exhaled. "For real?"

"For real."

"I have a favor to ask." Fuller tapped his pen against his open palm. "Do you think you could circle some of the run-on sentences and other issues? That way, after I get home from practice, I'll know what to work on."

"Sure." I accepted the red pen and began circling.

Several minutes later, I set the pen down and handed Fuller his paper. It looked like it was bleeding. But if he fixed all the errors, he'd totally impress Mrs. Brewster and earn a great grade. That, plus a few solid homework assignments, would all but secure his spot on the team.

"Oomph," he said, his eyes going wide. "That bad, huh?"

"I may have gone a little overboard, but if you get an A on this paper and do a good job on a homework assignment or two, it will definitely bring your grade up to a C or B. I figured you'd want to aim for that."

"You really think I could get an A on this paper?" Fuller's voice lacked confidence.

"I do." I wanted to reach out and give his hand a reassuring squeeze, but I stopped myself. "Writing a paper is like shooting a free throw. Sure, a big chunk of it is preparation and skill, but you know as well as I do, confidence plays an equal, if not bigger, part in nailing the end result."

Fuller smiled. "Thanks, Wren."

"You're the one who did the work. Be proud of yourself." I felt like I'd entered an alternate universe. One where at the drop of a DVD case, Fuller and I were getting along. I was even giving him compliments. I brought my hand to my forehead—nope, no fever. This was definitely happening.

Leafing through the pages, Fuller nodded. "Reading, well, listening to the entire book helps a lot, too." He chuckled. "It's just so hard to make time for anything other than basketball."

"At least you figured it out now and not next year," I offered.

As soon as I'd mentioned the future, Fuller's shoulders drooped and his jaw twitched.

"Did I say something wrong?"

Fuller ran his hands through his hair. When he pulled them away, his wavy locks stood up at a funny angle.

Pressing my lips together, I stifled a chuckle.

"Are you laughing at me?" Fuller's eyes crinkled in the corners.

Reaching forward, I ran my fingers through the unruly locks. "There you go."

Oh my gosh. Did I just touch his hair? What's wrong with me?

"Wh-What's the deal with next year? Why did you tense up?" I stammered, trying to get ahold of myself.

"I don't know if getting a scholarship to UGA is ever going to happen." I'd never heard him sound so dejected.

His confession left me stunned. "Why would you say that? You had scouts watching you last year, and they're supposed to be at the opener this year."

"AP isn't the only class I'm struggling in." He sank into his chair. "I'm doing okay in Ancient Civilizations and Physics, but Algebra Two…" He rubbed his collarbone with an open palm. "That's another story."

I'd taken that class two years ago. I'd earned an A each semester.

"What part is giving you trouble?"

He shook his head. "All of it. I'm totally lost."

"I could help you." The words tumbled out of my mouth before I could stop myself.

"No."

"Excuse me?" My face scrunched up in surprise.

"You've already helped me with enough." Fuller

motioned to his paper. "I can't ask you for any more of your time. Especially not after what happened yesterday."

"Shut up."

Throwing his head back, Fuller broke out in laughter. "Did…did you just tell me to shut up?"

With both elbows on the table, I propped up my head with my hands. "What if I did?"

He started laughing again. "People don't usually say that to me. Well, minus my little brother."

"Sounds like he and I'd get along well." This time it was my turn to laugh.

"Hey, you can totally say no. But, would you maybe want to come over after practice?" Fuller's shoulders went up slightly, and his head tilted to the left.

I'd never seen Fuller act shy before. I had to admit, it was pretty cute.

"You could meet Hudson and maybe help me understand polynomials and monomials?" His features had softened, and my breath caught in my chest, just for a second.

"Sure." *Dang it. Stop agreeing to spend more time with him.*

He flashed me a killer smile. The kind that took your breath away and made your knees go weak. "Thanks, Wren. You have no idea how much I appreciate your help."

A few minutes later the bell rang.

Fuller headed off to practice while I stayed behind to get my Calculus homework done. Sometimes doing my homework at school was easier than starting it at home.

Buzz. Buzz.

DAE: Where are you?

ME: Library.

DAE: Are you with Fuller?

ME: No.
ME: I wanted to make a dent in my Calculus homework before I head home for a quick run and to hang with Gramps.

DAE: I already did mine. ;)

ME: Lucky.

DAE: Want to come over for dinner?
DAE: My mom is making sundubu-jjigae.

ME: I'd love to, but I can't.

DAE: You're passing up sundubu-jjigae?
DAE: Are you feeling okay?
DAE: LOL!

ME: No.

ME: I've got a thing.

DAE: A thing?

ME: Don't judge me.
ME: Okay?

DAE: You're freaking me out.

ME: I'm freaking me out.

DAE: Why? Tell me what's going on.
DAE: What are you doing tonight?

ME: I'm helping Fuller with his math homework.
ME: At his house.

DAE: Clearly I slipped and hit my head.
DAE: In my confused state, I thought I read that

you're going to Fuller James's house tonight.

ME: You agreed not to judge me!

DAE: Wait, you're serious?

ME: Yeah, I know.
ME: I can't believe myself either.

DAE: I need details.

ME: Come meet me in the library.

DAE: Already on my way.

Chapter Ten

FULLER

"How was school today?" I tossed my duffel bag on the couch.

Hudson winked. "Aced my math test and got a note from Lydia. She thinks I'm cute."

"Ah, Little Romeo strikes again." I ruffled his dark brown hair. "Good job on the math test, buddy."

"That stinks." Hudson pointed to my bag and then pinched his nose. "You must have practiced extra hard, Betty."

"Betty?"

"Yeah, you're a Sweaty Betty." He held up his hands, palms facing the ceiling. "Get it?"

"I see someone has jokes for days." I grabbed my bag. "Maybe I should dump my practice jersey and shorts on your bed? Or I could hide them all over your room? It could be like a smelly treasure hunt?"

Pinching both sides of his nose, he proclaimed, "Gross."

"Yeah, yeah. Listen, I have a friend coming over to do

homework tonight. Try not to embarrass yourself, okay?" I copied his wink and pointing move.

"A friend?" Hudson raised an eyebrow. "Is it Marc?"

I could feel my cheeks starting to get warm. "Nope. A new friend. A smart friend."

"Who is it?"

"Her name is Wren."

Hudson sprang to his feet. "It's a girl? You're having a girl over to study? Ooh. I'm telling Mom and Dad!" He raced out of the room with me on his heels.

Flinging the duffel onto the floor, I finally caught up with him in the kitchen.

"Mom, Dad, guess what? Fuller's got a *girl* coming over." He stretched out the word into at least five syllables.

My dad turned toward me with concern written across his brow.

"Before blabbermouth made his little announcement, I was getting ready to come in here and ask if it's okay for my friend Wren to come over tonight." *That's twice now. Two times I've called Wren my friend.*

"No." My mom stood with her hands on her hips. "You aren't having anyone over until you pull your AP grade up."

Dang. They never tell me no.

"She's the girl tutoring me at school." I glared at my brother but winked before turning away. I could never stay mad at him. "She's going to help me with my paper tonight, and if we have time, we'll tackle our math homework." Technically we both had math homework. What my parents didn't need to know was that Wren was breezing through Calculus, while I was struggling in Algebra Two. "And, to make things clear, I'm not interested in her. She's just a friend."

Hudson immediately broke into Biz Markie's "Just a Friend" song.

I couldn't even be mad. Hudson was hilarious.

Mom's stern expression faded. "Oh. Well, I guess that's different. As long as she's working with you on schoolwork, she can come over."

"Thanks, Mom. I'm going to make a sandwich real quick and throw my clothes in the wash. She should be here in half an hour."

"There's leftover tuna casserole." My mom pointed to a large pan on the stove. "Would you rather have some of that?"

"Nah, a sandwich sounds good, but thanks." I turned toward my little brother. "We're going to study in the family room. Hudson, I need you to clear out, okay?"

My little brother giggled. "Why, so you two can make out?"

"You're dead," I shouted as I charged him, but we both knew I wouldn't touch him. Even though he had a mild form of brittle bone disease, he could still get hurt at the drop of a hat.

He screamed and darted around the corner.

"Be careful, Hudson!" My dad shook his head. "He's going to break his arm again if he keeps racing around like that."

Mom rubbed his back. "He'll be okay."

There was always this delicate balancing act when it came to my little brother. Half the time, we were doing our best to treat him like a normal kid. The other half, we were telling him to be careful and stop running everywhere.

I checked the time on my phone. "I better hurry up."

The refrigerator was stocked with everything necessary for the perfect sandwich. I grabbed the mayo, yellow mustard, salami, sharp cheddar cheese, tomatoes, and lettuce. My stomach grumbled as I started constructing the sandwich on the counter. "Anybody else want one?"

"I'm good, but thanks for asking, champ." Dad put his

arm around Mom's shoulders. "The tuna casserole was delicious."

"Mom?"

She rubbed her stomach. "I'm full, but thank you for the offer."

I didn't dare admit it, but the only reason I didn't want to have any of the tuna casserole was because I was worried that it would make my breath stink. I mean, sure, I could brush my teeth before Wren got here, but that stuff lingered.

By the time I finished making the sandwich, the grumbles in my belly were audible. Maybe I better make two.

Dingdong.

"Crap." With half a bite of sandwich in my mouth, I raced toward the front door, praying Hudson wouldn't get there first. Pausing in the hallway, I checked my reflection in the hanging mirror. Still chewing, I ran my hands through my hair. It always looked a mess after practice, and today was no exception.

"Helllllo!" Hudson swung open the door and grinned. "You must be Wren. Please, come on in." He held out his arm and motioned for her to come inside.

I inhaled sharply as Wren walked through the door. She'd changed into yoga pants that emphasized her legs and her firm butt. She'd pulled her long brown hair into a high ponytail that swung back and forth.

Damn, she's hot.

"You must be Hudson." Wren grinned and held out her hand. "It's very nice to meet you."

Hudson beamed as he extended his own hand and returned the handshake. "Ooh, a top-row-teeth smiler. Your favorite, Fuller." Hudson looked at me and winked. "And you're totally right, she *is* cute."

"Hudson!" I lunged at him but purposefully let him slip through my fingers.

"Nice to meet you," he called over his shoulder as he darted around the corner.

"Sorry about that." I motioned to my brother. "He's always trying to embarrass me."

"What's a top-row-teeth smiler?" Her lips curved up into a smile. The simple gesture sent my heart racing. Between those lips and legs, it was a miracle that she didn't already have a boyfriend. How did Dae and Brandon hang around her so much without falling for her?

"Ah, it's something Hudson always points out. I guess that makes us top- row twins." She winked.

"Oh, I guess I've never thought about that before. What kind of smile do you have?"

I smiled. "Top row, all the way."

"Two top rows... You know what that means." She winked.

Holy crap! Did she just wink at me?

Wren looked at her smartwatch. "I'm a little bit early, but Gramps wasn't feeling well and went to bed right after dinner. Hope that's alright?" Her long lashes swept up as she looked into my eyes.

"Is he okay?"

She rocked her head back and forth slightly. "He said that he felt dizzy. He's had plenty of water today, and he doesn't have a fever, so we're hoping it's something minor, like a little virus, that will pass quickly. My mom is keeping a close eye on him."

"I'm sorry he's not feeling well." Even though I'd only met him once, I already knew how important Gramps was to Wren and her family.

"Me too. Hopefully he'll feel better in the morning. If not, my dad will take him to the doctor. It's better to be safe than sorry."

Wren had no idea how familiar everything she was saying

felt. We were always worried about Hudson getting hurt, at home and at school. He'd broken his arm and collarbone last year after tripping on the top step of our staircase. A simple mistake had landed him in a cast and sling for eight weeks.

"So, you ready to do some math?" She adjusted the strap of her messenger bag.

"Oh, yeah. I just need to grab my stuff and put some clothes in the laundry. Can you give me two minutes?"

"Of course." She glanced around the entryway.

"Sorry. We can work in here." I led her into the room and toward the oversize sofa. "Can I get you a glass of lemonade or some water?"

"Water sounds great." Wren sat down on the sofa and opened up a large messenger bag. She began pulling out notebooks, a calculator, and her laptop.

My mom and dad popped around the corner. "Hi. You must be Fuller's tutor."

Wren stood up, tipping one of her notebooks off the couch in the process. "Oops."

I bent down to pick it up at the same time as Wren. When our hands brushed, sparks flew. *Dang, this girl is practically electric.*

Wren's cheeks turned pink. "Yes, I'm Wren. It's nice to meet you."

My mom smiled. "Fuller tells us that you're going to help him with his AP paper tonight and math homework, if there's enough time?"

"Yes, ma'am."

"We really appreciate you helping our son," my dad added. "He sure got himself in a pickle. Do you think he'll be able to raise his grade before the first game?"

My jaw dropped and my cheeks felt like they were on fire. *He didn't really say that in front of Wren, did he?* I'd literally never been so embarrassed in my entire life, which includes the time Marissa grabbed my butt in front of Hudson. I didn't hear the end of that for months.

My parents were talking about me like I wasn't even here.

"Yes, sir. Fuller is aiming for an A on his paper, which should pull his grade to a C or even a C plus. That, paired with solid grades on two homework assignments, will give him a B in no time."

Guilt sank into my stomach like an anchor dropping into choppy water. While I hadn't given Wren her terrible nickname in seventh grade, I did nothing to stop Marissa from mercilessly teasing her. I'd even joined in by calling her Wrentainer a few times. Of course, I'd stopped calling her that years ago, but I still felt like an asshole for going along with my friends as they made fun of her. Now, here she was, at my house, helping me, when she could have been anywhere else, doing anything else.

"That's wonderful news." My mom smiled. "I'm sure you know Fuller has his heart set on the University of Georgia next year. Have you picked out where you're going to school?"

"Yes, ma'am. I've already accepted early admission to the University of Georgia."

Wait. What did she say?

Why didn't she mention that to me before? The thought of seeing Wren walking around campus in those yoga pants next year made my fingers tingle.

My mom clapped her hands together. "Oh, how lovely. Maybe you and Fuller can continue to be study buddies next year."

The possibility made the corners of my lips twitch. Late nights, sitting next to Wren, hunched over a pile of books. My mind drifted to her cheering me on from the stands. It would be nice to see a familiar face next year…a really beautiful familiar face.

"What will you be studying at UGA, Wren?" My dad

never took this much interest in the girls I brought home. Not that I brought a ton of girls home, but there had been a few and he'd never had this kind of reaction to any of them.

The reality of the bet hit me in the face. If Wren found out, she wouldn't want to talk to me, let alone study with me. *I should suck it up and come clean…* But I knew that I couldn't. There was too much at risk. I needed to bring my grade up and that would be nearly impossible without Wren's help.

"I plan on going into engineering," Wren said. "They've got a great program at UGA."

My dad's eyebrows shot up. "They certainly do. I did my undergrad there. I still have a few contacts. Dr. Julia Klopp, the head of the engineering department, is a good friend. If you ever need me to put in a good word, let me know."

"Thank you very much, sir."

Mom looped her arm through Dad's. "Well, we won't keep you two from getting to work. Thanks again, Wren. It's very nice meeting you."

"It's nice meeting you, too."

"You're welcome to come over anytime. Fuller needs good influences in his life." My mom glanced in my direction. "Okay, come on, Charlie, let's let the kids get to their studying."

As soon as they left, I whispered, "I'm sorry about all of that." *And for everything else.* Too bad I didn't have the courage to say it to her face.

She waved my apology off. "No big deal."

I almost felt like I was in a parallel universe. There was a girl in our living room, and my parents actually approved. They totally hated Marissa. My mom even told me that she and my dad thought my ex-girlfriend was shallow and bad for me. Why hadn't I listened to her? They practically forbade her from coming over. Now they'd met Wren for all of two minutes and they were already inviting her a second time and offering to call in favors to buddies at UGA.

"I'll be right back, okay?" I said.

"Sure."

"I've just gotta grab a sandwich from the kitchen and toss my gym clothes in the wash. If I don't, we might need to call in a hazmat team to disinfect my room."

Wren scrunched up her nose and laughed. She looked really cute.

Wren held up her calculator. "Make sure you bring one of these when you come back."

"On it." As soon as I rounded the corner, I raced back into the kitchen and shoved a gigantic bite of the first sandwich into my mouth. Chewing frantically, I swallowed and took another bite. I definitely didn't want to keep Wren waiting, but I had to eat something or I wouldn't be able to concentrate.

"I like her." Mom winked at me. "And she's very pretty."

I pointed to my mouth.

"Don't worry, I'll ask you more about her later."

Of course she would. What would I say? *Oh, Wren? Yeah, I know she's beautiful. Why don't I spend more time with her? Good question. I guess she wasn't cool enough before…*

Pushing the thoughts from my mind, I finished chewing the last bite and swallowed.

The second sandwich I made a few minutes ago sat on the plate. There was no way I could shove that one down my throat at the same speed.

I frowned. I'd cut it in half and everything. I really needed to eat it, but I didn't want to keep Wren waiting. Deciding she wouldn't care, I poured two tall glasses of water. Balancing everything in my hands, I headed back to the family room.

"Guard this sandwich with your life," I joked.

"Huh?"

"Oh, I was trying to make a joke." *Stop acting like such a dork.* "Here's your water." Our fingers brushed as I handed her the glass. My fingers tingled. Two times in one night. I'd never felt that kind of intense reaction when I hung out with Marissa, which included plenty of make-out sessions in the back of her BMW.

"Okay, I just need to pop my laundry in the washing machine. I'll be right back. Oh, and help yourself to half the sandwich."

"All right." She eyed the sandwich with a grin. "If you have a tablet, bring that down, too. There's an algebra app I want to show you."

"Awesome. Be right back." I hustled out of the room and grabbed the duffel bag from the hallway. Taking the stairs two at a time, I dumped my smelly basketball clothes into the washing machine and added detergent. "These can go in, too," I said to myself as I added a basket of my little brother's clothing.

A few minutes later, I made it back down the stairs with my tablet, calculator, and everything else I could possibly need. "Ready." *Wait, when did she get the glasses?* The oversize black frames made her look even cuter than before.

Looking up, she totally caught me staring.

"Oh, yeah. I wear contacts to school." Wren pushed the glasses up. "When I get home, I switch to these."

"They look really nice." *What did you say to her? Get ahold of yourself before you spill anything else!*

"Um, thanks." Wren's fingers brushed against the frames and adjusted them slightly.

"I figured you didn't have much time to work on the paper since I marked it up in study hall, so I was thinking we could tackle math first?" Wren pulled out her tablet and powered it on. "Then, when you're done, all you'll need to do with your paper is clean up your citations and tighten up the sentences I marked. Sound good?"

"That would be great."

Forty-five minutes and one app later, I finally had a breakthrough. Wren had managed to explain polynomials and monomials in a way that actually made sense. We'd gone through more than half the problems I'd been assigned for homework, and after the lightbulb turned on, I'd gotten all of them right.

"Why didn't Mr. Osla explain it this way?" I set my math book down. "Seriously—the way you taught me makes perfect sense."

Wren shrugged and grinned. "I guess I'm the world's best tutor." She burst out laughing a second after the words left her lips.

I joined in. "I'm going to get that on a coffee mug for you."

A lock of Wren's hair had slipped free from her ponytail and fell across her face.

Before I could stop myself, I reached forward and tucked it behind her ear. It was as soft as I'd imagined. A little cool to the touch.

Her dark lashes swept up, revealing green eyes with swirls of gold. Even through the thick lenses, they were massive.

And tempting.

Her hand met mine, sending shock waves to my core as our fingers wound together.

My mouth went dry. "You're beautiful."

Wren's lips parted, but she didn't say anything. More importantly, she didn't pull away. She might have even leaned forward a bit. Wren freaking Carter leaning toward me? I couldn't believe what that little motion did to me.

Bringing my other hand up, I cupped her cheeks. Yep. Her skin was equally as awesome-feeling as her hair. Soft, smooth, silky. And it was exactly right that I was holding her like this.

I wanted to kiss her.

Scratch that, I *needed* to kiss her. Feel those lips on mine.

I leaned in until we were only inches apart. Her floral scent wrapped around me. A scent I'd never smelled before and never wanted to forget.

"Fuller," she whispered, the space between us shrinking even farther.

My heart slammed in my chest, stealing my breath. I'd never wanted to kiss someone more in my entire life. I knew it could be amazing. I needed to find out.

"Wren, can I—"

Buzz. Buzz. Buzz. Buzz.

Wren's eyes went wide. Pulling back, she patted the sofa around her. Once her fingers found it, she pressed it to her ear, never taking her gaze from me. "Hey, Mom. What's up?"

Holy buckets. What just happened? Did Wren and I almost kiss?

The color drained from her face, and she sat up straight. "Wait, what? What happened? Where are you?"

Frowning, I watched Wren whip off her glasses and rub her face. "Okay. Yeah, I'll be right there."

Wren let her hand fall into her lap. Tears welled up in her eyes.

"What happened?" I grabbed her hand.

"M-My grandpa. He was complaining of chest pain and fell." She put her glasses back on. "I've gotta go. My mom is riding with him to the emergency room. My dad is driving there behind the ambulance."

"Oh my gosh. I'm so sorry, Wren." I let go of her hand and helped her scoop everything into her bag.

"Please tell your parents. I, um, I—" Wren shook her head and glanced toward the door. "Um—"

Her hands trembled as she slung her bag over her

shoulder. She looked so small and fragile, I wanted to pull her into my arms and tell her that everything would be okay. "You shouldn't get behind the wheel right now. Please let me drive you."

Wren hesitated for a moment before nodding.

"Fuller? What's going on?" My dad stuck his head around the corner.

The almost kiss coupled with the bad news had left me breathless. "Wren's grandpa is having chest pain and he fell. She needs to meet her family at the emergency room, and I offered to drive her."

My dad looked down at his phone. He was an emergency room doctor at the main hospital in town. "I'll give Dr. Adams a heads-up that her grandpa is on his way in. He's on duty tonight."

"Thank you so much." Wren's voice was thick.

"Thanks, Dad. I appreciate it."

"Drive safe." He grabbed my car keys and wallet from the small glass dish in the hallway and tossed them to me. Snagging them both out of the air, I took Wren's hand and raced toward my car.

Chapter Eleven

Wren

"It's going to be okay." Fuller reached over and squeezed my hand.

Hot tears rolled down my cheeks and fell to my lap. "H-H-He's going to be so confused and scared."

"Your mom is with him in the ambulance though, right? That'll help. Your dad is right behind in his car, and we're only a few minutes away." Fuller's voice was calm.

The thought of Gramps strapped to a gurney in the back of an ambulance was almost too much for me to handle. "I can't believe I wasn't there to help. What if he's having a heart attack?"

"You do so much for your grandpa. You can't always be there. And chest pain can be anything from indigestion to heartburn, not always something serious. Hopefully it's only minor."

"What if it's not?" I asked, half to him and half to myself. I knew he was right, but I didn't want to believe it. Guilt settled in the pit of my stomach. Gramps wasn't feeling well earlier; I should have stayed home with him. Kept a close eye on him. I felt sick, like I was going to vomit. The only thing that would make me feel better would be seeing Gramps's face.

Still holding my hand, Fuller spoke softly. "I've been here before. Well, not rushing to the hospital for my grandpa, but with Hudson. The fear of not knowing what was wrong with him nearly caused me to have a full-blown anxiety attack. His screams of pain. Not being able to do anything that would make him feel better. The helplessness was overwhelming."

"How did you learn to handle it?" My voice shook.

"I don't think you're ever prepared or fully know how to handle situations like this, but taking deep breaths and trying to think positively really helps. Also, trusting the doctors to do what they do best lets me remain as calm as possible."

I wiped fresh tears from my face and forced a deep breath. It helped a little bit, but that all went out the window when the hospital came into view. Fuller followed the red emergency room signs until we entered a large parking lot.

I pulled my hand back, immediately missing the comforting touch. "Thanks for the ride. I really appreciate it."

"Wait." Fuller pulled into an empty parking space and turned off his car. "I'll come in with you."

"Are you sure?"

"Absolutely."

We got out of the car and raced toward the big glass sliding doors. Bright lights and an employee sitting behind a large desk met us as we entered.

My hands trembled. "Hi, my name is Wren Carter and I'm looking for my grandfather, Eugene Kaufman. He came by ambulance with my mom. My dad should be there, too."

A woman with big brown eyes and curly black hair typed his name into her computer. She had a plastic nametag that read "Sandra." "He's being evaluated right now. We have a two-visitor policy in each room, so we'll need you to wait out here." She motioned to the waiting room behind her. A handful of people sat scattered in wooden chairs with plastic cushions. Little kids in pajamas sat in the laps of their parents. One woman was in a wheelchair, a mask covering her mouth.

"But I need to see him. Make sure he's okay." The onslaught of fresh tears stung my eyes.

Fuller grabbed a few tissues from a box sitting on the counter. He handed me one, folded the rest, and put them in his pocket.

"You can switch places with your mother or father, but we can't have more than two people with the patient. Otherwise, there isn't enough room for the doctors and machines."

"Thank you, Sandra." Fuller touched my elbow and guided me to the waiting room. "Why don't you text your mom and dad that you're here? I'm sure one of them will switch spots with you as soon as it's possible. They're probably helping with paperwork and insurance details, you know?"

I nodded and dabbed my eyes with the tissue again.

We sat in a double seat. Reaching around to my back pocket, I grabbed my phone, opened up my messages app, and typed out a message to my parents.

ME: I'm in the waiting room.
ME: They won't let me come back.
ME: Something about a two-person limit?
ME: How is Gramps?
ME: What do the doctors think is wrong with him?

MOM: They're getting ready to take him in for X-rays.

ME: X-rays?
ME: What about the chest pain?

DAD: No signs of a heart attack.

ME: Thank goodness!

DAD: They'll keep running tests but want to get the X-rays done as soon as possible.

MOM: Doc thinks he may have broken a rib and possibly his wrist when he fell.

DAD: I'll switch places with you as soon as he's back.

MOM: Your friend's dad called and alerted one of the doctors on call.
MOM: He's taken very good care of Gramps.
MOM: Please tell him thank you very much.

ME: Thanks, Mom.
ME: Please tell Gramps that I love him!
ME: And that I have a super special basketball game to watch with him as soon as we get home.

MOM: Will do, honey.
MOM: We love you.

ME: Love you too.

"What did they say?"

I relayed the information to Fuller.

"That's great news about it not being a heart attack." Fuller sighed with relief and took my hand in his. "My dad has worked here in the ER for almost ten years. This is a really good hospital. Your gramps is in great hands."

I leaned against Fuller and let my head fall to his shoulder. Sobs racked my body. In any other situation, I'd be obsessing about our almost kiss. Scrutinizing every single detail, but all

I could think about was Gramps. I loved him so much, and the thought of him being scared and in pain was the absolute worst feeling in the entire universe. Tears blurred my vision as my body continued to tremble.

"Shhh. Shhh. It's okay." Fuller repeated the same phrase over and over while I continued to cry. He wrapped his arm around me for support. After what felt like a lifetime, my phone buzzed.

MOM: Grandpa's ribs are fine, but he broke his wrist.
MOM: The X-ray confirmed it.
MOM: He needs to have surgery, but they're going to wait until the morning when the orthopedic doctor gets in.

ME: Oh no!

MOM: Dad is going to come out so you can come in.

ME: Thank you!
ME: What about the chest pain?

MOM: Possible acid reflux, but they're going to check for gallstones with an ultrasound.

ME: Poor Gramps...

MOM: Try not to worry.
MOM: They are taking excellent care of him.

ME: I know, I just feel so helpless.

MOM: Everything is going to be okay, sweetheart.
MOM: Dad is on his way.
MOM: Love you <3

ME: Love you too <3

"They're still trying to figure out the chest pain. Might be acid reflux or gallstones. They are going to do an ultrasound. But he definitely needs to have surgery to fix his wrist," I told Fuller.

"What kind of surgery?" Fuller's eyes were full of concern.

"He broke it. I guess they're waiting on an orthopedic doctor in the morning." I glanced at the text message again. My vision clouded over with tears. "He must be in so much pain right now."

"I'm sure they've given him something for that. They have great orthopedic doctors here. Hudson's been seen by a few of them. I know I said it before, but I mean it—your gramps is in great hands."

I blinked back the onslaught of fresh tears that threatened to spill over at any moment.

My dad emerged from behind a large wooden door. He scanned the waiting room until he spotted me waving at him.

"Wren, and, um, who's your friend?"

"Friend." Oof, that was a loaded word. Our almost kiss flashed through my mind. How he'd cupped my face, how I'd leaned in and closed my eyes, and how I wanted his lips on mine more than anything I'd ever wanted before. My heart thumped and my palms suddenly felt damp. *No. Stop.* I couldn't think about that now. There was too much going on. "Hey, Dad. This is Fuller, the boy I'm tutoring. I was at his house when Mom called. I was too upset to drive, so he gave me a ride."

"It's very nice to meet you, sir. I'm sorry it's under these circumstances."

My dad held out his hand. "Thank you very much, young man. Dr. Adams is remarkable. Please tell your father we are incredibly grateful."

Fuller stood and shook my dad's hand. "Of course, sir."

"How do I get to Gramps?" I asked.

"Through those doors, down the hall, there's a little desk. The man behind it will take you to his room."

"Thanks, Dad." I turned toward Fuller. "Thank you. You have no idea how much all of this means to me."

"Listen, Wren, before you go back there," Dad said. "I'm going to run out to the car and grab a few things from the trunk for your mom. They're going to admit Gramps to the hospital and she's going to spend the night with him. I'm going to stay for a little bit longer, but I hate the idea of you sitting out here by yourself."

"I don't want to leave. I want to stay with Gramps." My voice caught in my throat.

"Visiting hours are nearly over in the main part of the hospital. Once Gramps is admitted, he can only have one family member with him." He placed his hand on my shoulder and gave it a squeeze.

"Oh." My head dropped.

"But you can see him tomorrow after school. He'll be out of surgery and feeling much better by then, I'm sure." My dad gave me what appeared to be his best reassuring smile.

Fuller stood next to me. His hands were clasped. "Sir, after Wren visits with her grandfather, I'd be happy to drive her home."

I chewed on my lower lip. "Are you sure? You still have math homework, and you need to clean up your paper."

"I'll be fine, I promise." Fuller nodded.

My dad put his hand on Fuller's shoulder. "Thank you very much. We'd really appreciate that."

We locked eyes. His were full of compassion and empathy. "Are you sure you don't mind waiting out here for me?" I asked.

Fuller shook his head. “Not at all.”

My stomach twisted into a knot as I gave my dad a quick hug before heading across the waiting room. Grabbing a squirt of hand sanitizer, I pushed through the swinging doors and headed down the hall and toward Gramps.

Chapter Twelve

Fuller

Moonlight streamed through the large leaves on the oak tree next to Wren's driveway. As I put my car in park, I stole a glance at her in the passenger's seat. She'd slid her shoes off and tucked her long legs underneath her chin. She pressed a balled-up tissue under her eyes, which were puffy from crying. Fighting the urge to reach out and pull her into my arms, I folded my hands in my lap. "You were really brave tonight, Wren."

She exhaled slowly, hugging her legs. "Seeing him in that hospital bed…" Her voice quavered. "He looked so fragile."

"Hudson was admitted last year after breaking his arm and his collarbone." I tried to control the emotion in my own voice. "My little brother is tough and he's been through more than most kids his age, but seeing him in a hospital bed was the absolute worst." My throat constricted as I recalled one of the many traumatic events he'd been through in his short life. "He didn't belong in those sterile rooms, wrapped up in the thin white sheets and scratchy blankets." Tears stung the corners of my eyes.

"Poor Hudson." Wren shook her head.

"The good thing is, he got better, and so will your grandfather." I gave her a sad smile. "You just have to stay strong."

"Yeah..." Wren looked down at her shoes.

We sat there in silence for several minutes. It was comfortable, unlike when Marissa and I were in her convertible. When we weren't making out, she would blab on about herself for hours on end. Why had I wasted so much time with someone so shallow? Because she looked good in those ridiculous shoes she teetered around in at school?

A stinging realization settled in my core. Sure, she was shallow, but was I any better?

Being with Wren felt natural, not forced. I could be real with her and she wouldn't rag on me for my insecurities. Our conversations were open, and they actually meant something. Most importantly, when I was with her, I wasn't just a dumb jock with a six-pack or Fuller, "Captain of the State Champions."

For the first time in years, I felt like I could shed the cocky exterior and just relax.

"Fuller, I know you've got a lot of homework, but is there any chance you'd come in and hang out until my dad gets back? I really don't want to be alone right now." Wren hugged her legs to her chest even tighter.

"Of course." I'd secretly been hoping she'd want me to keep her company for a little bit longer. "And don't worry about the homework. I can finish that up in the morning."

She sniffled and gave a thankful nod.

Part of me wanted to take her into my arms and kiss her. Like you'd see in the movies. A grand romantic gesture, literally sweeping her off her feet. But I knew better. Emotions were high right now, and Wren needed a friend.

Plus, if I was serious about something happening, I needed to tell Marc the bet was off and confess to Wren. I had to face the facts. Even though we weren't in one yet, our relationship would be doomed if I didn't come clean. Guilt clamped down on my heart. It was like a vise grip that I couldn't get loose.

She gave me a sad smile that pulled me out of my internal debate. "Thanks."

As we made our way to her front door, I pulled out my phone. "I'm going to send my parents a quick text. Let them know what's going on."

Wren nodded as she fished out her key and unlocked the front door.

A text from Marc flashed across the screen.

MARC: I stopped by your house.
MARC: Your parents told me you're with Wren?

He followed the text with a gif of Stanley from *The Office* laughing hysterically.

A suffocating sensation settled across my chest. I wished I'd never made that stupid bet.

"Everything okay?" Wren asked from inside her house. "You're frowning."

"Oh, um, yeah," I lied. I quickly typed out a message to my parents and hit send.

I followed Wren as she walked through her house, past the table I'd sat at and talked basketball with her Gramps, and into the kitchen. "I'm going to make a cup of tea. Do you want one?"

"Sounds good." The only time I'd ever drunk tea was when I had a sore throat. My mom would make a steaming mug and load it up with honey and lemon.

Wren's kitchen was small but warm. Bananas hung from

one of those hooks in the corner, next to an electric kettle. As Wren got to work on filling the kettle, I leaned against the blue Formica countertop. My eyes drifted to the refrigerator, where there were a series of magnets lined up. "Wait a minute, are all of these you?"

Wren's cheeks turned pink. "Oh, yeah. Those… Only child syndrome. All of the most embarrassing pictures are constantly on display."

She tugged the elastic out of her ponytail. As her hair fell to her shoulders, I caught a whiff of tropical flowers.

"You really don't have to look at them." Wren reached out to stop me, but I pivoted and spun around her, like a well-executed fakeout on the court.

"Oh, but I do." I grinned as I inspected the magnets. Each one contained a picture of Wren, from what looked to be about age five to last year. In the pictures, she wore either a track and field outfit or, in the more recent ones, a cross-country uniform. "You're adorable."

Oh, crap. Did I say that out loud?

"Ah, thanks." Her face went from a subtle shade of pink to bright red. "That shrine is kind of embarrassing, but my parents love it."

"My parents insist on displaying a picture of me in the bathtub. Which, when it's in a baby scrapbook, whatever. No big deal. But in reality, it's hanging on the wall across from my bedroom. So, yeah, I totally understand the parental embarrassment factor."

Wren let out a chuckle. A warm feeling rushed through my chest.

"You do know that if I ever come over to your house again, I'm totally swiping that picture and sending it to the anonymous Instagram account." Wren pressed her lips together, suppressing a smile.

I took a step away from the fridge and in one swift

motion, I wrapped my arms around her and tickled her waist. "You wouldn't dare."

Wren burst out in a fit of giggles, trying to wiggle away. She managed to trap my hands by pulling them behind her and pressing her body against the cabinets.

Holy buckets. My hands were on her butt. Her perfect, firm, round butt…

"Whoa." I pulled my hands back. "Are you okay with all of this? I mean, you've been through a lot tonight and I just want to make sure that—"

"Fuller, I'm completely okay with this. Actually, I've never wanted something more." Her tongue darted out and licked her lower lip. A flare went off inside my body, sending heat radiating from my fingertips to my toes.

I slid my hands down the back of Wren's legs and picked her up. Her mouth opened in surprise as I placed her gently on top of the countertop.

Wren reached forward and wrapped her hands around the back of my neck, pulling me forward in the process. Her dark lashes swept up and, for the second time that night, I wanted to kiss her more than I'd ever wanted to kiss anyone else.

Ever.

"Wren, I—" But I couldn't finish the sentence; the golden swirls in her emerald eyes had left me speechless. Screw that, I was mesmerized.

"Kiss me," she said breathlessly.

Closing the space between us, my lips brushed against hers. What started out as gentle and innocent soon turned into a desire-ridden hunger. Our tongues explored each other's mouths as my hands ran through her silky locks. She tasted like fresh spearmint.

Wren wrapped her legs around me, bringing me in even closer. I'd promised myself that I wouldn't let things go anywhere. I *couldn't* let them. Not unless I squashed this bet once and for all. I wanted to be completely honest with her, but I was too afraid she'd never speak to me again. Hurting Wren was out of the question, but as she ran her tongue across my lower lip, I forgot all about the bet and the terrible consequences that were sure to follow. All I wanted was to stay in this moment forever.

"Hey, Wren. I'm home."

I froze but found myself unable to pull away. My lips still yearned for Wren's touch.

With an intense shove to the chest, Wren pushed me back and hopped off the counter. She smoothed out her hair and took a deep breath. "We're in the kitchen, Dad." Grabbing three mugs from the cabinet, she poured boiling water and deposited a tea bag into each.

*Holy buckets. That was…*hot.

"Hey there, Fuller." Her dad gave us a tired smile.

"Hi, Mr. Carter."

"How's Gramps? Any changes?" Wren asked. Her voice was quiet but hopeful.

"Great news. The ultrasound came back and Gramps doesn't have gallstones. He's sleeping now. I think the pain medication will keep him out the rest of the night."

"Oh, thank goodness." Wren gave her father a big hug.

"My dad will be in around seven o'clock tomorrow morning. I'll make sure he checks on Gramps first thing," I said.

"That is awfully kind. Thank you, Fuller." Wren's dad placed a hand on my shoulder.

"Anytime, sir."

Wren turned around and used a small spoon to pull out the soaked tea bags from each mug. "I was making tea, Dad. Would you like some?"

"That sounds perfect. Thanks, sweetheart."

Wren grabbed a little bear filled with honey and squirted it into each of the three mugs. After a splash of milk, she handed one to each of us.

Wren's dad accepted the mug with both hands. "If you don't mind, pumpkin, I'm going to take this to bed. It's been a long night and your old dad needs to get some sleep." He paused and looked at me. "Oh, um. Are you two going to be out here for a while?"

"No, sir," I said. "I'm going to head out after the tea."

He gave me a nod of approval. "Thank you again for your help tonight. If it's okay, Wren and I will drive over to your house to collect her car tomorrow before school."

"Absolutely, sir."

"See you in the morning, Dad." Wren gave him a quick hug, careful to avoid the mug of hot tea.

"Let's, ah, go into the family room." Wren gestured with her shoulder. "This way."

I followed her into a cozy room with a couch and loveseat. The dark brown corduroy material looked comfy. It was the kind of furniture you'd lie down on to binge-watch an entire season of *The Office*.

Wren sat at one end of the couch. I wasn't sure if she wanted me to sit next to her or not, so I made my way to the opposite side.

"So..." She trailed off before saying anything else.

"Yeah." I switched the mug from my left to my right hand. It had a fluffy orange cat on it. I looked around Wren's house, wondering if she had any pets. I suddenly found myself wanting to know everything about her.

She set her cup down on the glass end table. "That was, um, nice."

My hands tingled. "Really nice." *Stop. Stop it right now.* Warring thoughts bounced around in my head. *That kiss. It was so hot. No. You can't do this to her. Wren deserves better.*

Eyebrows knit together, Wren frowned. "Is something wrong?"

"No. Not at all. It's just getting kind of late and I've got a five o'clock wake-up call tomorrow morning. Plus, I've got to finish my math homework and make those last-minute changes on that paper."

I immediately cursed myself for making excuses to leave Wren's house. While they were all valid points, none of them was more important than spending time with her. Time I'd never be able to get back if she found out about the bet.

Her shoulders drooped slightly. "Oh, right. I'm sorry. I totally spaced after we left the hospital."

I set my tea down and scooted next to her on the sofa. "No, don't apologize. There's a lot going on right now." *Yeah, like the fact that I want to kiss you again. And again. And again.*

Her shoulders were still down, but they stiffened up as my leg brushed against hers.

Okay, maybe one more kiss…

My heart started thumping wildly in my chest as I turned toward her. Tipping her chin up, I leaned forward. Her lips tasted like honey. Fire shot through my veins as she pulled me closer, running her hands through my hair, our bodies melting together. Tingles prickled the back of my neck and spine. I'd give anything to spend the rest of my night, screw that, the rest of the school year wrapped up on this couch with Wren.

Her hands worked their way down my back and to the belt loopholes in my jeans. *Holy buckets, this girl has me more worked up than I've ever been before.* I needed to get control of myself, STAT.

Think about your polynomials. That's not hot at all. Boring, boring math homework. Yes, polynomials and a cold shower.

Just when I thought I'd gotten control of myself, Wren's thumb brushed against the bare skin on my lower back.

"Wren, time to wrap things up," her dad called from the other room.

Using all my willpower, I pulled back. Lips parted, my chest heaved. It took everything in me not to continue the hottest make-out session I'd ever experienced. "Ah, yeah. I better get going."

"Right," Wren said breathlessly.

I stood, forcing myself to think of math equations. Otherwise I'd have a whole new reason to stay seated. "See you tomorrow?"

"Sounds good." Wren stood and led me to the front door. "And thank you. For the ride to the hospital, sitting there with me, and bringing me back here."

We stepped out into the chilly night. The air immediately cooled my skin, but not the fire that burned inside for this girl.

"You don't have to thank me for anything. I'm just glad I was able to help." I bent down and kissed Wren on the forehead.

A smile played on Wren's lips. Those perfect lips that tasted like honey and spearmint. *Dude, get a grip.*

"Okay, well, gotta go." My voice came out an octave higher than normal.

Wren's smile got even bigger. "Hey, Fuller?"

"Yeah?"

She stood on her tippy-toes and, in one swift motion, she kissed me. Pulling away, with parted lips, she whispered, "See you tomorrow."

• • •

The drive home only took a few minutes, but I needed every

second to get control of myself. All I could think about was Wren. The way she ran her thumb over my skin, her hands in my hair, the way her tongue licked her lower lip. I'd seen a whole new side of her tonight, one that I wanted to see more of but couldn't. Not until I got out of that stupid bet. And if I couldn't, tonight would be the last time anything ever happened between us.

To make matters worse, time was ticking. The game was next week. I needed to figure something out and fast, but it would have to wait until tomorrow. I had way too much homework to do, and I was getting a really late start.

My dad met me at the front door. "How's Wren doing?"

"She's pretty upset." I tossed my keys into the glass bowl next to the door. "Her family was really grateful you made that call to Dr. Adams. They asked me to thank you."

He nodded. "It's the least I could do for the girl who's helped you write this kind of a paper." He held up the draft of my Lit paper with red marks everywhere. "Now, I know you need to fix a few things, but this is amazing, son. Your mother and I are really proud of you."

Pride swelled in my chest. Mom and Dad were always proud of the work I did on the court, but it had been a long time since either of them had complimented me on my schoolwork. "Thanks. Wren is an incredible tutor. For the first time this year, I finally feel confident about turning in a Lit assignment." *Understatement of the year.*

Hudson appeared at the top of the stairs. "Fuller and Wre-en, sitting in a tree. K-I-S-S-I-N-G." He made kissing sounds and held his hands up like he was making out with an invisible girl.

"You're lucky I have homework to finish, turd."

Hudson giggled and raced off toward his room.

"You shouldn't call him names." My dad tried to appear firm, but the smile that crept up onto his face told another story. “Well, you said you have some homework to finish up. I won’t keep you.”

Sitting down on the couch, I opened my math book and sighed. Somehow, I’d have to find a way to finish my homework and then focus on fixing my paper. Yet all I could think about was Wren.

It was going to be a long night.

Chapter Thirteen

Wren

"I can't believe you made out with Fuller James!" Dae's jaw had practically dropped into his lap.

"I know." I was still in a state of shock.

He tossed a chip at me. "What is wrong with you? F.B.M.? Really?"

"Don't call him that." I laughed.

His eyebrows pulled together in suspicion. "Wait, are you just screwing with me? Making this whole thing up?"

"Nope. I'm telling you the truth. Cross my heart," I said, making an *X* motion over my heart.

Picking up my sub, I shrugged before taking a massive bite. What I didn't admit was that I'd been asking myself the same question and a few others, over and over again. *What's wrong with me? When can Fuller and I make out again? How perfect are his lips?*

Dae took a sip of his soda. We rarely left campus for lunch, but today I had to get away and spill my guts to him.

"Okay, pausing on this Fuller madness for a moment, how's Gramps doing?"

After I finished chewing, I gave him a thumbs-up. "He had surgery this morning. My mom said he did great. He has to have a cast on his arm for a few weeks, but the doctor thinks he'll make a full recovery."

"What about the chest pain?" Dae asked.

I chewed and swallowed a bite before responding, "Doctors can't find anything specific. They think it was just indigestion."

"Wow. That's great news."

Dae totally meant it. Sure, he was a typical guy's guy—he liked to talk about girls and farts, and he and Brandon were always wrestling around—but he had a heart of gold.

"Yeah. He has to spend one more night in the hospital, but he'll get to come home tomorrow. I can't wait. Fuller—" I cut myself off. Almost every single sentence I'd uttered today or thought that had crossed my mind involved Fuller.

Dae grinned. "Fuller what?"

"He gave me a DVD for Gramps. It's an old NBA championship game from 1957. Boston Celtics versus the St. Louis Hawks. Double overtime." A smile spread across my face. "Gramps is going to love it."

"Could he *be* any more adorable?" Dae did his best impersonation of me.

Tossing the chip back at him, I burst out laughing.

• • •

"Please place your papers in the basket on your way out." Mrs. Brewster pointed to the wire basket placed on a bookcase near the door. Several people groaned, but she ignored them. "You can expect them back next week." She was one of the only teachers who still expected us to print out everything. Most of the time, we just submitted our assignments electronically.

I'd already turned my paper in and received an awesome grade, but I knew the anxiety that came with turning in a big assignment. I stole a glance at Fuller. He had his paper in his hand. He'd even put it in a report cover.

As the class shuffled out, I got up and made my way toward the door. Fuller and I met up in the hallway. "You did it!"

He grinned. "I totally did. I feel like the paper is so good. My mom and dad read it last night and said it was the best thing I'd ever written."

"Well, I don't know what else you've written, but I'm really proud of you."

"I couldn't have done it without you, Wren."

"True." I chuckled. "But your hard work is what's going to earn you that A."

Fuller laughed as he opened the library door for me.

We found our regular table and got seated. I bit my lower lip as Fuller's arm brushed against mine, my thoughts drifting back to last night. The way he'd held my hand in the hospital. Our intense make-out session. Scratch that, make-out *sessions*, plural. I could feel heat pooling in the apples of my cheeks. I wasn't sure how Fuller and I had ended up in this situation or how we could ever make it work—I mean, we were practically on opposite ends of the popularity spectrum—but I wanted it to more than anything.

"More importantly," Fuller said, plopping his backpack on the table, "any new updates on Gramps?" His brow creased with concern.

We'd been texting each other on and off all morning. "Yes, he ate some pudding and a piece of toast. The doctors said that it's a really good sign that he has an appetite."

"That's amazing. I'm so glad his recovery is off to such a

great start."

"Me too. I'm visiting him after school. I'm going to bring my laptop and the DVD you got him. I figured that would put a smile on his face." I patted my backpack, where I'd safely tucked the DVD away. "Oh, that reminds me, I picked up something for your brother." I unzipped my backpack and pulled out a Deadpool laptop sticker. "I found it at the gas station this morning."

Tingles shot through my fingertips as I handed him the sticker.

Fuller's eyes lit up. "Wren, this is awesome. He's going to love it."

The way my name rolled off his tongue sent shivers down my back.

"Seriously, thank you."

I grinned. "You're welcome."

"Wren, Fuller, what a coincidence meeting you two here."

Snapping my head around, my gaze landed on Dae. He was wearing a cheesy grin and waving.

"What are you doing?" I mouthed.

Ignoring me, Dae pulled out the chair across the table and plopped down in it. "I finished my Ancient Civilizations paper early, so Mr. Norman gave me the okay to come here and pick out some books for the end-of-quarter research project." He kicked his feet up onto an empty chair.

"Well isn't that nice of Mr. Norman." I gave Dae a sarcastic smile. He and I were a lot alike, including our preference for turning in our assignments early.

"Dude, you've already turned in your paper and started on your research project?" Fuller's eyes went wide. Fuller and Dae both had Mr. Norman, but at different times during the school day.

"Yup." Dae chuckled. "I'm not the type to leave things until the last minute."

Fuller laughed. "Last minute? The paper isn't due until next week and the project isn't due for another month. That's, like, a lifetime away."

For a moment, I thought Dae might be offended. But instead he joined in the laughter.

After what seemed like forever, Fuller and Dae stopped chuckling.

"Aren't you two hilarious." I rolled my eyes but burst into laughter in the process. That set the two of them off again.

The librarian appeared from nowhere. "You three are being way too loud. If you can't lower your voices, I'm going to have to ask you to leave." Her lips turned downward into a disapproving frown. "This isn't a roast on Comedy Central."

I slapped a hand over my mouth, stifling a giggle as I pictured Mrs. Parsons settling down in front of Snoop Dogg roasting Justin Bieber. "Yes, ma'am."

We all waited for her to disappear behind a stack of shelves before saying another word.

Dae leaned forward and whispered, "You ready for the season opener against the Falcons?"

Fuller hesitated for a moment before nodding. "It's going to be a tough game, but I think we can pull off a win."

He had on a maroon polo today and dark wash jeans. My mind wandered and I pictured our second kiss last night. I wanted to slide my fingers through his belt loops again and pull him in for a kiss. Dae's voice snapped me out of my daydream and brought me back to reality. As long as Fuller brought his grade up, he'd be playing in the season opener. Which meant our tutoring sessions would be ending soon.

Will he still want to hang out with me? Or is whatever we're doing only happening because it's convenient? No, he wouldn't do that.

Would he?

"Their point guard, Nate Branson, is a total beast." Dae's

eyes were wide. "But he's not as quick as you or TyShaun."

Fuller flinched but quickly replaced it with a smile. "Coach has us running in the off-season and it's really helped." He checked over his shoulder, ensuring the librarian wasn't still watching. "We've been working on sprints and long distance. I've always been pretty good at short distances, but I was absolute crap at running anything longer than a mile. Now, I can run five miles in under an hour."

"Not too shabby." The corners of my lips twitched. I had no idea that Fuller had been running in the off-season.

"Not too shabby?" Fuller's eyes lit up. "Okay, Miss Professional Runner, how many miles do you run in an hour?"

"Seven on a decent day. Eight on a good day."

Fuller's jaw dropped. "You're seriously that fast?"

Dae chuckled. "She's that fast."

Fuller exhaled and pressed himself back from the table. His chair teetered on the back two legs. "Maybe you can give me a few tips sometime?"

"I could do that." I pictured running alongside Fuller. Sweat dripping down our bodies, muscles pumping in unison, and our endorphins rushing. Tingles shot through my body as the scene played out in my mind.

"All right, well, I better get those books and get back to class." Dae winked at me. "Good talking to you, Fuller."

"Same, Dae."

A few seconds later, my friend disappeared into the reference section of the library.

I pulled out my Calculus textbook. "Since we don't have any Lit homework, I'm going to try to knock out my math before I go visit Gramps."

"Good idea. I've got some, too." Fuller slipped his Algebra Two book out of his backpack and set it on the wooden table with a thud. "I don't think I've ever finished all my homework before heading to practice."

"Speaking of, how did the polynomial and monomial assignment go last night?"

Fuller opened his notebook and tapped the top of the page.

"Wow, thirty-eight out of forty? That's ninety-five percent."

"How do you know it's ninety-five?" Fuller looked down at his paper.

I shrugged. "I did the math in my head."

"Wow, I had to figure it out with my calculator." He chuckled. "You're seriously the smartest person I know." Fuller ran his hand through his hair. "I'm totally jealous."

I cocked my head to the side. "You're jealous of me. Yeah right."

"Um, yes, I am right." Fuller nudged my arm with his.

I arched an eyebrow. "You're like the most popular guy at our school. Plus, you're the best basketball player who's come through Magnolia Valley in, like, a century. You're the only prep basketball player to have over ten triple doubles under your belt going into your senior season. People practically worship you."

"Just because I'm popular and good at basketball doesn't mean I can't be jealous of you. You're seriously smart. Sometimes, it takes me twice as long to pick up on new concepts. It can be super frustrating."

I paused and took in what Fuller had admitted. I had no idea he felt that way.

Fuller's leg brushed against mine, but instead of pulling it away, he kept it there. "I know things started out pretty rough between us, but I'm really grateful for all your help."

"I'm glad things worked out between us, too." As soon as the words left my lips, I realized how open-ended they sounded.

"So am I." Fuller's blue eyes twinkled.

My heart skipped a beat as he took my hand in his. "Really glad."

"Ahem."

Spinning around, I saw the librarian frowning at us and shaking her head.

I pulled my hand away from Fuller and gave the librarian a sheepish look.

"Right," Fuller said, winking at me, "about that math homework."

She made a clucking sound with her tongue as she headed back to a cart of books that needed to be returned to the shelves. "This is *not* the back row of the movie theater, Miss Carter and Mr. James."

Cheeks blazing, I reached into my backpack for my calculator. Man, Mrs. Parsons's superpower had to be her ability to pull out a "This is not," example at any given moment.

"Hey, Wren."

I turned my head just in time for Fuller to steal a quick kiss.

As he pulled away, he whispered with an eyebrow raise, "Maybe we can go to a movie sometime and sit in the back."

Chapter Fourteen

Fuller

"Fuller, my man." Spinning around, I came face-to-face with Marc.

"Oh, hey, Marc." The high from kissing Wren faded as my teammate slapped his hand on my shoulder. "What's up?"

"Word on the street is that you're spending a lot of time with Wrentainer." He grinned and motioned with his hips. "A lot of time."

I shoved him, hard. "Don't call her that."

We used to joke around with each other all the time. Now I realized how immature we'd been.

"Sensitive subject I see." He held up his hands in a surrender position and laughed. "Well, you've already got step one of the bet done. How's the second part coming along? Is Wren ready to walk down the hallway holding your hand?"

"I want out of the bet." I kept my voice low and calm.

Marc's eyebrows shot up in surprise. "Why?"

My mouth went dry. "It doesn't matter. I want out, and Wren can never know about it."

"No way!" Marc said with a grin. "You're just trying to get out of wearing the wrestling singlet."

"It's not like that, but I need you to drop it. I'll wear that stupid outfit for forty-eight hours straight if you promise me that you'll never mention the bet to anyone ever again."

"Holy crap," he said in disbelief. "You actually like her. You've got it bad for Wrentainer."

"I said, don't call her that."

Marc blinked several times before shaking his head. "So it's true."

"What is?"

"I never thought you'd fall for Wrenta— I mean, Wren. Marissa is going to blow a gasket when she finds out. You do know that she's telling everyone you're going to ask her to the Fall Harvest Dance."

"I don't give a crap." Ignoring the cluster of freshmen in the hallway, I leaned in to my best friend. "I need to get out of the bet—now."

"Like I said: no way." Marc laughed and shook his head.

Losing my cool, I shoved Marc up against a locker. "Why the hell not?"

Marc's eyes shot open. "What's your problem?"

A girl with black hair and braces stared at me, her mouth agape.

Aware that we had an audience and that I had one of my closest friends up against a locker, I let go of Marc's shirt. "We'll finish this later."

As I stormed down the hallway, I tried to figure out how I could convince Marc to forget about the bet. A sinking feeling spread in my stomach. It wasn't just him I'd need to convince, though—TyShaun knew about it, too.

I shoved the locker room door open. It rebounded off the

wall with a *thwack.*

Get your crap together, Fuller. You can figure this out, but slamming doors open and throwing teammates up against lockers isn't going to help anyone.

Forcing myself to take a deep breath, I made my way to my locker.

Just as I opened it, a hand reached out from behind me and smashed it shut.

"Marc, I'm sorry about earlier. I—"

Much to my surprise, Brandon's face appeared instead of Marc's. His features were tight and his entire face was beet red.

"Now's not a good time, Edwards." I tried to remain calm, but my adrenaline was already raging and my heart was thumping wildly in my chest.

Brandon grabbed me by the shoulder. "We need to talk."

"Get your hands off me." My chest heaved with each word.

"Somewhere private." He let his hands fall to his sides.

I nodded toward the opposite side of the locker room. "Equipment room." People were rarely in there. Especially once practice started for the season.

Flipping on the light, I waited for Brandon to pull the door shut behind us.

"I thought I told you to stay away from Wren." He pushed his shoulders back and puffed out his chest. "She's my best friend, and she doesn't need some jackass leading her on."

"It's not what it looks like."

"Really? Well then, explain what the hell it *does* look like, because I, for one, am confused."

Rubbing my face with both hands, I exhaled loudly. "Look, I like her. A lot." A huge weight lifted from my chest. "Seriously. I'm really into her."

Brandon took a step back and blinked several times.

"You're what?"

"It's complicated, though."

Brandon jutted out his chin. "Complicated?"

"Brand, I'd never hurt Wren. All I need to do is get through this next week and a half. Then everything will be fine." I took a step back, bumping into a net-like bag holding at least fifteen soccer balls.

"I don't believe you." Brandon shook his head.

"That's on you. All you need to know is that I care about Wren."

He crossed his arms. "All *you* need to know is that I'll beat your ass if you do anything to hurt her."

"Understood." I only knew about one fight Brandon had ever been in and the other guy ended up with a black eye and bruised ribs. He didn't mess around, and if I did anything to hurt Wren, I'd be in big trouble.

Chapter Fifteen

Wren

"I still can't believe he kissed you in the library." Dae chuckled. "That's some nerdy shit, Wren. Even for you."

Shoving Dae's shoulder, I popped a grape into my mouth and chewed. We'd snagged a spot at a table in a quiet corner of the cafeteria. Luckily, we were the only two sitting there and no one else could hear our conversation.

"I told myself over and over again that I'd never fall for someone like Fuller James. I mean, he's so not my type, but the more I get to know him, the more we have in common. Plus, he's so sweet. He sent me a text as soon as he got home from practice to check and see how Gramps was doing. That stupid tough guy act he puts out there isn't the real him at all."

"I'm glad Gramps is doing better. My mom's making a gigantic batch of kimchi this weekend. She wanted to know if she could drop some off for everyone on Saturday?"

My mouth watered at the thought of Dae's mother's cooking. "Yum. His favorite. That's really sweet. I'll let my mom and dad know." I reached down and rubbed the back of my leg; my hamstrings were a little tight. I made a mental note to do a longer warm-up on my next run and to do a better job of stretching afterward.

"Good deal." Dae dunked a carrot stick in a small cup of ranch dressing. "So, not to dwell on the negative or anything, but what about the whole Marissa thing?"

My shoulders sank. I'd heard the whispers in the hallways. I'd seen the picture of her from last year, wearing the Fall Harvest Princess crown on that gossip Instagram account. There were dozens of comments about her and Fuller winning the princess and prince titles back to back. "I know."

My eyes wandered to the wall behind Dae. Posters advertising the dance had been plastered across every square inch. The LGBTQIA+ committee had been in charge of organizing the dance this year. They'd secured the best DJ in town and the dance was going to be epic. I closed my eyes for a second, and pictured Fuller and me slow dancing in the middle of the gym.

Dae crunched on the carrot, bringing me back to reality. "She's telling everyone that Fuller is going to ask her to the Fall Harvest Dance. Has he said anything about her?"

"No, we never talk about Marissa." A bitter taste filled my mouth as I said her name.

"But don't you think you should talk to him about it? Make sure you're both on the same page. Maybe ask why he was such a jerk to you in middle school?"

Dae meant well, but I wasn't going to fall for the rumors and I definitely didn't want to bring up the past. It had been five years since Marissa had told me that we couldn't be friends. *Fuller doesn't want me to hang out with you anymore.* Recalling her words stung. But they were just that: words. All three of us were different people than we had been in middle school. "Nope. Rumors are rumors and the past is the past."

Dae shifted in his chair. "All right. If you really think that's what's best."

Guilt tugged at my heart. I didn't admit it to Dae, but part of me did want to confront Fuller. I'd gone over it a hundred times in my mind. I'd ask him what was going on with Marissa and why he was a jerk to me back in middle school, he'd explain and apologize, and I'd accept. But every time I replayed the scene, I'd only end up feeling worse. What was the point? I couldn't hold a grudge forever. That wasn't healthy.

Plus, I was falling for Fuller.

"All right, if you feel that way, I respect it." Dae shoved a carrot into his mouth. "I wasn't going to tell you this, but…"

"But what?" I grabbed a box of Nerds from my backpack. Best dessert ever.

Dae grinned.

"Come on, tell me."

He swallowed. "He messaged me on Instagram last night."

"He who?" I reached across the table. "He Fuller?"

"Maybe." Dae shrugged.

"Dae!"

"Chill, chill." He chuckled.

"Chill? Are you kidding me? Spill it, Dae." I tore off the perforated top of the Nerds box and dumped a few of the bright pink, sugary sweets into my hand.

He grinned. "He may or may not have inquired as to what kind of movies you're into."

I slapped a hand over my mouth to contain the squeal that threatened to come out, spilling the Nerds all over the table in the process. "Wait, why did he want to know that?"

"It sounds like he may be getting ready to ask you out."

Excitement shot down my spine. "Wait, what? Like on an actual date?"

"I'm not going to ruin his game."

"Dae!" I quickly swept up the candy and tossed it into a napkin.

The bell rang, signaling that we had five minutes to get to class.

"Gotta go." He picked up his tray and bolted from the table.

"Dae, wait." But it was too late. He'd purposely dropped a truth bomb on me and run away. *He's lucky he's my best friend.*

A few minutes later, I'd thrown away my garbage and made my way to AP. Fuller was already in his seat. He smiled when I walked in, and butterflies took flight in my stomach and refused to calm down. I snuck a few Nerds while Mrs. Brewster took attendance on her computer.

I loved AP and it usually flew by, but today time practically stood still. All I could think about was Fuller asking me out. Would it be an official date? Did he want to take me to a movie? Or did he want to watch one together at his house? Would he try to kiss me again? He'd left abruptly after our second kiss. But he had a ton of work today, so even though I didn't like it, I understood.

Finally, after what felt like an eternity, the bell rang.

Mrs. Brewster motioned for Fuller to stop by her desk after class. I headed to the library with a fluttery feeling in my stomach. I was pretty sure she wanted to talk to him about his paper. He'd worked really hard on it, but would he earn a grade high enough to pass AP?

A few minutes later, Fuller walked through the door with a report cover in his hand. His expression was neutral, which caused my stomach to clench in anticipation.

"She graded it." He tossed his paper on the table.

Holding my breath, I waited for him to tell me his grade, but instead, he motioned to the paper with his eyes.

Reaching across the table, I grabbed his paper and flipped open the cover. In the upper right-hand corner was a long note from Mrs. Brewster, but more importantly, his grade. Fuller had earned a ninety-seven percent. A massive smile spread across my face, and my chest swelled with pride. "You did it!"

He came behind me and wrapped his arms around my shoulders. "It's all because of you." His arms lingered for another few seconds before he pulled out the chair next to me.

"I helped you get organized, but you did the work. This is really awesome, Fuller." I read over Mrs. Brewster's note. She praised him for his excellent thesis and grammar, and for his overall approach to the paper. She used words like "insightful" and "reflective."

"My parents are going to freak out." Fuller's smile was so genuine; he looked like a little kid on Christmas morning. "And, best of all, Mrs. Brewster said that this already brought my grade up to a C plus. We're getting an assignment and homework next week, so if I do a good job, my grade is going to go up to a B minus or even a B. Can you believe it? I'm going to be able to play in the season opener and I'm getting a freaking C plus in Advanced Lit!"

"Of course I can." I smiled. "You did a great job. I'm really proud of you."

I handed him back his paper. Fuller always looked good, but the authentic smile plastered across his face took his hotness to a whole other level.

"Listen, I, um, I was wondering if maybe you'd like to come over tonight?" He carefully placed his paper back into his backpack. "We could watch a movie? Celebrate my awesome grade?" His shoulders rose slightly, and he bit his lower lip.

"That would be really nice." I tried to remain calm, but

I was freaking out on the inside. I felt like one of those little cars that kids played with when they were younger. The kind you would pull backward, revving it up in the process. Then, as soon as you let it go, it would race across the floor.

Fuller definitely revved me up.

"Really?"

His voice sounded unsure. Did he think I might turn him down? I mean, it wasn't like he was taking me out to dinner or a movie in public, but still, Fuller James invited me over to his house on a Friday night, to watch a freaking movie. I thought about the freshman girl I'd stood next to in the cafeteria line. The one who said she would invite Fuller in and make out with him. If she were in my shoes, she'd probably squeal so loudly she'd burst people's eardrums.

"I was thinking we could watch one of the best Avengers movies of all time." His blue eyes peered into mine. "If that's okay? We could totally watch something else instead."

I grinned. "I love the Avengers." Dae for the win. "But, serious question, which Avengers movie is the best of all time?"

"*Infinity War*, duh." Fuller rolled his eyes. The corners of his lips twitched.

"I'm glad we're on the same page." I fought the urge to wrap my arms around his neck and kiss him. *No, stop. You're still in the library.* I'd have to wait until tonight. Tonight, when I was at Fuller James's house watching a movie.

"Awesome. I have practice until six. Maybe you could come over around seven?"

"I can do that." I felt like jumping up and sprinting around the room. I also felt like vomiting. Definitely a combination of both. Sure, I'd been over to his house once before, but that was for tutoring. Well, tutoring that led to an almost kiss, that eventually ended in the best make-out session ever. What was going to happen when I went over tonight? Would we kiss again?

My stomach churned. Wait, what if this wasn't a date? What if he wanted to thank me for helping him with his paper and we were just going to hang out, like when Dae or Brandon and I watched movies? Oh my gosh. What if I had it all wrong?

Distracting me from the whirlwind of thoughts bouncing around in my mind, Fuller pressed his lips together. *Those soft lips.* He looked like he was trying to suppress his grin.

Reaching under the table, he squeezed my hand. "How about we get some math homework done? You know, so we have all night to hang out." He emphasized the words *hang out*.

Butterflies exploded in my stomach.

"Deal?"

My doubts melted away. "Deal."

• • •

"I don't know." I twirled around in the floral dress. It was still casual, and the jean jacket I wore on top was super cute, but was it too much? I never wore stuff like this to school. I was strictly a T-shirt and jeans girl.

"Come on, you look great, Wren." Dae sat on my bed with his phone in his hand. He'd been texting someone nonstop since he came over.

"Are you sure it isn't too much?" I frowned and flipped my braid over my shoulder. "I don't want to make it look like I'm trying too hard."

"You look good," Dae said with a smile.

I smoothed out the dress with my hands. "Thank you."

He set his phone on my nightstand for a moment and met my gaze. "You're welcome."

I tilted my head to the side and glanced at my own reflection in the mirror. "I do look pretty cute. Okay, I'll wear it. But I'm throwing on these." I held up my favorite pair of white, low-top Chuck Taylors.

"Good choice. It's totally you."

My bedroom door swung open, and Brandon strolled in. "Hey, hey, hey." He plopped down on my bed. "My legs are killing me."

"What's up?" I asked, turning away from the mirror.

"Coach had us do ladder circuits like twenty times. We've been working on improving our overall speed as a team all preseason, but today was the hardest."

"Did you know that Russell Westbrook could get from one baseline to another in 3.36 seconds?" I asked.

Brandon laughed. "I did not know that, Wroogle."

Scrunching up my nose, I said, "Huh?"

"Wren plus Google equals Wroogle."

Brandon burst out laughing and I joined in. Dae, on the other hand, did not. Instead, he had his phone glued to his hand.

"Who are you texting?" I asked.

Dae set his phone down next to him on the bed. "Huh?"

I tossed my shoes on the carpet and sat down next to Dae. Catching him off guard, I grabbed his phone and sprang to my feet.

A wide grin broke out across my face. "Are you serious?"

He tried to grab his phone back, but I spun away and tossed it to Brandon.

"Are you flirting with Jenna Marie and keeping it a secret from us?"

Dae tilted his head to the side and shrugged. "Maybe?"

Brandon grinned and tossed the phone back at me.

"Maybe? You think this is maybe talk?" I waved his phone over my head. "I knew you liked her, but I didn't know you two had become so…extra friendly over the phone." She was hands down one of the nicest and prettiest girls at Saint

Catherine's, a nearby Catholic high school. Dae and I met her at a cross-country meet. I must have totally missed the sparks between them.

Dae's dark brown eyes flashed with happiness. "I'm going to ask her out."

I tossed him his phone. "Dae, that's awesome."

"Yeah, man. That's good stuff," Brandon added.

Dae tucked his phone into his back pocket. "Thanks."

Brandon turned his attention toward me.

"Something you want to say, Brandon?" I asked.

"Are you sure you want to hang out with Fuller? His head is so big, I'm amazed he can get in and out of the gym for practice." His tone usually had a bite to it when Fuller's name came up, but unless I was imagining it, it seemed a bit softer today.

"He's not that bad. I promise." The words sounded foreign as they left my lips. Never in a million years would I have expected to be sticking up for Fuller James.

Dae nodded in agreement with me. "I've only talked to him a few times, but something about him has changed. He's a lot more down-to-earth."

Brandon opened his mouth to respond, but before he could say anything, Dae's phone buzzed, giving me the perfect excuse to change the subject.

"Jenna Marie?" I asked.

Brandon's rigid jaw loosened, but only slightly. He had to put up with cocky basketball captain Fuller. I didn't blame him for not liking him, but I was hoping that, if things with Fuller and me continued, Brandon would give him a shot off the court.

Dae grinned as his fingers flew across the keyboard of his phone. "Yup, and guess who has a date tonight?" He moved his shoulders and neck from side to side in an impromptu celebratory dance.

"Eek!" I jumped up and down. Dae dated a lot, but I hadn't seen him this geeked about someone in a while. "Maybe if things work out with Fuller, we can all go on a double date sometime?"

I ignored Brandon flinching in response to my suggestion.

"Deal." Dae stood and stretched his arms above his head, causing his sculpted abs to peek out from under his shirt.

"Damn, Dae. Looking good."

"Who me?" he joked, tucking his phone into his pocket.

Dae and I had kissed once freshman year. We bumped foreheads and our teeth clinked together. It was hands down the most awkward experience ever. Luckily, we both decided that it should never happen again. We were way better friends than anything else. Same with Brandon, minus the whole kissing thing. Always had been, always would be.

"Whatever, you're a Grade A hottie." I chuckled and checked the time on my phone. "Oh my gosh! It's six thirty. I need to leave for Fuller's in like twenty minutes."

Brandon grimaced but remained silent.

Dae placed his hands on my shoulders. "Don't freak out. Tonight's going to go great."

Ignoring Brandon, I spun around in my dress and grinned. "For both of us!"

A flash of doubt raced through my mind as I looked at my reflection in the mirror. My lack of dating experience left me totally uneasy about tonight. Excited, but worried that something would go wrong. I'd read a sub thread on Reddit about terrible first dates. Bumping faces while kissing and breaking a nose in the process, dumping a hot coffee on the guy's lap and sending him to the emergency room with second degree burns in the worst place possible… What if something like that happened tonight?

I pushed my fears aside.

Tonight's going to go great.

Chapter Sixteen

Fuller

The carpet squished under my toes as I paced back and forth across my bedroom floor. "It's no big deal, Fuller. She's coming over to watch a movie. It's like any other date you've had before." My pep talk left me only more flustered. Partially because it was a lie. This wasn't like any other date I'd had before. This was a date with Wren Carter. The girl who I hadn't given the time of day to for years, only to fall for, hard, in less than two weeks.

I closed my eyes and flopped onto my bed. How had I missed it before? She'd been the same person since seventh grade, but now, all of a sudden, I was seeing her in a new light.

Opening up my Instagram app, I clicked on her account. Since she accepted my request over the weekend, I could finally see more than her profile picture. She'd posted a new picture yesterday. It brought a smile to my face. She sat with her arm around Gramps, both wearing matching Bulls jerseys. The caption read, "My favorite guy and me."

I scrolled through the rest of her pictures, pausing on a selfie of her running. She was wearing her Magnolia Valley High School cross-country uniform and a pair of running shoes. She'd taken the picture just over two weeks ago, and captioned it with the hashtags #LastMeetAsACougar, #GCC, and #Runner4Life. The girls' team had just missed out on qualifying for state this year, but that didn't seem to bother Wren. Besides telling me that she listened to audiobooks on long runs, she never mentioned running or the team. She was always more focused on academics.

I zoomed in on her face. Those hazel eyes, the way they twinkled when she got excited, and those lips. Man, those lips. They were perfect.

I'd been thinking about kissing her all day. Especially when we were in the library. The way her face lit up when I asked her to come over… Hopefully Hudson and his friend would keep each other occupied while Wren and I watched our movie. The last thing I needed was two nine-year-olds interrupting our kiss with one of their Nerf Gun battles.

At least my parents wouldn't be looming over us. They were heading out to dinner with some friends. Normally, they didn't let me have girls over when they weren't home, but, since Hudson would be there, and it was Wren, they were more than okay with it. They really liked her. In fact, even though they'd only met her once, she was the first girl they'd actually asked me to have over again.

I closed my eyes and let my phone fall onto the mattress. I hadn't felt this happy or hopeful in a long time. My feelings for Wren were real and, like I'd told Brandon, I'd never do anything to hurt her.

I'd even come up with a plan to get Marc and TyShaun to drop the bet. Things had progressed way past the point where I could be honest with Wren; I knew there was no way she'd accept my story and forgive me. Everything that had happened between us was based on a lie. I'd already hurt her once; I couldn't risk doing it again. My best chance was to cancel the bet, but I was running out of time. The season opener was next week.

Cringing, I imagined myself telling her tonight while we were sitting on the couch. It would be like middle school happening all over again. She'd never forgive me.

That's why things had to work with Marc and TyShaun. It was pretty simple—I'd pull them both aside before our next practice. Unlike earlier with Marc, I'd talk to both of them calmly. I wouldn't lose my cool. I'd tell them that I really liked Wren and that I'd do anything to get out of the bet. I didn't care if they wanted me to do all their math homework until the end of the year, just as long as they never spoke about the bet again. I had a backup plan, too, in case that didn't work, but I really didn't want to have to use it. I had dirt on both of them. Pictures of them drinking at Marissa's massive end-of-the-summer party. They were both obviously wasted and double-fisting beers. It would get them suspended and possibly kicked off the team.

I refused to go there, unless I was desperate. But Wren was worth it.

My bedroom door cracked open and Hudson stuck his head through. "Fuuuuuuuuller, your girlfriend is here!" He giggled and then raced down the stairs with his friend Davion.

"Hudson, don't you dare get that door!" I sprang out of bed and raced after him.

When I got to the door, I frowned. Hudson and Davion were nowhere to be seen, and the door was still shut. I tentatively reached for the handle and opened it. Greeted with the chilly air and an empty doorstep, I shut the door. "You little dweebs."

Hudson cupped his hands around his face and shouted, "Fuller's got a crush! Fuller's got a crush!"

Davion joined in, laughing the entire time.

I placed my hands on my hips. "Listen, I know you two think you're adorable and all, but you can't say that in front of Wren. For real."

"Why?" Hudson moved his hips from left to right. "Because you liiiiiiiiike her?"

Before I could respond, the doorbell rang.

"Both of you, upstairs. Now. Understood?" I tried to sound serious but couldn't help cracking a smile.

Davion turned around and raced up the stairs.

"Hey, Fuller." Hudson stayed put. "I really like the way you are with her around."

"What?" I had my hand on the doorknob.

"Wren makes you really happy. I like it."

A warmth radiated from my chest to my fingertips. "Thanks, buddy. That means a lot."

Hudson smiled and then raced up the staircase.

The doorbell rang a second time. Twisting the knob, I pulled the door open.

"Hey." Wren smiled.

"Wow." I inhaled sharply. She stood in front of me wearing a dress that cut off mid-thigh and accented her long legs.

"Thanks." Her cheeks turned pink, but she didn't look away.

"Oh, um, sorry. Come in." *Real smooth, Fuller.* I'd never had trouble talking to girls before. Now I sounded like an awkward middle schooler trying to talk to his crush for the first time. I stepped back and wiped my damp palms on my jeans, making room for Wren to walk past me. As she did, the tropical scent of some kind of exotic flower floated through the air. A smile tugged at my lips.

"How was practice?" Wren asked as she slid off her shoes.

"Great."

"Are you guys ready for next Friday?" She stood with her arms wrapped around her waist.

"I think so. Coach has been working us really hard."

"How are the free throws coming along?" She arched an eyebrow. "Josh and Logan really struggled with those last year."

I nodded. "Way better."

She smiled and let one of her hands fall to her side. "Awesome. If you can get the team's percentage up, that's really going to help you win games. Especially Marc."

I nodded in agreement. "Totally."

"So…"

A few seconds passed before I realized that we were still standing in the hallway. "Oh, right. There are some snacks in the kitchen. Want to help me bring them into the family room before we get the movie started?"

"Sure." She reached up and tugged on her braid.

"Kitchen's this way," I said, holding my hand out. Wren walked alongside me as we made our way through the hallway. "You look awesome, by the way."

Wren's arm brushed against mine. "Thanks. I wasn't sure about the dress. I don't usually wear them."

Reaching down, I wove my fingers through hers. "I like it, but you look just as nice in jeans and a T-shirt."

Wren stopped walking, our hands almost coming apart in the process.

"W-Was that not the right thing to say?" My heart was pounding. I'd never had feelings this strong for someone before, and I didn't want to take any missteps.

She stepped forward, our bodies only inches apart. Her black lashes swept up, revealing those emerald and honey colored eyes. "It was the perfect thing to say."

My hands found their way to her waist as hers linked around my neck. Our lips met and quickly melted together.

Not only did she smell like tropical flowers, her lips tasted like coconut. Closing my eyes, I got lost in the kiss. Her tongue explored my mouth, sending shivers down my back.

A shrill giggle interrupted our moment.

My eyes flew open as Wren jumped backward, bumping into the wall in the process.

"Hudson, I thought I told you to stay in your room." I put my hands on my hips, but my face was burning. He'd caught Marissa and me making out once or twice, but this was something different.

With Wren, there were feelings. Intense feelings.

"Hey, Wren! Thanks for the Deadpool sticker. It's super cool." He grinned.

I put my hand on his shoulder. "That's great," I said, "now, back to your room, please."

"Davion and I wanted something to drink." He grinned from ear to ear. "I didn't know you'd be down here making out!"

I shooed him toward the kitchen. "Come on, Nosey McGee."

He tried to stifle a fresh round of laughter by slapping a hand over his mouth.

I turned and squeezed Wren's hand. "Sorry," I mouthed.

She smiled.

Hudson's eyes went wide as they landed on Wren and me holding hands.

Ignoring him, I walked to the fridge and grabbed two cans of LaCroix. "Here you go, Hud."

"Thanks." Smiling, he stole one more look at Wren before sprinting out of the room.

"Slow down, Hudson," I shouted as his little feet pounded up the stairs.

I brought Wren's hand to my lips and kissed it. "That was kind of embarrassing."

"Yeah. Not going to lie, I've never been busted like that before. But he's too adorable to be mad at." She smiled and shrugged.

"It probably won't be the last time." I chuckled, wrapping my arms around her and kissing the top of her head. She fit so perfectly in my arms. Like a piece of a puzzle that had been missing for far too long.

"Okay, let's talk food," I said. "I made popcorn, and there's a batch of chocolate cookies Dad made yesterday in a plastic container over there." I pointed to the counter. "I also have M&M's with and without peanuts, Nerds, Reese's Pieces, Red Vines, and I got us a few of these." He pulled out two heart-shaped lollipops covered in sprinkles.

Wren's heart beat a little bit faster. "Nerds, my favorite. I'm cool with the rest, too."

She was so easygoing. "Sweet. I've got some sparkling raspberry lemonade. Want to have some of that to go with the snacks?"

"That's my all-time favorite drink. How did you know?" Wren arched an eyebrow. "Did Dae have something to do with all this?"

I bit my lower lip and tried to suppress a chuckle. "Maybe he did. Maybe he didn't."

"Well, you'll have to tell him that he did a good job." Wren grinned. "How about I grab the drinks and the popcorn, and you pile all the candy on top of the container of cookies?"

"Perfect," I said, loading up the candy.

Wren grabbed the cans from the fridge and a large bowl of popcorn from the counter. "Avengers time?"

"Let's do it." My eyes went wide. "I mean, let's watch the movie."

The corners of Wren's lips twitched.

We made our way into my family room. The overstuffed couch pushed up against the wall loomed in front of me.

Swallowing my nerves, I set the food on the coffee table and sat down in the middle. I wiped my sweaty palms off on my jeans.

Tucking a leg underneath her, Wren sat on the cushion next to me. “Here you go.” As she handed me the can of lemonade, her fingers brushed against mine.

“Thank you.” My voice cracked slightly, which I immediately tried to cover up by clearing my throat and patting myself on the chest. Trying my best to avoid any further embarrassment, I grabbed the Apple TV remote and brought up the movie on the screen.

“Here we go.” Wren licked her lips and grabbed a handful of popcorn.

Her smile was totally contagious.

I pressed play and tossed the remote next to me on the couch. Normally, I’d be totally into the movie, but tonight, I couldn’t concentrate. All I could think about was Wren and that kiss we’d shared in the hallway. She must have coconut lip balm. From this point forward, that flavor would always put a smile on my face.

Shifting her body, Wren grabbed a pillow off the floor and plopped it onto her lap. She rotated her shoulders back and moved her neck from the left to the right.

“Everything okay?”

Wren reached her hand back to her neck and frowned. “Ah, my neck is a little bit stiff. I think I slept in a funky position.”

“That’s the worst. If you want, I could try and get some of the knots out.”

She bit her lower lip. “Really? That would be great.”

I pushed the coffee table back and patted the floor.

Wren got up and settled down in the space between my legs. “One sec.” She tugged the hair tie out of her hair and pulled her braid out. A moment later, she bunched up her hair in a bun on top of her head, the scent of her shampoo filling the air. My eyes closed momentarily as I inhaled the tropical scent. "Okay, good to go."

I covertly wiped my hands off on the sofa before I started massaging her neck. I began with her shoulders and worked my way up to her neck. "Yikes. You're really tight."

"Yeah, I guess I've been a little extra stressed with everything that happened to Gramps. When things get really intense, I clench my jaw in my sleep. I also get headaches and sometimes, if I'm super stressed out, I come down with migraines. The dentist wants me to wear this mouth guard thing. It's pretty dorky." She laughed.

"That isn't dorky." She was so open. The complete opposite of Marissa, who used to ask me at least twice a day if I thought she was fat. The girl barely ate and was like a twig. Even though I tried to reassure her, she continued to ask. It was like a routine we had to go through. One time I mentioned talking to a therapist or school counselor about it—I thought I was being helpful. Turns out, I wasn't. Marissa made me grovel for two weeks for that one.

"Wow. You're so good at this." Wren let her head fall from side to side.

I grinned. "Thanks. I tweaked my back during freshman year. Five massages and a few physical therapy sessions later, I was good as new." My fingers continued to work in unison, making quarter-sized circles going up both sides of Wren's spine. With each minute, the tight knots loosened up.

Ten minutes passed. Wren had completely relaxed. A few strands of hair had fallen down and tickled the backs of my hands. I would have gone on forever, but I stopped when Wren's head fell to the side.

"Oh my gosh! Did you kill her?" Hudson's voice squeaked out from around the corner.

My head snapped to the right. At the same time, Wren

lifted her head and rubbed her eyes. "Oops, did I fall asleep?"

"Did you put her in a sleeper hold?" Hudson smiled as he pretended to put an imaginary person in the same move we'd watched professional wrestlers do on TV.

Davion popped out around the corner. "Are you guys watching an Avengers movie?"

"Yes." I didn't want to sound annoyed, but my little brother was totally messing up my movie date with Wren. "What do you two need? You're supposed to be up in Hudson's room."

"Oh, um, Davion said he hasn't seen this movie yet." Hudson turned around and threw his arm over his friend's shoulders. "So, we were wondering if we could, um, if we could watch it with you guys?"

Pausing the movie, I jutted out my chin and drew my eyebrows together. He knew better than to come down here and ask to join us. Mom and Dad explicitly told him to stay upstairs. They trusted me to follow their rules and be respectful.

Wren stood and rolled her neck to the left and right. "I don't know. Do you two think you're tough enough to handle it? There are some pretty intense scenes."

My heart sank. I loved my little brother, and Davion was a really good kid, but I selfishly wanted alone time with Wren. Time to talk to her, hold her hand, and most of all, time to pull her into my arms for another make-out session.

"I'm not a crybaby." Hudson put his hands on his hips. "I watch *Deadpool* all the time."

Davion nodded, his eyes going wide. "Yeah, and they even say the f-word in that movie—like, a lot."

"Hmmm." Wren appeared to eye up Hudson and Davion. "I don't know, Fuller. What do you think? Should we let them crash our movie night?"

I rubbed the back of my neck. "I don't know."

Hudson clasped his little hands together. "Please, Fuller. Pleeeeeease."

Davion followed suit.

Wren turned toward me, tilting her head to the side. "I think we should let them. Just this one time." She winked at me, instantly turning my knees to jelly. Thank goodness I was sitting down.

Patting the sofa, Wren motioned for the boys to come over.

"YES!" Davion cheered.

Hudson punched his little fists in the air. "Wren, you're, like, the coolest girl Fuller has ever had over. You're *way* better than Marissa. She used to tell me to get lost all the time." He rolled his eyes. "She's a total Regina George."

My jaw dropped and heat rushed to my face.

"Did you just reference *Mean Girls*?" Wren started laughing. In fact, she laughed so hard she snorted, which only caused her to laugh even harder. Hudson and Davion joined in. I tried to keep a straight face but failed. A moment later, I burst out in laughter right alongside them.

Nearly three hours later, the movie credits rolled. Davion and Hudson sat in silence. They'd both blinked back tears when Spider-Man had turned to ash. Luckily, Wren reminded them that Spider-Man was okay and that there were more movies starring the web-shooting hero, so they didn't have to worry. She'd ended by saying, "Remember, guys, Peter Parker always finds a way to beat the bad guys."

I didn't know how she did it, but Wren made everything better. Even hanging out with my little brother and his friend had been more fun with her there. Wren had them eating out of the palm of her hand.

"I wish Groot had his own movie," Hudson said, resting his head on his hand. He let out a yawn. "After Deadpool, he's the second best."

"But he only says one thing." I chuckled. "Wouldn't that make for a boring movie?"

"Nope! I am Hudson. I *am* Hudson. *I* am Hudson. See how different it sounds?" He let out a high-pitched laugh.

Wren grinned. "Did you know that he's played by Vin Diesel, who happens to be a top-row-teeth smiler?"

"Nice," Hudson said, returning the smile.

"Okay, guys. Mom and Dad will be home soon. Head upstairs, brush your teeth, and get your pajamas on, okay?"

Hudson saluted me. "Yes, sir."

Davion stood up with a straight face and repeated the same gesture. "Sir, yes, sir."

"It was fun hanging out with you two." Wren smiled. "How about we do it again sometime soon? Maybe watch *Ant Man and the Wasp* together?"

Hudson's eyes lit up. "That would be awesome!"

"Totally." Davion looked like he'd been given a puppy.

"Okay, night."

Hudson rushed over to Wren and wrapped his arms around her. "See you soon!"

"Yup," Davion said, gently reaching over and hugging Wren and Hudson at the same time. All his friends knew to be careful around Hudson, but Davion was always the most vigilant. He was a good little guy.

The boys let go and raced up the stairs.

"Wow." I shook my head in disbelief.

Wren looked at me. Her eyes were full of concern. "Is that a good wow or a bad wow?"

I smiled and pulled her into my arms. "A very good wow." I placed a kiss on top of her head. "No one has ever been that cool to my brother before."

"Oh, good." Wren looked up at me, her eyes sparkling.

"Hey…" I licked my lips. Like my mouth, they were dry.

"Yeah?"

"I really like you, Wren Carter." The words came out as soft as a whisper.

Wren bit her lower lip. The corners of her eyes crinkled. "I really like you, too, Fuller James."

Chapter Seventeen

Wren

"Wren, Dae, come sit with us." Fuller motioned us over.

Dae's eyes went wide for a second, but then he played it cool by giving Fuller a nod of acceptance.

The cafeteria tables were lined up in long rows and the air smelled like hamburgers. Groups of students sat with their cliques and gossiped about the day's events. Judging by the momentary silence, followed by the buzz of excited voices right after Fuller invited us over, I was pretty confident the topic had shifted. I didn't care, though—people could talk all they wanted. Fuller and I liked each other. If anyone had a problem with it, that was on them.

A smile played on my lips. Fuller was wearing a navy blue T-shirt and jeans. His dark hair was swept to the side thanks to some gel. He was hands down the best-looking guy at our school. Not to mention, I now knew he was an amazing kisser.

I raised my fingers to my lips, remembering our kiss in the hallway at his house on Friday night.

As we made our way across the cafeteria, Dae elbowed me in the side and whispered, "I should have asked—are you cool sitting over there with Fuller and his friends? I mean, you know what they say when you make assumptions."

"Yeah, yeah. It's totally fine." Balancing my tray, I bumped my best friend with my hip.

"I'm glad you two are... Well, whatever you are." He grinned.

"Me too, Dae." I returned the smile. "Before we head over there, serious question." We stepped past a group of sophomores crowded around a table. "When are you seeing Jenna Marie again?" I bit my lip and grinned.

Dae winked at me. "Wednesday after school."

"Ooh." Dae didn't normally fall for girls at the drop of a hat, but he'd been gushing about all things Jenna Marie over the weekend. I'd heard on repeat how pretty, smart, and funny she was, but I didn't care. I was happy for my friend. Especially after his nasty breakup with Eva last year.

"Yeah, yeah," Dae said, rolling his eyes.

The cafeteria was already buzzing with people, but as Dae and I changed course and headed over to Fuller's table, it got even louder. People weren't even being nonchalant about it. Some straight-up pointed at us.

Ignoring the circus, Dae gently tapped my arm with his elbow. "For real, Wren. I'm happy for you and Fuller."

"Thanks, Dae." I bumped his arm back with my own elbow. "I wish Brandon was, too."

"Maybe it'll just take him some time to come around." Dae shrugged.

"True, but hopefully not too long," I said as we approached the table. Taking a deep breath, I set my tray down next to Fuller. A few of the guys at the table glanced at us. Wide eyes, arched brows, and general looks of shock and confusion had settled across their faces. Dae took the seat directly next to me.

"Nico, Jeremy, you guys know Wren and Dae, right?"

Fuller must have cut them a look, as the surprise on their faces dissolved.

"Oh, yeah. Hey, Wren. Dae," Nico said. "What up?"

"Not much, man," Dae responded. "You guys ready for the game on Friday?" They were juniors and two of the best defenders on the team.

They both nodded.

"We are going to crush the Falcons." Jeremy took a bite of his hamburger. A blob of ketchup hit his tray in the process.

Fuller reached across the table and bumped fists with them. "Yeah we are."

He was passing AP and his math grade had gone up, too. Nothing was going to stand in the way of him taking the court Friday night, and I couldn't be happier for him.

"Oh, look what I picked up at the gas station this morning." Fuller pulled a box of Nerds out of his backpack.

I grinned. "Thanks, Fuller."

"Welcome." He winked, sending tingles throughout my body. He took a bite of cooked green beans. "Dae, how did you do on that Ancient Civilizations paper?"

"Aced it." Dae unwrapped his grilled cheese sandwich. "How about you?"

Fuller grinned. "Solid B. So, basically, I aced it, too."

He and Dae laughed.

I was relieved but not surprised. Fuller told me that he'd been doing well in Ancient Civilizations. Everyone loved Mr. Norman. He'd been voted the school's favorite teacher by the students five years in a row. He actually made learning history fun. Last year, he'd dressed up in chainmail in order to teach a lesson about armor worn during medieval times. That was dedication. Plus, he had a great sense of humor, including laughing when Breccan Slater, the school prankster, hid spring-loaded, life-size cutouts of Mr. Norman around the school. They were literally popping out of doors, springing out of closets, and dangling from the ceilings all over school. Well, allegedly it was Breccan Slater; he never confessed, and there wasn't any evidence linking him to the prank, but everyone knew it was him.

Flipping open my lunch container, I pulled out an assortment of small jars. The contents consisted of raw sugar snap peas, carrots, and a chickpea salad. I also had a small glass bowl of kimchi from Dae's mom. My mouth watered as I opened it.

"Looks good." Fuller stabbed a chickpea and popped it into his mouth. "Mmm. That's delicious."

"Did you steal some of my chickpea salad?" I arched an eyebrow.

"I did, and I don't regret it." Fuller put his arm around my back and kissed me on the cheek.

My body tensed up but then relaxed. Everyone in the cafeteria had probably witnessed Fuller kissing me, but who cares? We liked each other. That's what people who liked each other did.

Leaning against him, I took a bite of one of my snow peas. "That happens to be Gramps's favorite recipe. Well, that and Dae's mom's kimchi." I motioned to the small glass jar.

"I've never had kimchi before. Can I try it?"

"Sure." I slid the jar over to him.

Fuller took a bite. A moment later, his face lit up. "Now, *that* is one of the best tasting things I've ever put in my mouth."

"Ah, TMI, Fuller." Nico shook his head.

Jeremy chuckled as Fuller asked for another bite, but before I could say, "Sure," a familiar voice interrupted us.

"Hey, Fuller."

I spun around, nearly choking on my sugar snap pea. In

front of me stood Marissa. She scowled before turning her attention to Fuller.

"What do you want?" he asked.

She flipped her perfectly straight blond hair over her shoulder. "What are you wearing to the Fall Harvest Dance?"

Fuller's face scrunched up like he'd smelled something rotten. Then, sighing, he let his head fall to the side. "Marissa, why do you need to know what I'm wearing to a dance two weeks from now?"

"Well, because you're taking me, and I don't want my dress to clash with whatever you're wearing." She playfully reached out and pushed his shoulder. "Obviously."

I recoiled. Fuller and I weren't going out, and I didn't even know if he considered whatever we were doing to be dating, but I hated watching Marissa putting her mitts all over him. I knew I should suck it up and ask him point-blank what was going on with us, but a small part of me was scared of the rejection that could follow. I was having fun with Fuller, and I wanted to keep it that way. Bringing up the future could ruin everything.

"Um, Marissa, I'm not taking you to the Fall Harvest Dance."

Marissa's face turned a deep shade of red. "Excuse me?"

Fuller shook his head. "It doesn't matter what I'm wearing, because I'm not going with you."

"We have to go together. We're obviously going to be crowned Prince and Princess of the Fall Harvest Dance again." She shot daggers at me. "That used to be important to you."

Fuller shook his head. "I took my name out of the running. And you're wrong. That stuff just isn't important to me anymore."

"Ooh," Nico said, banging his hand on the table. "Denied!"

Fuller slipped his arm around my back. "In fact, I haven't done it yet, but I was going to ask Wren to be my date."

The air whooshed out of my lungs. *Did Fuller just ask me to be his date to the dance? And did he just do it right in front of* Marissa*?*

Marissa glared at me and then licked her lips. "I *bet* you're going to regret this, Fuller."

Fuller's arm stiffened before leaving the small of my back. *Why did he do that? Is something going on between him and Marissa, or is she just in my head?*

The air was thick with tension, and I wanted nothing more than to bolt, but I refused to move. I'd never give Marissa that kind of satisfaction. Plus, Fuller asked me to be his date to the dance, not her. She was just trying to get under my skin. I deserved to be here, sitting next to him and Dae. Marissa was the one who was out of line and out of place.

Without saying another word, Marissa stomped away, her heels clattering against the linoleum floor.

"I'm sorry you got caught in the middle of that," Fuller said.

My heart was still racing. "It's not your—"

The two-minute warning bell rang loudly, stopping me before I could tell Fuller that I didn't blame him for Marissa's actions.

He leaned forward and kissed me on the cheek. "I've got to run to my locker and grab my books for Lit. Meet you there?"

Wait… Did he actually ask me to the dance? He said he was going to. Should I answer before he leaves? Completely torn, I stammered, "S-Sounds good."

Dae looped his thumbs around his backpack straps. "I gotta jet too, or I'm going to be late. See you after school?"

"Deal."

I ducked into Mrs. Brewster's class, mentally replaying

what went down at lunch as I made my way to my seat. I wished Marissa hadn't butted in on what should have been a super romantic moment, but instead of feeling bad about myself, for the first time in five years, I genuinely just felt sorry for her.

I glanced toward Fuller's desk. It was still empty.

As I turned around, Lyla caught my gaze. She looked me up and down and then scowled.

"Problem, Lyla?"

She must have been shocked that I called her out on her nasty look, because instead of saying something back to me, she crossed her arms over her chest and looked away.

"Guess not." Spinning around, I felt the corners of my lips twitch. Standing up to her hadn't been that difficult, and it gave me a rush, like I'd slammed a double espresso latte.

Fuller raced in as the final bell rang. He hurried past me but let his fingers linger on my desk for a moment. After he was in his seat, I looked down. A small piece of paper folded up into a little square sat on my desk. Sliding my hand over it, I brought it under the desk and opened it. *I meant what I said in the cafeteria. Will you go to the dance with me? Fuller x*

Oh. My. Gosh.

Fuller James officially asked me to the Fall Harvest Dance! I mean, he did before, kind of, but this cemented the fact that it was real. It took everything in my power not to squeal, the knot that had formed in my stomach over the whole Marissa thing at lunch loosening. Yes, I'd gone to school dances with guys before, but not someone I had feelings for like Fuller. Plus, no guy had ever sent me a note like this. I mean, sure, I'd had texts from guys, but never an old-school note on a piece of paper. It somehow felt extra romantic.

I carefully folded it back up and slipped it into my backpack, sneaking a glance at Fuller in the process. I nodded and mouthed, "Yes."

Fuller clenched his fist and pulled his elbow back against his body like he'd dunked the winning basket. His blue eyes pierced mine, twinkling as they crinkled at the corners.

For the second time in my academic career, I struggled to focus in class. My thoughts kept getting jumbled up in my brain. What dress would I wear? Should I wear high heels or flats? How should I do my hair? Maybe I should go get it done. *Gah!* I had less than two weeks to figure everything out. My hands shook with excitement as I jotted down a list of things I would need for the dance.

After what felt like an eternity, Mrs. Brewster wrote our homework on the whiteboard, her marker squeaking the entire time.

I finished scribbling the assignment into my planner and closed it as the bell rang. Zipping my backpack, I stood up and made my way out into the hallway. I paused and glanced over my shoulder.

"Looking for me?" someone whispered in my ear.

Spinning around, I came face-to-face with the guy I couldn't stop thinking about.

"Want to walk to study hall with me, Fall Harvest Dance date?"

"Eh, I guess I can make space in my calendar," I joked. "But on the way, there's something I want to talk to you about, okay?"

"Of course. Is everything okay?" Fuller cocked his head to the side and peered into my eyes.

"It's—"

I stopped talking as a group of boys on the lacrosse team walked by us.

Fuller paused alongside me and wove his fingers through mine. "We can talk in the library."

I looked down at our intertwined hands and inhaled.

He started to pull away. "Oh, is this not okay?"

I tugged his hand back toward me and nodded. His thumb brushed over the back of my hand, sending shivers up my arm.

I struggled to keep my composure as we made our way down the hall.

We walked by Benjamin, a junior on the team. He high-fived Fuller and said, “See you at practice.”

Fuller pulled me closer. “This is really nice.”

“Yeah, it is,” I said in agreement.

Our shoulders bumped together as we made our way toward the library.

“Oh, wow,” I heard from behind us.

Fuller stopped in his tracks, tugging me backward in the process.

Turning around, TyShaun came into view.

“Well, if it isn’t Fuller James and Wren Carter holding hands.” TyShaun’s laughter shot through the crowded hallway. He held up two fingers and wiggled them back and forth.

Why did he do that? My throat went dry and my stomach flip-flopped. *No, don’t let him make you feel this way.* “TyShaun, why don’t you mind your own business?”

He stifled a laugh. “She’s feisty.”

“You need to quit it.” Fuller stepped in front of me, gripping my hand tighter. “Now.”

His teammate threw his head back and continued laughing. “Sure thing, Fuller. Oh, and don’t worry, I’ll let Marc know.” He slapped the locker to his left before spinning and walking away. His laughter continued to ring throughout the hallway until he turned the corner and disappeared.

“Wren, I’m so sorry. They…they just like giving me shit, but it’s not fair to you.” Fuller’s dark lashes swept down as he dropped his gaze. “I’m going to talk to him and Marc after school.”

“Screw him,” I said. “His percentage from the three-point line is the worst on the team. He should watch who he's making fun of."

"Stone-cold, Wren," Fuller said with a chuckle. "Remind me not to piss you off."

"Whatever, we both know it's true."

Fuller pushed on the library doors. We made our way past a cart full of books and toward our regular table. Mrs. Parsons glanced down the long, thin bridge of her nose and frowned. "You do know this is the library and not the roller rink, Miss Carter and Mr. James."

"Oh, whoops." I let go of Fuller's hand and gave her my best apologetic smile.

She gave us a curt nod before getting behind the cart and rolling it over to the young adult fiction section.

"Did she say the roller rink?" Fuller whispered. "Do those even exist anymore?"

"Be nice." I gave him a slight push as he pulled out two chairs, side by side.

Fuller plopped his backpack on to the table. "Okay, but before we get started on our homework, I have one serious question for you, Miss Carter."

"What's that, Mr. James?"

He gave me a lopsided grin. "What do you think of my three-point shooting percentage?"

Chapter Eighteen

Fuller

"Eh, it could be better." Wren cocked her head to the side and shrugged.

I brought my hand to my heart. "Ouch, Wren. That hurt."

"I could give you some tips, if you're interested?"

"Oh really?" I arched an eyebrow.

"Totally."

"Okay, lay it on me." I lifted my palms and wiggled my fingers.

She leaned in, letting her elbows rest on the table. "Your balance is a little weak. You need to focus on squaring up your feet and being completely balanced before you let the ball go."

"Well, damn." She was totally right.

"Steph Curry did an interview about it back in the day." She winked at me, sending shivers down my spine. How could one little action cause such an intense reaction? I shook my head.

"Wren, you never cease to amaze me."

Her smile faltered. It was as if she was suddenly holding something back from me.

"So, what's up? What did you want to talk about?" My leg brushed up against hers under the table.

She twisted her lips to the side.

"You can ask me anything." I leaned forward. *Yeah, right. Anything but why TyShaun and Marc are acting like jerks.* Guilt gnawed away at my conscience.

"Are you one hundred percent over Marissa?" Wren's emerald eyes were full of concern. "I know you two have a history, and she seemed so confident that you were going to the dance together..."

I reached under the table and grabbed her hand. "One hundred and fifty percent. Marissa is just trying to get under my skin. I think I need to man up and call her after practice. I'll be honest, tell her that I care about you and that we don't need her interfering in our relationship. I don't know if she'll listen, but it's worth a try."

The thought of calling Marissa made my skin crawl, but there didn't need to be any more blowups or confrontations between me and her or her and Wren. The call probably wouldn't go over well, but it was the least I could do. We'd gone out on and off for more than two years. She was manipulative and cruel, but I was hoping our past would mean something to her.

She did weirdly emphasize the word "bet" in the cafeteria. What if Marissa knows about it? Would TyShaun tell her? They've been friends since middle school. Then again, we all used to be friends... All of us except Wren. The sickening possibility sank into my stomach. *No, no way. She would have already thrown it in my face and used it against Wren.*

"I guess it couldn't hurt." Wren's jaw tightened. I hated that she was stressed because of me. The worst part was that she already felt like this and she didn't even know about the worst part.

My inner angel and demon rehashed the possibility of laying everything out on the table for the millionth time. The thought of hurting Wren and letting Coach down was too much to bear. I'd brought my grades up, I was playing in the season opener, and I had Wren Carter in my corner. My only option was to sweep any and all evidence of the bet under the rug and work up the courage to ask Wren Carter to officially be my girlfriend.

"You know what?" she asked, pulling me out of the rabbit hole I'd temporarily fallen into.

"What?"

"You're a great guy, Fuller." Wren tucked a strand of hair behind her ear. "I'm really glad I hit you with mashed potatoes in the cafeteria."

Grinning from ear to ear, I squeezed her hand under the table. "Me too, Wren. And you know what else I'm glad about?"

"What's that?" She'd propped her elbow on the table and was resting her face in the hand I wasn't holding.

"That you agreed to go to the dance with me." I sounded like a lovestruck fool, but I didn't care. I'd fallen for Wren Carter, hard.

"I'm glad you asked." Wren bit her lower lip. "Are you really okay taking your name out of the running and giving up your chance of being the back-to-back Fall Harvest Prince?"

"That isn't important to me anymore." I looked into her hazel eyes. "I meant what I said to Marissa. I'm over the popularity contest."

"Are you sure?" Wren asked.

"Totally."

Her head tilted to the left. "I have to make a confession."

Letting out a shaky breath, I pretended everything was

fine. "What's up?"

Wren's eyes lit up. "You know, I've never gone to a dance before with someone I actually liked."

My chest swelled with pride. "Is that so?"

She nodded.

"Well, I have a confession to make, too." I took a deep breath. "I've been wanting to ask you something... But I haven't worked up the nerve to do it yet."

Wren leaned back in her chair. "Fuller James, nervous? No way. I don't buy it."

My shoulders rose and then fell. "It's the truth. While I may have never stumbled across this problem before...I seem to have fallen into a sandpit of doubt."

"Do you need Westley to jump in and rescue you?" Wren asked me with a giggle.

"Westley? I'm lost."

Wren's brow furrowed. "*The Princess Bride* reference. Please tell me you've watched that movie before."

I shook my head. "Nope, sorry."

Wren let out an audible gasp. "Fuller James, that's inconceivable!"

"What?"

"Okay, hold the phone. Before you explain your sandpit of doubt, please tell me that you've watched my second favorite movie, *Say Anything*."

"Um, say what?"

Wren's eyebrows shot up as she inhaled. "It's only the best classic romantic comedy of the nineteen eighties. John Cusack and Ione Skye, the boom box scene? He plays her the 'In Your Eyes' song?" Wren looked at me like I was some kind of alien.

"Okay, well, how about this." I leaned in closer, screw Mrs. Parsons and whether we're in a library or a roller rink or whatever. "You come over on Saturday and we'll watch both those movies."

"I'd love that." Wren hadn't stopped smiling since we stopped talking about Marissa. Unfortunately, that was about to change. There was something I had to talk to her about before our movie date and before we could take the next step. Something that could change everything…

"Wren, I'm so sorry." The words tumbled out of my mouth so fast, I'm not sure they were even intelligible.

Her face scrunched up in confusion. "What?"

"I'm really sorry for how I treated you in middle school." My heart went into overdrive, thumping so wildly I was sure she could hear it. I'd never been this nervous before.

She inhaled softly.

Hands pressed against the table, I continued. "I was a huge jerk. I thought being popular was more important than being a decent human being. I…I was a coward and a bully."

When Wren didn't respond, my chest deflated. Had I blown it by bringing up the past? Would Wren suddenly remember what an asshole I'd been and cut me out of her life?

Finally, after what felt like an eternity, she spoke. "Thank you for the apology. I really appreciate it."

"If I could take it all back, I would in a heartbeat." I meant every single word, but had I done enough since falling for Wren to convince her that I had changed? Assured her that I wasn't *that* guy anymore?

"I believe you." She paused; her voice didn't sound as sad, but her smile still hadn't returned. "It's weird, you know?"

"What is?"

She looked up, her eyes meeting mine. "This whole situation. You and me. I never would have thought in a million years we'd be here."

"Me either." I smiled. "But I'm really glad that I was failing AP Lit."

"That makes two of us."

There it is! Her smile had finally returned. But just as quickly as it had popped up on her face, it vanished again.

Wren shifted her weight in her seat. "Sometimes I wonder what if would have been like if Marissa and I'd stayed friends. You know, if you hadn't told her to stop hanging out with me."

"Wait, what?"

"I'm not mad. I was just thinking how different my life would be if Marissa and I were still friends. Could you imagine me wearing high heels to school?" She let out a soft chuckle.

My nose scrunched in response. "Wren, I never told Marissa to stop hanging out with you."

"Seriously?" Wren asked.

"Cross my heart." I made an *X* over my chest.

Her head moved from right to left as she exhaled. "I don't know why I'm surprised… It's yet another lie from Marissa. I guess it was easier for her to put the blame on you than to tell me that she didn't want to be my friend anymore."

"I'm sorry you had to go through that," I said. I meant it, too. "And…there's one more thing."

She froze, probably afraid to hear what I'd share next.

"It's my fault you got that terrible nickname. If I just would have kept my mouth shut, things would have been a lot different."

"What do you mean?" Wren asked.

I sighed. "That night, no one laughed until I repeated it. It's my fault it caught on." His voice was full of remorse.

Her eyebrows pulled together. "Until you *repeated* it?"

"I feel like by saying this, it sounds like I'm trying to blame someone else, but I want to be completely honest with you." I looked deep into her eyes. "Marissa came up with the nickname. I was being an ass and I repeated it, loudly. That's when everyone else heard it and started laughing."

She let out a slow breath. "I'd always thought it was you…"

"I'm still responsible." The muscles in my jaw clenched.

Wren sat with her hands folded and her gaze averted. "You know what? Knowing that it was Marissa isn't a shock. But I still appreciate you being honest with me."

I winced. "I'm really sorry, Wren."

"I forgive you." Wren's words felt light and airy.

"You do? For real?" I didn't want to sound desperate, but I had to know if she still cared about me. And there was something else I wanted to ask her… Something big.

"For real. And if it's okay with you, I still want to watch my favorite movies with you this weekend." She smiled, a big, contagious smile.

"You have no idea how happy that makes me." I reached forward and squeezed her hand. "But you're only invited over under one condition." It felt like all the air had been sucked out of the room. It was ballsy, but I hoped it would pay off.

"What's the condition?" Wren arched an eyebrow.

Running a hand through my hair, I looked her in the eye and blurted out, "That you agree to go out with me."

Wren's eyes shot wide open. She looked like she'd seen a ghost or maybe LeBron James walking down the street, I couldn't tell. But if that wasn't terrifying enough, she just sat there, speechless.

"I was just joking! I swear. I mean, you totally can still come over, if you don't want to um, be my, I mean, be my girlfriend or whatever. Or if you don't want to come over at all, that's okay, too. It would suck, but I'd understand." My cheeks burned as the words tumbled out of my mouth. It was like I'd suddenly come down with some kind of terrible case of verbal diarrhea.

"Yes." Her smile returned.

My jaw dropped. "Wait, are you sure?"

"I'm sure." Wren reached forward and took my other hand in hers. "Fuller, I'd love to be your girlfriend."

My heart drummed in my chest. I wanted to kiss her, but I also had the urge to get up and sprint around the block in celebration. *She said yes!* I beamed as our fingers intertwined. The fact that the bet was still looming over my head put a slight damper on things, but I was going to take care of that next. Then everything would be perfect.

"Wow, I'm dating the leading free throw and soon-to-be leading three-point shooter in all of Magnolia Valley High School's history." She smiled and bit her lower lip.

Adrenaline shot through my veins. Breathless, I cupped Wren's face with both hands and stole a quick kiss. As I pulled away, I could taste coconut lip balm.

Luckily, we hadn't gotten caught, but I wouldn't care even if we had. I couldn't help myself. I was the happiest guy in the whole school, because Wren Carter had agreed to be my girlfriend.

• • •

After giving Wren a kiss in the hallway and ignoring several gawking sophomores, I jogged to practice. Even though I was dreading it, it was finally time to squash this bet situation once and for all.

Luckily, Ty and Marc had gotten to practice early. I glanced at the clock in the gym. We had ten minutes before we needed to be changed and on the court. Plenty of time to clear the air.

"Hey, guys. Can we talk?"

Marc tensed up and took a step backward. I didn't blame him. The last few times we'd talked, things had been heated.

"Out there," I said, pointing to the side doors of the gym. "It'll only take a minute."

They both nodded and followed me outside.

Mountains towered around us as a subtle breeze raised goose bumps on the back of my neck. I was equal parts nervous to come clean and excited to finally have the secret squashed for good.

I rubbed the back of my neck. "Look, I've been an asshole. I never should have made the bet; it was a jerk move. Ty, I shouldn't have threatened you with those pictures of you and Chantel, either—that was a jerk move, too. The truth of the matter is, I was struggling in AP. Principal Davis and Mrs. Brewster assigned Wren as my tutor. They basically had to force her to do it, which was super embarrassing, and Coach didn't want you guys to know there was a chance I'd be riding the bench for the season opener. He was scared it would screw with the team's mojo, so I tried to cover it up with the bet."

Inhaling and exhaling slowly, I continued. "The thing is, I really like her, and I'd do anything to keep her from finding out about the bet. Seriously, anything. Ty, I'd walk Bear every single day after practice until we leave for college next year. Marc, I'd hunt down Fabian Nicieza and Rob Liefeld and get them to sign all your *Deadpool* comics."

It felt like a three-hundred-pound weight had been lifted off my chest. I took a deep breath. My confession felt more freeing than my early morning runs. The best part was, I didn't need to act like an even bigger jerk and threaten my friends.

TyShaun shook his head. "You don't need to do all that, man. We'll drop it. I mean, that's what friends do, right?"

Marc nodded in agreement.

"You guys have no idea how much better I feel right now. This crap has been eating me up."

"You think you should come clean about the bet?" TyShaun asked. "I mean, to her."

It felt like cold hands clamped on my lungs and squeezed the air out of them. "No. I can't. She'd never forgive me. And it doesn't matter anyway—my feelings for her are real."

"Understood." Marc cocked his head to the side and scrunched up his nose. "Wow, man. I had no idea. You really like her that much?"

"Yeah, I do." Hearing myself admit out loud that I liked Wren for the second time today felt good. Scratch that, it felt amazing.

"But she's so…"

"Trust me, guys. I know I was a huge jerk to her in the past, and I've already apologized to her about that, but I really like her. I was wrong about so many things." I held out my hands, palms facing up toward the sky. "It's that simple."

Chapter Nineteen

Wren

"We're so glad you could join us, Wren." Mrs. James smiled and passed me a giant bowl of salad.

"Thank you so much for inviting me." I accepted the bowl and used the salad tongs to transfer the leafy greens to my plate.

"Pregame dinners are my favorite." Fuller loaded his plate with pasta and smothered it in homemade spaghetti sauce.

"Same. We usually have pasta at my house before cross-country meets. We always use my grandma's sauce and meatball recipes. Gramps loves those dinners." Nostalgia tugged at my heart. Family dinners were the best.

Fuller caught my eye and smiled. "Gramps is a great guy."

"We're really glad he's feeling better," Fuller's mom added.

"Thank you. So are we." I handed the salad bowl to Hudson's outstretched hands.

"We're also incredibly grateful that you helped our Fuller

recognize his potential in AP," Fuller's dad said, clapping his son on the back. "Thanks to you, he'll be starting the game tomorrow night."

Fuller's cheeks turned dark red. "Thanks, Dad."

"Anytime, champ."

Hudson grabbed a breadstick from a basket in the center of the table. "Is the UGA coach still coming tomorrow?"

Fuller finished chewing a big bite of pasta before answering. "I think so, Hud. There might even be a few scouts there from other schools, too."

Hudson's eyes shone with admiration. "Wow."

"Wren, are you coming to the game?" Mr. James asked.

"I wouldn't miss it for the world." I grinned broadly.

Fuller's mom gave his dad a knowing look.

Twenty minutes later, after we were all stuffed from salad, pasta, and breadsticks, I helped Fuller clear the plates from the table.

"Hey, I have a little something for you." Fuller winked at me.

"A present?" My skin started tingling.

"Yup." Fuller scraped the remnants from his little brother's plate into the trash can.

A smile played on my lips. "Are you going to tell me what it is, or do I have to wait?"

"Oh, you definitely have to wait."

I playfully shoved his shoulder. "Not fair."

He shrugged. "My present. My rules."

We made quick work of the rest of the dishes until only the bowls of pasta, sauce, and salad were still out.

"Lunch for tomorrow," Fuller said as he filled up a container with the leftover pasta. He dolloped on three big spoonfuls of sauce. "Gotta carb up."

I placed the last dirty dish in the dishwasher and shut the door. "That pasta sauce was really good. It might even give Dae's mom's kimchi a run for its money."

"Mmm, kimchi. I can't believe I've been missing out for so many years." Fuller rubbed his stomach. "Thanks for sharing with me the other day."

"Hey, that's what girlfriends are for, right?" I grinned.

"Mm-hmm." Fuller peeked his head around the corner of the open kitchen doorway.

Apparently satisfied that his parents weren't going to walk in, he pulled me into his arms and ducked his head. His lips met mine; they were warm and tasted like spaghetti sauce.

The sounds of footsteps pulled us apart. Fuller darted back over to the plastic container he'd filled for lunch tomorrow and snapped it shut. "You sure I can't make you one?"

His mom walked into the kitchen. "Oh, Wren, please, take some leftovers home. We made enough to feed a small army tonight."

"Are you sure?"

"Of course. Let me grab you a container." She hummed as she made her way over to the cabinet to the left of the sink. "Here you go, sweetheart."

"I need to run upstairs and grab something. I'll be right back." Fuller flashed a grin at me before disappearing around the corner.

Mrs. James and I were left together in the kitchen.

"Wren, I wanted to tell you, we really are so incredibly grateful for everything you've done for Fuller." She laid a hand on my shoulder. "Charlie and I are so proud of the changes Fuller has made since meeting you. His grades have improved, but also his overall attitude is better, too. Even Hudson has noticed."

I was so happy, I felt like I could float right out of the kitchen. "I'm glad I could help."

"Mom, are you telling Wren embarrassing things about me?" Fuller had popped back into the room with a Magnolia Valley High School tote bag in his hand. "She already knows about the picture of me in the hallway."

"Who? Me?" She pulled her hand to her chest. "Also, that picture is one of my all-time favorites. I keep a copy with me always." She pulled out her phone and unlocked the screen.

"Ah, Mom, trust me, Wren doesn't need to see that," Fuller said, stepping in front of me and blocking my view of his mother's cell. "If things are good in the kitchen, do you mind if I steal Wren for a few minutes?"

His mom checked her watch. "Not at all. Just don't make it too late. You've got a full day of school tomorrow and then the game. You need a good night's sleep."

Fuller smiled. "Don't worry, Mom. We won't be long."

She handed me the two containers filled with food. "Sounds good, kids."

"Thank you again for dinner, Mrs. James," I said to Fuller's mother. "It was delicious."

Reaching down, Fuller took my hand in his and led me into the family room. Anticipation shot through my veins.

"What's in there?" I asked, arching an eyebrow and pointing to the bag with my other hand.

"Oh, in here? Eh, nothing." Fuller shook his head, but his grin was unmistakable.

I tried reaching around him to grab the bag, but he twisted in the opposite direction and then held the bag above my head.

"Hey, that's not fair! You're, like, a foot taller than me." Balancing the two containers in my hands, I jumped for the bag, but he somehow managed to lift it even higher.

Fuller laughed. "Okay, okay, I'll trade you. Hand over

the containers and I'll give you what's in the bag."

"Here you go." I handed him my lunch for tomorrow and held out my hand.

"And here you go." He held out the bag, but just out of reach.

I jumped up, but he held it even higher.

"Hey! Hand it over, mister," I said with a smile.

"Okay, okay." Fuller smiled as he passed me the bag and waited for me to open it.

There were two things inside. I pulled out a box of strawberry and grape Nerds first. "Ah, my favorite."

"Sweets for my sweet." His dark lashes swept up and his gaze met mine, sending the familiar rush of shivers racing through my body. "There's something else in there, though…"

I reached in and pulled out a maroon and gray T-shirt. On the front, it read "Magnolia Valley Cougars."

"Turn it over," Fuller said, biting his lower lip.

I flipped the shirt, and a massive grin spread over my face. On the back was Fuller's last name and the number eleven, the same number he'd had since freshman year.

"I was thinking you could maybe wear it to the game tomorrow?"

I held the shirt to my chest. "This is really sweet."

He grinned. "So you'll wear it, then?"

"Of course I will." I sprang forward, the box of Nerds jiggling in my hand, and wrapped my arms around his toned midsection.

He hugged me back as I laid my head against his chest. I felt so safe in his arms, like nothing could ever go wrong, just as long as he held me this close.

He kissed me on top of the head. "Wren, you're the best thing that's ever happened to me."

…

The next day at school flew by in a blur. I'd thought about wearing his shirt to school but decided on the floral dress I'd worn to Fuller's house for our first date instead.

I had plans to Dutch braid my hair, add maroon and gray ribbons, and get all decked out for the game. Fuller's shirt would be the cherry on top.

After the last bell rang, Fuller kissed me and then headed off to practice. I smiled as I made my way to my locker to meet Dae.

All my happiness evaporated the moment I saw Marissa heading toward me. She had on a black skirt and shiny pink lip gloss.

I held my breath as she drew nearer. Marissa used to have a hold over me, but that was because I let her. No more. I was done shrinking down in front of Marissa. Holding my shoulders back and raising my chin, I prepared to ignore whatever insult she'd choose to throw at me.

"You look nice today, Wren."

The words came out of Marissa's mouth as if she handed out compliments like that to me all the time.

Flustered, I adjusted my backpack, tightening the straps under both arms. "Oh, um, ah, thanks."

"No problem. Will you be at the game tonight, cheering on Fuller?"

"Yeah." My voice quavered slightly. I braced myself for the nasty insult that was surely coming my way.

"I guess I'll see you there." She smiled before walking past me.

As her stilettos clicked down the hallway, I stood perfectly still. *Did that really happen? Did Marissa talk to me without making fun of me or calling me Wrentainer?*

Fuller had told me that he'd called Marissa and that they'd cleared the air. I figured that would prompt her to come at me with even more venom, but maybe hell had frozen over and she'd decided to be nice instead.

"Hey, Wren. Wait up."

I spun around and came face-to-face with Brandon and Dae.

"You're never going to guess what happened a few seconds ago." I shook my head in disbelief as I recounted my interaction with Marissa.

Dae leaned against a locker with a look of disbelief plastered across his face. "Yeah right. There's no way Marissa would be nice to you. No offense or anything."

Brandon stood next to me, listening intently but not saying anything.

"None taken and I'm so not kidding. It was literally the first time she's been nice to me since seventh grade. Wait, do you think she's screwing with me?"

"Probably," Brandon grumbled. "She's always trying to mess with *someone*."

"She could be faking it," Dae agreed. "Or maybe she really is capable of change? I mean, you did say that Fuller talked to her, so maybe what he said actually resonated?" He didn't sound confident in what he was saying.

"Yeah, maybe she finally realized that she and Fuller aren't getting back together and that she's wasting her time?" Now I was the one who didn't sound confident.

"I've gotta head to our pregame meeting," Brandon said. He shifted his weight from side to side before looking me directly in the eyes. "I just wanted to get something off my chest first. You know Fuller isn't my favorite person, but if you trust him… Well, if you trust him, then I'm happy for you."

Finally!

"Aw, thanks, Brand." I gave him a quick hug. "That really means a lot to me."

He shrugged and appeared to attempt a smile. "All right, I gotta go before I'm late."

"We'll be there cheering you on tonight," I said, patting him on the back.

"Yeah, man. Good luck," Dae said as our friend made his way through the crowded hallway.

"Looks like Brandon's come around," Dae said.

I nodded and faked wiping sweat from my brow. "Talk about a big relief." *Best-friend-hating-boyfriend scenarios never work out. Thank goodness that's fixed!*

"Anyway, enough about him," I said. "Are you still bringing Jenna Marie to the game tonight?"

He grinned. "Yup, I'm picking her up around six fifteen. We should get back to school by quarter to seven."

"Perfect." We'd planned to sit next to each other, but I hadn't told Dae about the shirt that Fuller had given me yet. It was going to be a surprise, not for Dae but for everyone. I would officially show up as Fuller James's girlfriend. I'd planned out my entire outfit last night after getting home from Fuller's house. A pair of ripped dark wash jeans, the maroon and gray shirt with Fuller's name and number, and a cute pair of hoop earrings.

I shoved my Calculus book into my locker and grabbed a thick Physics book from the bottom shelf. Even though all I wanted to do during study hall was flirt with Fuller, we'd made a pact to continue to study together and do our homework in the library. That way, we could hang out or talk after he got done with the team's pregame meeting. Thanks to our productive session, all I had to do this weekend was study for my AP Physics test next week.

Dae and I made our way toward the parking lot. Freshmen scurried by to get to their buses in time, while juniors and seniors talked about their weekend plans on the way to their cars.

I tightened my backpack straps; the strain of carrying heavy books all day hurt my back. "I'm nervous for the guys.

Sounds like there are going to be at least three scouts at the game. Brandon was kind of freaking out. I don't blame him, though…there's a lot of pressure on the team tonight."

Dae moved his head up and down in agreement. He appeared to be paying attention, but I saw him looking at his phone.

"Do you think Brand's going to get drafted into the NBA next year?" I said, trying to keep my voice even.

"Yeah, totally," Dae said, still looking at his phone.

"Is that before or after he runs for president?"

No response.

"Or destroys the alien invaders taking over our planet?" I suppressed a chuckle.

His eyes were still glued to his screen. "Ah, yeah. Sure."

"Dae," I said, shoving my friend's shoulder.

He tucked his phone into his back pocket. "Huh?"

I shook my head. "You've got it bad for Jenna Marie, huh?"

He grinned. "I do."

"Why don't you ask her to be your girlfriend? Make things official?" I elbowed him lightly in the ribs.

"Well…" Dae trailed off as a massive smile took over his face.

"Dae Kang, what are you hiding from me?" I stopped and placed my hands on my hips.

He stopped walking and spun around. "I asked her last night."

I let out a loud squeal. "Did she say yes?"

Arching a brow, he ducked his chin. "Do you think she would say no to all this?" He pointed to his muscular abdomen.

"You're ridiculous, you know that, right?" I joked.

"That's not what Jenna Marie said last night."

I sprang toward him and gave him a massive hug. "Yeah,

yeah, enough with the jokes." Letting go, I couldn't stop grinning. "I'm really happy for you, Dae." We walked side by side to the back row where we'd both parked this morning.

Dae ran a hand through his black hair. "My mom wants her to come over for dinner tomorrow night."

My eyes lit up. "Aw, meeting Mommy and Daddy Kang. That's a big step. You haven't brought anyone home since..." I softened my tone. "Well, since Eva."

The perma grin on Dae's face flickered. "Let's not talk about her."

I held up my hands. "My bad." It had taken him months to get back on his feet after Eva doused their relationship in gasoline and lit the match. He'd been a lot more guarded since then, going out on dates but never getting serious with another girl. Jenna Marie had changed all of that, and I couldn't be happier for the both of them.

I flipped my key ring around my finger. "All right, I'm going to head home and get ready. See you back here at quarter to seven?"

"Sounds good. Meet by the concession stands?"

"See you there."

...

"Wow, kiddo. You look great."

"Thanks so much, Gramps," I said, spinning around. "Check out Fuller's shirt. Pretty cool, huh?"

Gramps scratched his head. "Isn't he that nice boy who came over? We talked about Charles Barkley."

My heart swelled with happiness at the small memory achievement Gramps had displayed. "Yup."

"I'm sorry I can't make it to the game." He looked down at his cast. "Doc wants me to take it easy."

I put my hand on his shoulder and gave it a gentle

squeeze. "We'll be sure to go to a game together as soon as you're feeling better." My heart broke as I said the words out loud. Gramps and I never went to games anymore; they were too much for him. "But if you're feeling up for it, would you like to watch the game on TV with me tomorrow morning? I have the DVR set up and ready to record it."

"That sounds great, Wrenny."

The nickname made me smile. He and Grandma had called me that when I was a little girl, but he rarely used it anymore. I thought he'd forgotten it for good. "Sounds great. I'm going to head out now, Gramps. I'll see you later."

"Night, sweetheart."

I grabbed my coat and shouted goodbye to my parents before heading outside and slipping into my car.

It was only six fifteen, but I was too anxious to wait around the house any longer. I'd get to school before Dae and Jenna Marie, but I didn't mind. I might even be able to see the guys warm up.

The drive through town felt different. Almost like the perfect light during the golden hour had settled down on our little mountain town and stayed there. I'd started to see places as opportunities for cute dates with Fuller. I looked at the quaint general store on the corner of Main and Third Street. *Maybe Fuller and I can grab a malt next weekend?*

I let out a chuckle as I drove by a new business called Escape Me! Allegedly, there was a guy dressed up as a zombie inside and, if you didn't solve the clues to escape the room fast enough, he'd pretend to attack you. I bet Brandon and Dae would love that place. I wondered if Fuller and I could set up Brand with someone. That way, we could triple date.

By the time I got to school, I had a huge smile on my face. I never thought I'd be one of *those* girls who got all mushy when she started dating someone, but Fuller brought it out in me.

Leaving my coat in the car, my hands trembled slightly as I locked my car and headed into the school. Trying to shake the nerves, I gave myself a little mental pep talk. *Fuller is going to do great tonight. He's going to be super excited to see you in the stands. Dae and Jenna Marie are going to be there, too, which is awesome.*

Everything is going to be perfect.

Posters for the game lined the school walls. Our basketball games usually drew in a huge crowd, but tonight's would be an even bigger spectacle than usual. We were playing the Falcons, our rivals. We'd lost our only game to them during the regular season, and they'd almost knocked us out of the state tournament in the playoffs. The competition would be tough, but I knew the guys could take them down. Especially with their improved free throw percentages.

The familiar sounds of basketballs being dribbled up and down the court echoed off the brick hallway leading to the gymnasium. Ducking inside the door, I scanned the court. Fuller stood with a basketball in his hands, getting ready to take a shot from the three-point line. His feet were totally squared, and his balance was perfect. A grin spread across my face. *Looks like my advice has helped already.*

As the ball sailed through the hoop, he looked over at me and waved. I waved back as giddy excitement shot through my body.

"Nice shirt," he shouted before catching a pass from TyShaun.

Brandon nailed two layups in a row, grinning as the ball rebounded off the backboard and swished through the net. He was hands down the best point guard in our entire division. Fuller and the other guys on the team were lucky to have him.

With pride bursting in my chest for Fuller and Brandon, I decided to play it cool. Turning around, I exited the gym and made my way toward the concession stands. I ordered some Red Vines and a bottle of water. That would keep me occupied until Dae and Jenna Marie got here.

Twenty minutes later, students, parents, and teachers had flooded the commons, where the concession stands were set up. The crowd buzzed with excitement as basketball fans of all ages milled about.

Dae and Jenna Marie showed up right at six forty-five. After waiting in line for popcorn and soda, we made our way toward the gym.

"Wren, your outfit is super cute." Jenna Marie smiled.

"Thanks." I grinned. "Fuller gave me one of his basketball shirts last night."

"Totally adorable." Jenna Marie squeezed Dae's hand.

I wasn't sure if she was talking about my shirt or Dae, but either way, it made me happy.

As we entered the gym, I smiled. The atmosphere was perfect, from the sound of squeaking sneakers, to the smell of popcorn, and best of all, the excited buzz of the students and parents getting ready for tip-off.

"Magnolia Valley Cougars! Magnolia Valley Cougars," the cheerleaders shouted in unison. They stood at the far end of the gym, waving their pom-poms in the air. The fans chanted along and clapped.

We made our way up and across the crowded bleachers, taking a seat at the half-court line. It was my favorite spot to watch the game.

Fuller and his teammates appeared to be finishing their warm-up. They'd switched from shooting hoops to dribbling and passing drills.

"Hey, Wren."

I froze. I knew that voice, and it sent shivers down my back, even if she'd been abnormally nice to me earlier in the day. Dae scowled.

Spinning around, my eyes landed on Marissa and Courtney. They were wearing matching maroon tank tops that left nothing to the imagination, and super-short jean shorts. The pockets were sticking out by at least three inches. Shockingly, they must have forgone their high heel death contraption rules for the game. Instead, they wore bright white sneakers.

"Hey, Marissa. Courtney." I greeted them with abundant caution, unsure of what they wanted or why they were talking to me.

Marissa smoothed out her shirt before sitting down on the bleacher behind us. Which, of course, meant I had to look up at her as she continued the conversation.

"That's a cute shirt." She flipped her hair over her shoulder.

"Thanks, Fuller gave it to me." I kept my voice level, trying not to give her the satisfaction of making me nervous.

"Listen, I think it's really sweet that you and Fuller have this little thing going on." She looked at Courtney and laughed. "But there's something I think you should know."

The air whooshed out of my lungs, and just like that, I felt like we were back in seventh grade again. The confidence that I'd felt the night before in Fuller's family room vanished.

"Marissa, why don't you go sit somewhere else?" Dae's eyes narrowed in on her.

"Oh, trust me, I wouldn't be caught dead sitting next to the three of you. The only reason I'm here is to let Wrentainer in on Fuller's little secret." She leaned forward, locking eyes with me.

My blood turned to ice. "What are you talking about?"

"Well, see," she said, brushing something off her leg, "Fuller and the guys…" She stopped and shot a snide look at Courtney before bursting into laughter.

"Stop dragging it out, Marissa. Say what you need to say and then get out of here." Adrenaline rushed through my body at light speed. My fight-or-flight reflex was in full force, but I refused to give in.

"All right, all right. You know when you were assigned to be Fuller's tutor?"

"What about it?" My stomach flip-flopped. *How did she know I was tutoring him?*

Marissa's lips twisted into a wicked smile. "He didn't want anyone to know that he was being forced to work with *you*. You know, because you're Wrentainer and all."

Dae scooted closer to me and put his arm protectively around me. "She's lying, Wren. Ignore her."

My heart hammered in my chest and the walls suddenly felt like they were swaying back and forth.

She shot Dae a nasty look before continuing. "Fuller lied about the tutoring sessions and covered it up by telling Marc that you two were hooking up in the AV room." Marissa's lips turned up in a wicked smile. "Marc obviously didn't believe him, so they decided on a bet to prove it."

"A bet?" My voice sounded hollow. I knew I was sitting in the stands of the gym, but it suddenly felt like I was in another dimension where only Marissa and I existed. "I don't believe you. Fuller wouldn't do that to me."

She laughed. "You don't have to believe me. Ask Fuller yourself. Also, how would I know the details unless he blabbed everything to TyShaun and Marc?"

Ice radiated through my veins. She had a point.

"Fuller bet that he'd be able to get proof of you two hanging out—which the picture on the Instagram account covered quite nicely—that he could get you to do some kind of PDA thing with him in the hallway, like holding hands, and the final step, that you'd show up at tonight's game as his girlfriend. I guess you were supposed to wear his letterman jacket, but I'm sure his T-shirt counts."

My heart pounded in my chest and my temples throbbed.

"Here's the best part. After the game, he's going to break up with you in the parking lot. Marc is supposed to ask you out after and take you to the Fall Harvest Dance next week, but Courtney wants to go with him, so I figured I'd do you a little favor and give you a heads-up."

I couldn't breathe, let alone respond to what my ex–best friend had spat at me in front of the crowd.

"Oh," Marissa continued, feigning a sad facc. "You thought he actually liked you?"

"You poor girl," Courtney chimed in.

Dae scooted so close to me that our arms were touching. "There's no way Fuller would ever make a bet like that. He cares about Wren. We all know you're jealous, Marissa. You're probably just making this whole thing up."

"Don't believe me? Fine, look at this," she said, holding up her cell phone.

I scanned the screen. It was a text message between her and TyShaun.

TyShaun: He's got two weeks to convince Wrentainer to be his girlfriend.
TyShaun: Otherwise he loses the bet with Marc.

Marissa: What a loser.
Marissa: He can't stand her.
Marissa: Nobody can!

TyShaun: She's actually kinda hot.

Marissa: Shut up!

TyShaun: You're hotter?

Marissa: A question mark?
Marissa: Are you serious?
Marissa: Whatever, not like it even matters.

Marissa: Everyone knows Fuller and I will be back together by the Fall Festival.

Marissa pulled her phone back and sneered, "You didn't really think that he liked you, did you, Wrentainer?"

"Don't call me that." My voice shook as the words left my mouth.

"What? You don't like the nickname Fuller gave you in seventh grade?" She rolled her eyes.

I stood up, my body quaking with anger. "He didn't give me that nickname. You did!"

"You're such a loser," she hissed as her face scrunched up and turned crimson with anger.

She and Courtney got up without saying another word. They climbed down the bleachers and headed out the gym door.

My chest heaved as tears welled in the corners of my eyes. I didn't want to believe what she was saying, but it made sense. Everything from Fuller giving me his shirt to wear to the game, to the picture on Instagram, to TyShaun holding up two fingers when he saw us holding hands in the hallway.

The worst part was that he was going to dump me in the parking lot after the game. I was nothing but a joke to him. A stupid bet.

"I, um, I gotta go," I mumbled to Dae and Jenna Marie.

"Wren, wait," Dae pleaded.

I shook my head, bolting out of my seat and racing down the bleachers.

The stares and whispers of my classmates were almost too much to handle, but they didn't even hold a candle to how it felt when Fuller looked at me from across the court.

I felt like he'd reached into my chest and torn out my beating heart.

His smile disappeared once he saw the tears running

down my face. I wanted to scream at him from the sidelines, to tell him what an asshole he was—but I didn't want to give him the satisfaction. He didn't deserve one more second of my time or attention.

Vision blurred from hot tears, I raced through the crowd of people waiting to get into the gym and down the hall leading to the parking lot.

"Wren, sweetheart. Is that you?"

I stopped dead in my tracks.

Less than a foot away stood Fuller's parents and his little brother.

Wiping the tears from my cheeks, I tried to smile and pretend everything was okay.

"Oh, Wren, honey. What's wrong?" Fuller's mother took a step toward me.

Fresh tears burned my eyes and dripped onto my cheeks. "Ah, I'm not feeling very well. I need to go home."

Without another word, I sprinted down the hallway and into the fresh air.

Sucking it in, my legs propelled me forward toward the corner of the parking lot. *How could I have been so stupid? Why would I ever believe someone like Fuller James would actually like me?*

I reached into my small crossbody purse and fumbled through its contents. Finally, my fingers felt the loop of the key ring.

"Wren." Dae's voice cut through the crisp air.

Shaking my head, I unlocked the driver's side door. "I-I can't talk right now, Dae."

I felt his hands on my shoulders. "Wren, I'm so sorry."

Collapsing into his chest, I began sobbing. My entire body shook. Dae held me up as my knees turned to jelly.

"I should have seen right through him." Dae whispered. "I never should have trusted that asshole."

Hot tears streaked down my face, forming a wet patch on his shirt.

"I'm so stupid." My voice choked with emotion.

Dae shook his head and held me tighter. "He fooled both of us."

Sniffling, I pulled back and wiped my face with trembling hands.

The pain in my chest had been replaced with a numb sensation, and I suddenly felt exhausted. "I'm going to head out. You should go back in and be with Jenna Marie."

"No way." Dae leaned against my car. "She's waiting by my car. Come with me. We'll drive you home."

I shook my head. "I'm fine. I just need to crawl into bed and pretend none of this ever happened."

"Are you sure?" Dae spoke softly as he pulled me in for another embrace.

"Yes. I'm sure. Thanks for offering, though."

Dae gave me one final squeeze before I stepped away and got into my car. My best friend stood with drooped shoulders, watching me drive off.

Twenty minutes later, I pulled up in front of my house. Somehow, I'd managed to stop crying on the way home. I searched my glove box for something to wipe the mascara off. Coming up empty, I used the bottom of Fuller's T-shirt. It didn't matter if I stained it. It was going in the trash.

I checked the mirror and sighed. While I managed to get all the black smudges off my face, I couldn't hide my puffy red eyes.

Deciding that waiting wouldn't make things any better, I grabbed my purse from the passenger's seat.

Forcing myself to breathe, I walked through my front

door and popped my head into the family room.

"Wren, is that you?" Gramps asked from the sofa.

"Hey, Gramps."

My mom and dad frowned. "What are you doing home so early?"

I held my hand to my head. "Um, I'm not feeling so good. My head hurts and I feel…funky. I decided that it was best to come home and rest."

"Oh, honey. I'm sorry. I know how much you were looking forward to watching Fuller at the game. Can I bring you a cup of tea or some Tylenol?" my mom asked with a still-furrowed brow.

"I'm going to grab a glass of water. I'm sure I'll feel a lot better after I get some rest," I lied.

Nothing would make me feel better about what happened tonight. Ever.

"All right, well, feel better, pumpkin," my dad said.

"Night night, Wrenny," Gramps added.

I walked into the kitchen and grabbed a glass from the cabinet next to the fridge. After filling it at the refrigerator, I made a beeline for my bedroom, the chilled water sloshing around with every step.

Setting the cup down on my nightstand, I tossed my phone and purse on the floor.

That's when I caught a glimpse of myself. Wearing Fuller's stupid basketball shirt. I yanked it off and threw it across the room. Tears streamed down my face as my knees gave out. Reaching back, I caught myself on the edge of my bed. Pulling myself backward, I collapsed on top of my duvet. "How could I have been so stupid?" The words came out in between the sobs that shook my body.

Rolling over, I closed my eyes and vowed never to speak to him again.

I hate you, Fuller James.

Chapter Twenty

Fuller

My alarm went off at exactly five o'clock, but it didn't matter; I was already awake.

I picked up my phone and unlocked the screen for what felt like the thousandth time since I went to bed. I'd sent her more than twenty texts starting Friday night and ending last night after dinner, but she hadn't replied to a single one. I didn't even know if she'd read them, since they all said only, "Delivered."

Opening my Instagram app, I typed in her username and clicked on her profile picture. *Blocked.* I sighed and let my phone fall to my chest.

I wanted to drive to her house and apologize in person, but if she wouldn't pick up my calls or answer my texts, there was no way she'd let me inside her house.

The darkness in my room matched my mood. As I lay there with my eyes closed, Friday night's events played through my mind on an endless reel. Wren running out of the gym, my parents telling me that she left because she was sick, the worry in my gut that it was something else coupled with the helpless feeling that I was stuck at school until the game was over…

Then finding out the truth afterward.

I rubbed my face with my hands. I was furious with Marissa, and I'd called her out on it as soon as I'd heard what she'd done, but how mad could I be? *I* was the one who made the bet in the first place. No one forced me to do it. Then, instead of being a man and confessing everything to Wren, I made my friends promise to keep my secret. I'd been pissed at TyShaun for blabbing to Marissa, but ultimately it wasn't his fault. Everything that went down was my fault. Plain and simple. Marissa had simply been the final nail in the coffin.

Wren's feelings had been crushed because I was a cocky jerk who always put himself before others. My friends knew it, my teammates knew it, and now the girl I'd fallen in love with knew it.

I rolled over onto my stomach and slammed my fist into the mattress.

Holding my breath, I cursed myself over and over again. *I love her. I freaking love Wren Carter and I lost her! What is wrong with me? Why couldn't I buck up and be honest with her? Why did I have to continue to hide the truth from her? I'm such a loser!*

Desperate to let off some of this pent-up emotion before school, I got out of bed and changed into a pair of shorts and a T-shirt. My house was still as I slipped out the front door. Locking it behind me, I rolled my neck to the left and then the right before I started jogging down the sidewalk.

An hour later, sweat dripped down my body. While I felt exhausted from pushing myself to the max, I still felt like the world's biggest asshole. Normally, I'd already have gone back to the house to take a shower and head to the gym to shoot some hoops, but I couldn't possibly go back to the scene of the crime. Instead, I decided on heading in the opposite direction. I doubted anything would make me feel better, but an extra thirty minutes out here couldn't hurt.

Friday was supposed to be one of the highlights of my senior year. The UGA Coach had shown up as well as three scouts from other teams. I'd played my heart out and managed to pull off a triple double, scoring twenty-three points and getting fourteen rebounds and eleven assists. Coach slapped me on the back after the game, congratulating me on my personal best. I'd been an animal on the court, and everyone had noticed.

Well, everyone but Wren. I knew she wouldn't leave pregame unless something had happened. I was worried that her gramps had gotten sick again, but when I'd checked with Brandon at halftime, he didn't know what was up, either. It had thrown me, but I managed to play through it. I figured Wren would want that…

Little did I know that she probably wanted me to trip on the half-court line and break my ankle. No… Wren wasn't vindictive. She wasn't like Marissa. *Ugh! Marissa.* It wasn't really her fault, though. It was mine. I did this. Nobody else was responsible.

I raised my hands to my head. I was driving myself mad. Replaying the same things over and over in my head. There was only one thing that could make it better. Seeing Wren and apologizing face-to-face.

The pavement pounded under my shoes. If I could rewind time and take it all back, I'd do it in a heartbeat. I'd give up any of my possessions to be able to undo the pain I'd caused Wren.

That's when I saw a figure racing across the street, a long braid bouncing off her back. She was hands down the fastest person I'd ever seen in real life. That's when my conversation with Wren dawned on me. She could run seven miles in an hour. Praying it was her, I crossed the street. "Wren? Is that you?"

The figure skidded to a halt and spun around.

Wren's face twisted into shock and then horror as her eyes landed on me. "Did you follow me here?"

"No, I wanted to get in a longer run. So, I, ah, I took a new route this morning." Even though I didn't want to believe it, the level of disgust in her voice hit me like a cannonball to the gut. "I've been trying to get ahold of you all weekend." I took a step toward her.

She stepped back. "Get away from me."

Her eyes were dark, and she wore a deep scowl on her face. My heart ached to undo the pain I'd caused. "Wait, please. Let me—"

She held up her hand, cutting me off mid-sentence. "No."

I wanted to reach out and pull her into my arms. Kiss those soft lips that tasted like coconut. Make things better. But that wasn't an option anymore. Wren didn't want anything to do with me. I'd screwed up everything and lost her in the process.

"I know it's going to be tough, seeing as we go to the same school, but listen to my words. I *never* want to see your face or hear your voice *ever* again. Understood?"

My heart thumped wildly in my chest. "I never meant to hurt you."

Wren rolled her eyes. "You want to *bet*?" The word hung in the air between us, causing me to wince as though she had slapped me. Without another word, Wren took off and disappeared into the misty morning air.

• • •

"Fuller?"

A soft knock on my bedroom door followed. I caught the basketball I'd been shooting into the air.

"Can I come in?"

"Now's not a good time, Hud." I'd been staring at the ceiling for hours, trying to come up with a way to fix the destruction I'd caused.

"It'll only take a minute," his little voice called through the door.

He sounded so grown up. Like a younger version of our dad. When did that happen?

"All right, buddy. Come on in." I tucked the ball under my arm and sat up.

Hudson came into my room and sat next to me on my bed. "Do you want to talk about it?" He placed his little hand on my shoulder and gave it a squeeze.

My heart broke into a million pieces with this simple gesture. As soon as the game was over, he wanted me to check in on Wren, make sure she was okay. When she refused to take my calls, he told me to go over to her house. At the time, I didn't have the heart to explain to him what happened. He looked up to me. By admitting I made a bet about Wren, I'd be letting him down, too. The fact that he adored her would only make things harder. "It's complicated, Hud."

"She left your game before it even started. She blocked you on Instagram." He scooted closer to me and wrapped both arms around my midsection. "I like Wren. So do Mom and Dad."

My little brother's concern cracked the tough facade I'd been putting on since I found out what happened on Friday night.

He squeezed me tighter. "Why isn't she talking to you anymore?"

Blinking back the tears that had welled up in my eyes, I carefully hugged Hudson back. "It's not good, little man."

He tilted his face up toward mine. "Did you do something wrong?"

I let my head fall into my hands. "I screwed up. Bad."

"Why doesn't Wren want to be your girlfriend anymore?" His voice cracked, which almost sent me over the edge.

My hands fell into my lap. "I totally blew it. I acted like a complete jerk, and I hurt her."

Hudson crossed his legs. "Tell her you're sorry. Maybe make her a card. Bring her flowers or something. Girls in the movies always like that kind of stuff."

Completely dejected, I leaned against the headboard of my bed. "I tried, but she didn't want to talk to me. Honestly, Hud, I don't know if she'll ever forgive me."

Hudson shrugged. "What if you did something big? Like, you know, when Vanessa had that thing taken out of her so she and Deadpool could have babies?"

"Dude!" I gasped. "That's definitely not something you should be talking about! You're nine!"

My little brother rolled his eyes. "Whatever. Do something big. Maybe at the dance, so everyone will see how sorry you really are? Something that'll win her back."

I chewed on my lower lip. "You know, while that's a wildly inappropriate example, you might be onto something."

His eyes lit up. "Really?"

"Really."

He clenched his fist and pulled his elbow backward. "Yes. Hudson for the win!"

I ruffled his hair. "I'm going to need some ideas, though. Think you could help me come up with a plan?"

"Duh! Like you could do it without my help." He rolled his eyes again and, for the first time since Friday, I felt a shimmer of hope in my heart.

"Do you think it would be all right if I called two friends to help us out?" I asked Hudson.

Hudson put his little hand on my arm. "I think we're going to need all the help we can get."

• • •

Five hours later, Dae, Brandon, Hudson, and I looked at one another.

"Okay. What did we learn by watching those movies?" I asked.

I couldn't believe they'd agreed to come over. I thought for a minute that they might show up at my front door and punch me in the face, but, after I all but begged them, they agreed.

Brandon stood up and stretched. "I learned that my butt fell asleep midway through *Say Anything*."

"Very funny." I turned toward Dae and Hudson. "These are Wren's favorite movies. But we need to figure out how I can use them to win her back."

"The grand gesture in *Say Anything* is pretty epic. I think you could pull off something like that at the dance," Dae said. "But you need to incorporate *The Princess Bride*, too."

"I have an idea! Be right back." Hudson hopped off the couch and raced out of the room. A few seconds later, his feet thundered down the stairs.

"What are you doing?" Brandon asked with a chuckle.

Hudson had put on his Deadpool mask.

"You gotta dress up as Westley," he said enthusiastically. "They go through heck and back as a couple, right? But he never loses hope. If you dress up like Westley and tell her that you haven't lost hope, maybe that will win her back?"

"Dang. That was deep, little man," Dae said with a smile.

Hudson winked at him. "Trust me, I know all about girls."

We all burst into laughter.

"Hey, Hud. Can you do me a favor?"

He pulled off the Deadpool mask. "Sure."

"Can you give me a few minutes with Brandon and Dae?"

"Yeah. I'm going to go play some Fortnite. Call me if you need any more help."

I ruffled his hair. "Thanks, buddy."

Once Hudson headed back upstairs, I turned my attention back to Wren's best friends.

I took a deep breath. "I know this wasn't easy for either of you, but I really appreciate you coming over here and hearing me out. I care so much about Wren, and I royally screwed up. A lot of people would have written me off permanently."

Brandon nodded. "Not going to lie, Fuller, I wanted to punch your lights out, but there's no way we'd make it to State without you, so I reconsidered. Also, Wren obviously cares about you and, even though you did a bunch of stupid crap, I think it's obvious you really like her, too."

"Thank you."

"We hate seeing her so upset," Dae added. "And if I thought even for one minute that she was one hundred percent over you and never wanted to see you again, I wouldn't be here."

"Wren is really lucky to have you two for best friends." I thought about my own relationships. Would Marc or TyShaun go to bat for me like this? Would I do the same for them? I definitely needed to reevaluate how I treated my friends.

"Okay, so back to the plan," I said, standing up. "I think I've got an idea, but I'm going to need your help in order to pull it off."

Chapter Twenty-One

Wren

"Thanks for keeping me company tonight. It's the first time I've missed a game in four years." I took a long swig of raspberry lemonade. "Friday night without basketball… So weird."

Dae and Jenna Marie both gave me empathetic smiles. They were sitting side by side in the hard plastic booth across from me.

"Minus that jerkwad, I still want them to win." I let out a sad chuckle.

Dae stole a glance at his phone. "Want to know the score? Brandon just texted me."

"The game is already over?" I tucked my knees under my chin.

"Yeah, they won, sixty-five to thirty-two." Dae set his phone down. "Brandon is going to meet us here in ten minutes."

My heart ached. My chest ached. Missing the game had

been bad enough, but the planet-sized hole Fuller had left in my heart felt like it would never be repaired.

Jenna Marie dunked a French fry in ketchup. "It's hard."

"What?"

"Having someone betray you." She took a bite. "But I can tell you one thing. It will get better."

Taking another sip of lemonade, I shrugged. "I was stupid for ever thinking someone like Fuller James could be a decent human being. I've learned my lesson. The rest of my senior year is going to be all about spending time with my friends, acing my AP tests, and graduating as valedictorian."

Jenna Marie shook her head. "You don't have to swear off finding someone forever. I promise, there are a few good ones out there." She glanced up at Dae.

Guilt washed over me like a powerful wave. "There might be, but I'm done looking until I get to college."

"If it makes you feel any better, Fuller feels terrible," Dae said cautiously.

My eyebrows shot up in surprise. "How do you know that?"

"Oh, well, you can just tell." Dae stole a quick glance in Jenna Marie's direction. "You know, because—"

"Hey, guys." Brandon's voice interrupted our conversation.

"You getting something to eat?" Dae asked, cutting our talk of Fuller short. It was probably for the best. I didn't need to waste any more time thinking about him.

"I already ordered." Brandon scooted next to me in the booth. "I'm starving."

Pushing Fuller to the back of my mind, I laughed. Brandon was always hungry.

"I probably went a little overboard with three chili dogs and a basket of fries." He gave me a lopsided grin. "I may need some help eating all of it."

"Heard you won. Congrats." I wanted to ask him more about the game, but the tightness in my chest prevented me. I hadn't cried since Wednesday after school, and I didn't want to start again now.

Brandon threw his arm over my shoulder and squeezed me into the nook between his armpit and his side. "We totally kicked their butts."

"Proud of you." I let my head fall onto his shoulder. "Also, thanks for showering."

He chuckled and stole one of Jenna Marie's fries. "What's on the agenda for tonight?"

"*League of Legends* and popcorn at my place?" Jenna Marie suggested.

Dae and Brandon nodded in agreement.

When I didn't say anything, everyone turned their eyes toward me.

"Wren?" Brandon asked.

Shrugging, I took a long sip of my drink. "I was thinking about heading home after this— I have that AP Psychology paper due next week."

Jenna Marie shook her head. "No way. I need your opinion on my dress for tomorrow night."

A dance I'm no longer attending… I stared out the window, my eyes landing on a yellow Jeep with a Magnolia Valley basketball bumper sticker. It reminded me of Fuller. Everything reminded me of him.

"Wren?" Jenna Marie's shoulder lifted slightly.

"I'm sure it's awesome." Jenna Marie was stunning; she could wear a black trash bag with some duct tape to the dance and look perfect.

She stuck out her lower lip. "Please? I have two dresses and I totally need your help picking the right one."

Dae looked at her and grinned. My heart stung as I watched him tuck a fallen lock of Jenna Marie's hair behind her ear. He was smitten. Just like I used to be with Fuller.

"I…I loved him."

As the words left my lips, Brandon and Dae shot each other a look I couldn't decipher. *Was it an "I told you so" glance or maybe one of pity?*

"Oh, honey." Jenna Marie got up and wrapped her arms around me.

"I loved him, and he played me." I hadn't said the words out loud, but I'd thought them plenty of times. They stung even more when they left my lips.

Brandon's shoulders fell. "I'm so sorry, Wren."

I picked up a fry but then threw it down in disgust. "He's always been a jerk. Believing that he had changed was such a stupid move."

Jenna Marie shook her head. "He fooled all of us."

I tried to focus on the anger coiled in the pit of my stomach instead of the agony tightening in my chest.

"Hey, I've got an idea," Dae said. "How about after the dance, we have a movie night? Just the four of us? We could watch *The Heat*."

A sad chuckle escaped my lips. Dae loved that movie; it always made him laugh. We'd watched it, like, twenty times after Eva had broken up with him.

"I don't want to bring the rest of you down," I said. "You should all go to the dance and have fun. I'll hang out at home with Gramps."

"We aren't going without you. Period." Dae picked up his drink and took a long swig.

"All right, all right," I responded. "I'll go."

Jenna Marie clapped her hands together. "Yay!"

Turning my head, I gazed out the window and allowed my mind to drift to the source of my pain.

How could you do this to me, Fuller James?

Chapter Twenty-Two

Fuller

"Are you nervous?"

I looked up at Marc and TyShaun. "More nervous than I've ever been before any game."

TyShaun put his hand on my shoulder. "You got this and hey, I'm sorry again. I never should have told Marissa anything."

"Thanks, Ty." I ignored the nausea swirling in my stomach. "I appreciate it, but this is my mess, and I'm the one who needs to do the apologizing, not you."

"Wren's going to think you're the coolest." Hudson grinned, displaying a large gap where he'd lost his most recent tooth.

We stood outside the school building. A cold wind whipped through the parking lot, but I didn't mind. The costume I was wearing kept me plenty warm.

"All right, guys. Let's do this."

I adjusted the facemask and the tight leather pants as we made our way to the front door. Hudson walked next to me. He'd dressed up, too. In fact, this whole plan had been his idea. Marc and TyShaun carried all the supplies as we walked through the front door. Once I'd explained the plan to them, they'd jumped on board, too. It had taken everything in Dae and Brandon's power just to get Wren to the dance, but luckily, they'd pulled it off. Having my friends by my side gave me the confidence I needed to go through with everything. I was a really lucky guy. After everything that had happened, these guys really had my back.

Luckily, the DJ for the dance was a family friend. He'd given my plan the okay. He'd even agreed to set up a special wireless microphone.

My gloved hands shook as the music floated down the hallway. Holy buckets, was I nervous. Part of me wanted to chicken out and turn around and run, but if I did that, I'd never get Wren back. And that was all that mattered.

"You got this, Fuller," Hudson's voice squeaked. "Stick to the plan. Just like we rehearsed."

His words of confidence gave me the extra boost I needed. For a nine-year-old, he was pretty wise.

And creative, the little stinker.

As I walked toward the gym, a group of junior girls spotted us and began laughing. Their dates, Jeremy and Nico, frowned.

"Dude, what are you wearing?" Nico asked, tilting his head as he looked me up and down.

I didn't respond. Instead, I motioned for the small group to follow me toward the gym. I felt like the Pied Piper.

"Fuller. There you are." Marissa grabbed onto my arm but loosened her grip once she got a look at my outfit.

"Back off, Marissa."

She looked me up and down, scrunching her nose in the process. "What are you wearing? Where's your tux?"

"What you did last week was unforgivable. You owe Wren an apology and you know it." I waited for her to release my arm.

"An apology? Seriously?" She released her grip and placed her hands on her hips. "Look, I did you a favor by telling Wrentainer about your stupid little bet. Forget her. Let's go in together, and you can be my Fall Harvest Prince."

"I took my name out of the running, Marissa. I already told you that. I'm finally getting my priorities straight, and Wren is way more important to me than a popularity contest."

Her smile disappeared and was instantly replaced with a scowl. "You know what, Fuller? You've changed so much, I barely recognize you. You and that loser deserve each other!"

"You're right, I have changed—for the better. Oh, and you know, there are better ways to get attention. This whole act you put on, it's too much. I didn't call you out on it while we were dating, and that's my bad. But you deserve to know and, honestly, I hope you can change. Because if you don't, no one is going to want to be your friend." Without another word, I turned around and made my way to the stage.

Marissa took one step after me before I heard a snap. Taking a quick glance over my shoulder, I saw her balancing on one stiletto, as the heel on the other one had broken. Courtney rushed to her side and helped her to a chair on the opposite side of the hall.

"You know what they say about karma." Marc smiled and gave me a pat on the back.

TyShaun nodded. "Good luck, man."

"Thanks, Ty."

We walked through a balloon arch to get into the gym. Bales of hay and pumpkins masked the bleachers, which had been pushed up and secured against the walls. There were tables scattered around the perimeter as well. They each had ornate centerpieces with red and orange leaves, pinecones, and a lantern in the middle. Battery-operated candles flickered, giving the space a special ambiance.

Okay, it's now or never.

Chapter Twenty-Three

Wren

My jaw dropped as I watched Fuller make his way to the DJ booth. He had on the tightest black pants I'd ever seen, and he wore this billowy black shirt that was open at the chest. Hudson, who was at his side, was wearing a Deadpool costume. I shot a glance at Dae and Brandon. They both shrugged.

I'm outta here. If this was Fuller about to pull off some over-the-top ridiculous stunt, I didn't need to see it. I took a step to the side, planning to sneak out the back of the gym without being noticed, but stopped when Jenna Marie linked her arm through mine.

"I think you're going to want to stay for this," she whispered with an encouraging smile on her face.

The DJ cut off the song that was playing. "Sorry for the interruption, Magnolia Valley Cougars, but we have a special announcement that will only take a few moments. If everyone could please turn their attention to the stage, that would be great. Thank you!"

My heart started to hammer in my chest. I wanted to turn and run, but my feet stayed cemented to the gym floor.

Fuller grabbed a wireless microphone and put his hand in the air. A moment later, blinding floodlights were aimed at him.

"Um, wow. Those are bright." He held his hand up, peering into the crowd. "All right, some of you may not recognize me in this outfit, but it's me, your varsity basketball captain, Fuller James."

He swung what appeared to be a homemade sword in the air, waving it back and forth. *Are those Nerds boxes? What is he doing?*

The crowd emitted a mixture of gasps and laughter.

"I'm here tonight, dressed up as Westley from *The Princess Bride*, for several reasons. The first is to admit that I'm a complete jerk." The crowd fell silent. "I was failing AP and too embarrassed to admit that I needed help. Principal Davis and Coach Carter found out and told me if I didn't bring my grade up, I wouldn't be able to play basketball."

My chest rose and fell quickly. Even though my classmates booed loudly, I suddenly felt like it was just Fuller and me in the gym.

Fuller waved his sword. "No, don't boo. It was my fault. I'd been so focused on basketball and training that I wasn't putting in the effort. Plus, I was being an asshole. On and off the court. I thought I was untouchable. So I made a terrible decision. I made a bet with a teammate to cover up the fact that I was failing and that Wren Carter had been assigned to tutor me until I brought my grade back up."

A sophomore in front of me shouted, "Is that a rodent of unusual size in your pants?"

Someone behind me whistled, while other students in the crowd howled with laughter.

My throat went dry.

"I'd disappointed Coach big-time. He didn't want me to tell anyone about the tutoring, because he was afraid that it could throw the rest of the guys off their game. The bet helped me cover all of that up.

"Instead of taking it like a man, I bet my friend that I could trick Wren into becoming my girlfriend. He said that would be too easy to pretend, so he and I came up with three stupid steps, proof that we were hanging out, witnessed PDA, and Wren had to come to the first game as my girlfriend, wearing my varsity jacket."

The crowd fell silent. I could feel people staring at me, but I didn't dare take my eyes off Fuller. I was afraid that if I did, I'd either burst into tears or throw up.

"Once I completed all three steps, the plan was to break up with Wren after the season opener, in the parking lot. If I won, my friend would have to ask her to this dance and give me his *Deadpool* comic book collection. He's my little brother's favorite superhero."

I gulped and glanced around me. *What is he doing? Is he trying to embarrass me even more?* The humiliation was almost too much to handle. I'd already started mentally preparing for my exit. There was a door in the corner of the gym that led to the tennis courts. As long as it wasn't locked, I could cut through and make it to the parking lot in about thirty seconds.

"You're an asshole," someone shouted from the crowd.

Surprisingly, a bunch of my classmates nodded in agreement.

"You're right. I am an asshole. From the very first day I spent with Wren, something inside me started to change. I realized I was a cocky jerk who belittled people and bossed them around. My behavior was unacceptable. Through tough talk and setting high expectations, Wren showed me that I could not only turn my grades around, but I could also become a better person. On top of that, Wren Carter is the smartest, kindest, and most beautiful person I've ever met."

A group of girls in the front row let out a collective "Aw."

"The second reason I'm dressed like this is because I have another confession. Before I got to know Wren, I made fun of her. I was a bully. I called her by a terrible nickname. I should have known better back in seventh grade, but I didn't. I thought being popular was more important. Kind of like I thought being the best basketball player in the history of Magnolia Valley was more important than passing my classes. I thought I could ride the 'Fuller "the Jock" James' wave this year and skate by without putting in any effort."

The crowd booed again.

"I know, I definitely didn't have my priorities straight. But, thanks to a bit of luck and a handful of mashed potatoes, I got to know Wren Carter, and you know what? I fell for her, hard. But then I screwed up. I didn't come clean with her, and she found out about the bet at the game last week."

Brandon placed a reassuring hand on my shoulder and whispered, "You okay?"

I stole a glance at my best friend. "I…I'm not sure."

"If you want to leave, just say the word, okay?"

Nodding, I turned back toward the stage.

Fuller took a deep breath and exhaled. "After she found out, she wouldn't talk to me or respond to my text messages, and she even blocked me on Instagram. Not that I blame her. My actions hurt her. Desperate for her forgiveness and willing to do anything to win her back, my little brother and I came up with a plan."

Jenna Marie took my hand. My heart pounded so intensely I was sure she could hear it.

Hudson waved to the crowd in his Deadpool costume. People around us clapped and hollered.

"Wren told me once that her favorite movies were *The Princess Bride* and *Say Anything.* After I made a complete ass of myself, I sat down with my little bro and watched them both. Then, I read the *The Princess Bride* book. Well, I listened to it, but you get the gist. Tonight, I'm dressed up as Westley. He goes through hell and back for the woman he loves. I'm willing to do the same for Wren."

My hand flew to my chest. *Love? Did he just say love?*

TyShaun came on stage and handed him an old boom box.

"In her other favorite movie, there's a grand sweeping gesture." He hoisted the boom box up over his head with one hand and gestured toward the DJ with the other. A few seconds later, "In Your Eyes" by Peter Gabriel started blasting out of the massive speakers on either side of the stage.

Tears welled up in the corners of my eyes, and my breath caught in my chest.

Marc handed Hudson a huge stack of poster boards. Fuller's little brother tilted them toward the crowd.

Fuller began reading them, one at a time. "Wren, I'm sorry. I acted like a complete jerk."

Hudson let the first poster fall to the floor of the stage. "A HUGE jerk," he shouted.

Several people in the crowd laughed.

"Correction, Hudson is right. I behaved like a *huge* jerk." Fuller nodded at his little brother. "Wren, I didn't take your feelings into consideration when I made the bet, and by the time I knew I'd done something stupid, I was too scared to come to you with the truth."

Hudson let the poster fall.

"I made the biggest mistake and I regret my actions more than anything."

Fuller stared out into the sea of people, and even though

I doubted he could make out anyone's faces due to the spotlight shining brightly on him, it felt like he was looking directly at me. A warm sensation spread through my chest.

"Wren Carter, I know I don't deserve you." Fuller's voice cracked with emotion. "But I had to get up here and tell you and everyone here tonight that I'm sorry."

Hudson let the last poster fall, revealing the final message.

Gasps and applause broke out from the audience.

"I have one thing left to say. To be honest, I've never said it to anyone before." Fuller paused, his chest rising and falling. "Wren Carter, I love you."

My classmates erupted into wild cheers.

Heart slamming, I looked at Dae and Brandon. They both gave me a quick nod and genuine smiles. *Were they in on all of this? How could they have kept it a secret from me?*

Fuller's voice drew my attention back toward the stage. "If there's any way, deep in your heart, that you can forgive me, Wren, I promise, from this point forward, I'll always be honest with you, no matter what."

Girls around me dabbed at their eyes with tissues while some of the guys from the basketball team started chanting, "Wren. Wren. Wren."

I swallowed the lump in my throat and took a step forward. The crowd went berserk as I continued to make my way toward the stage.

Fuller squinted and held out his hand, trying to block the bright light. He didn't have a clue that I was almost to the stage.

Knees trembling, I climbed the steps. That's when he turned around, our eyes locking. "You did all this for me?"

"Yes." He took my hand in his and pulled me into his arms. "I am so sorry, Wren."

The cheers were deafening.

Fuller took a step back, setting the boom box down

and letting the microphone fall to his side. "Wow. You look beautiful."

A hush fell over the students in the audience.

My eyes were glossy and my heart was beating so fast it felt like it was going to spring out of my chest. "Did you really mean what you said?"

"Every single word."

As if we were the only two in the gym, I reached up toward Fuller's face and touched his mask. "I can't believe you dressed up as Westley."

He brought his hand to mine and let it slide down his face, stopping at his shoulder. "Wren, I love you, and I'd do anything for you. Absolutely anything."

A murmur of excitement fell over our classmates, who'd crowded around the stage.

"Will you give me a second chance?" His palms were damp.

Anxiety coupled with pure bliss coursed through my body as I looped my hands around his neck. "Fuller James, I'll give you another chance. But under one condition…"

I beckoned him closer. As he leaned down, I whispered my terms into his ear.

He pulled away, lips parted. "Seriously? That's your condition?"

I grinned and shrugged. "It's your call."

Fuller leaned down and whispered into my ear, "As you wish."

Epilogue

Wren

"You ready, guys?" I asked with a smile.

Fuller and his teammates gave me thumbs-up.

It was hard to believe it had been a month since the dance. The thought of Fuller dressed up as the main character from *The Princess Bride* and making a grand gesture like in *Say Anything* still brought a smile to my face every time I pictured it.

I picked up a megaphone and held down the button on the handle. "The car wash to benefit the Alzheimer's Association is officially open!"

Several cars behind me honked their horns in excitement as I began waving them through to the basketball players.

I'd divided them up into groups of three. Fuller, TyShaun, and Marc got to work on their first car. The people behind them hopped out of their car and started taking pictures.

Fuller stopped and spun around. "Yeah, yeah. Enjoy it while you can."

I stifled a giggle. I'd given Fuller one condition at the dance last month. That he go through with his end of the bet by wearing the mesh wrestling singlet, but he had to do it outside of school and while doing a good deed. He insisted on hosting a car wash to raise money for people with dementia and their caregivers. The money would be donated in Gramps's name.

Of course, he'd agreed. But I'd tossed in a pair of sweatpants and a jacket to throw over the singlet. After all, it left very little to the imagination and, with the chilly buckets of water and the temperature hovering around forty-five degrees, I didn't want him to come down with pneumonia.

As Fuller and the rest of the guys got to work, I stopped by the driver's side of each vehicle in line to collect the $5.00 car wash fee.

A few leaves clung to the trees surrounding the parking lot, but most had fallen. Normally, winter kind of bummed me out, but not this year. This year, I had a whole different outlook. Chilly mornings would be spent holding hands with Fuller on the way to class and late Friday nights would be reserved for eating popcorn and Nerds after his basketball games.

Smiling, I walked up to the side of a blue truck.

"We'd like to donate an extra fifty dollars," my dad said with a smile. He handed me the money.

"Thanks, Dad." I shoved the money into a plastic container. "I really appreciate you coming out."

"We wouldn't miss it for the world," Gramps added with a grin. "Great seeing these young men do something good for the community."

"Definitely. After the car wash, are we still on for watching the game?" I asked.

Gramps gave me a thumbs-up. "I'll pop the popcorn."

"Is it okay if Fuller and his little brother Hudson come

watch with us?"

"That sounds like a lot of fun. He's a good ball player." Gramps tilted his head to the side. "Though…that's an awfully strange outfit he's wearing."

I let out a chuckle. "It sure is, isn't it, Gramps?"

He nodded.

My dad smiled. "Thanks for putting this all together, sweetheart. We are so proud of you and Fuller."

For the first time in ages, he looked well rested. After Gramps's fall, my parents had a serious discussion. In the end, they decided that it would be smart to have some extra help around the house in order to keep Gramps safe. A certified nursing assistant now came to our house from ten at night until ten the next morning, five days a week. Even though it'd only been a month, it had already made a lot of difference in our lives, and best of all, Gramps was safer than ever.

"Thanks, Dad." I glanced up. "Looks like it's your turn. See you guys later today." I stepped back and tapped on the cab.

As Dad drove up, I waved the next car forward. Jenna Marie sat in the driver's seat. A girl with curly red hair sat next to her.

Jenna Marie rolled down her window and grinned. "Hey, Wren. Everything looks great."

"Aw, thanks." I reached forward and accepted a five-dollar bill from her.

"This is Anna. I wanted to introduce you two. She's going to the STEM Academy Camp over winter break, too."

"Hey, good to meet you," Anna said. "Do you know what dorm you're going to be in?"

"Jasper Hall. How about you?" I asked.

"Same," she replied with a smile. "It'll be nice to see a familiar face."

"Definitely."

Three of the guys finished up and tapped the side of the car. "We're ready."

"Looks like you all are up." I pointed to the farthest car-washing station to the right. "Thanks again for stopping by."

"No problem. I'm just so glad everything worked out." Jenna Marie smiled before putting her car back into drive and heading toward the guys.

I took a step back. I'd hoped the event would be popular, but I had no idea it would bring in this many people. The line of vehicles stretched from outside the gymnasium, where we had the hoses hooked up, to the entrance of the school.

Halfway through the line was a raised truck covered from wheel to wheel in dried-up mud. I chuckled. That was going to take the guys forever to clean.

We'd gotten the okay from Principal Davis to host the car wash at school. He loved when our students performed community service. Not only did the kids benefit, but our school did as well. He'd shown up in a Magnolia Valley High School track suit and had agreed to sit on a donated dunk tank. For five dollars, you could throw three balls and try to knock him into the water. Coach and a few other teachers had signed up as well.

A broad smile stretched across my face. Amazed at how quickly everything came together and the people who helped to make it happen, I beamed with joy.

I had to give the basketball team huge props. The players had done a great job hyping up the fundraiser. They'd made signs, told hundreds of classmates about the event, and they were even raffling off a signed basketball.

But, without a doubt, Fuller had done the most to advertise the car wash. Using his good news of receiving a scholarship offer from the UGA Coach, he'd made calls to appear on the local news and radio stations; plus, he'd recruited the JV boys' and girls' basketball teams to set up a bake sale and run the school's gigantic popcorn maker. They had coffee and lemonade available as well. Everything you could want on a Saturday morning.

The cheerleaders had gotten on board, too. They lined the street outside school, waving their pom-poms and encouraging people to stop.

After I'd collected money from all the cars in line, I fished my phone out of my pocket, ready to snap some pictures of the event. *That's strange*, I missed a text from Fuller. He must have sent it right before the car wash opened. I tapped on the message.

Fuller: Hey, Wren.
Fuller: Just wanted to say…
Fuller: I love you <3

Warmth radiated through my chest as I typed out my reply.

Me: I love you too, Fuller James.

Acknowledgments

In elementary school, I devoured books. Everything from The Boxcar Children to Goosebumps to *Jurassic Park*. My parents constantly took me to the library, where I could find new books and worlds to get lost in. When I wasn't reading, I was coming up with my own stories. Exciting adventures that took place in the Amazon, a thriller that sent the main characters racing across a farm and taking refuge in a silo, and a historical thriller featuring swashbuckling pirates.

My love for reading and writing has continued to grow. It has also made my dreams come true. Publishing books for readers to fall in love with brings so much happiness to my heart, it's unreal!

Becoming an author and publishing books is something I couldn't have accomplished without loads of amazing people who have helped me along the way.

I Hate You, Fuller James came to life thanks to my wonderful agents, Jennifer Wills and Nicole Resciniti. Their unwavering support in my journey is beyond appreciated. A massive THANK-YOU is owed to the best editor on the planet, Stacy Abrams! With her guidance, my manuscript transformed into something that I am so proud of, it makes me want to cry. I'm also incredibly grateful for Lynn Rush. My critique partner, agency sister, co-writer (on different projects), and friend, Lynn played a massive part in helping me shape this book. Another thank-you to my friends Ali Novak, Alex Evansley, and Kristi McManus. They're always there to bounce ideas off and help along the way. They are the greatest!

Mad love for the rest of my #WattFam as well. We've all come so far and I can't wait to see what's in store for us next! To the Sprinters United (Writing) crew, thank you for all of the motivation. I wrote this book in record time thanks to your help! Thanks to two of my biggest cheerleaders, Fiona Simpson and Andrew Cole-Bulgin! To my mom and dad as well as my mother-in-law and father-in-law, thank you! You all serve as such wonderful role models! Because of you, I work hard and find joy in life.

Thank you to the entire team at Entangled, led by the brilliant Liz Pelletier. I know that my books are in the best hands in the business. I love working with everyone and I'm excited for my future with this amazing publisher!

Lee Roy, you are such a caring husband and wonderful dad to our sweet Bells. Thank you for supporting me on my journey of becoming an author. Accomplishing my goals with you and our little family by my side is simply the best!

To my darling Bella Rose, this book came to life shortly after I found out that I was pregnant with you. For the first three months of your life, you kept me company as I wrote this story. Curled up on the couch with your fur siblings, typing away, with steaming cups of peppermint tea, I knew that I had a partner in this journey. Your first birthday will come shortly after this book is published. I hope that as you grow up, it brings you pride that your mommy loves you with her whole heart and has shown you that it is possible to live your dreams!

Lastly, I want to thank my readers. Without you, none of this would be possible! You literally inspire and motivate me each and every single day. The joy I get from writing for you is nearly unmatchable. I appreciate you all so much! THANK YOU!

About the Author

Kelly Anne Blount is a *USA Today* bestselling author of young adult novels. She loves to alternate writing sweet romances, gritty thrillers, and fantasy books. She's a firm believer in balancing light with dark.

When she's not writing, she's probably lost in a book, watching *Twilight*, or having an adventure with her sweet family, which includes her handsome husband, their darling daughter, and their five furry loving rescues.

After living in a palace in Scotland, across from the Caribbean Sea, and in the snowy land of Wisconsin, Kelly and her family reside in beautiful Asheville, North Carolina.

Kelly loves connecting with readers on social media! Stop by and say, "Hi!" or ask a question. You can find her everywhere @KellyAnneBlount.

Discover more of Entangled Teen Crush's books...

Stuck with You

a *First Kiss Hypothesis* novel by Christina Mandelski

Catie Dixon got over her hot childhood frenemy Caleb Gray ages ago. So when he unexpectedly shows up at their families' Texas beach house, as unsettled about his future as she is about hers, she's irritated by the draw to let him back in. A forced week of togetherness sparks more than an understanding, but what do you do when the person standing in the way of your future is the one person you suddenly don't want to live without?

Announcing Trouble

a novel by Amy Fellner Dominy

I may know everything there is to know about baseball, but that doesn't mean I have to like it. Or like *him*. Garrett Reeves: sidelined player and the embodiment of everything I've learned to hate about baseball. When Garrett convinces me to call games alongside him, our chemistry heats up the booth. But when he has to decide between our future and a new shot at his dreams, I know baseball will win out every time.

The Bookworm Crush

a novel by Lisa Brown Roberts

Shy bookworm Amy McIntyre is about to compete for a dream scholarship, and that level of confidence doesn't come easy. Her solution? A competition coach. But the best person for the job is the guy she's secretly crushing on...local surfer celebrity Toff Nichols. To her surprise, Toff agrees to help. Then their late night practices become less about coaching and more about making out. But does Toff really like her or is this just another lesson?

Printed in Great Britain
by Amazon